2084

a novel of the future upon us

by Robert Wintner

2084 / by Robert Wintner
ISBN: 979-8-9865304-7-5

1.Republican—Politics. 2.Overpopulation—Hunting—Mandate. 3.Dystopia. 4. Suburban—The Future—Novel. Printed in the USA

Cover photo by the author: *Arrgghh*, in which Commerson's frogfish endures the evening news.

Contact at RobertWintner.com or Robert Wintner Author on FB.

Twice-Baked Books

$15.00
ISBN 979-8-9865304-7-5
51500>
9 798986 530475

For George (R)

Author's Note

Disinfectant injections and distraction first ruled the "all-out war on COVID," as bio-crisis went to sandbox politics, as millions perished, and media consoled with thoughts and prayers.

Most boxers say they never saw the last punch coming.

Oh, say, can you see?

In 1960, *The Weekly Reader* for kids ran a story on overpopulation. The cover was a sketch of Earth so crowded that people were falling off. The caption said, "Six billion in our lifetime." Mr. Whaley's sixth graders worried more about recess but world pop not so much at three billion.

Two years later, Mrs. Albin told her eighth graders at Plaza Park Elementary to write a story of the future. I wrote of a World Championship on a huge court with twelve-foot baskets and nine-foot players. One guy drank gallons of hot tea for steam pressure, to spew the ball from his huge mouth. A kid could dream in simpler times. Mrs. Albin, a dour woman, wrote: *A+ Very funny!* I sensed sarcasm. I thought she'd called me a punk, in her way.

2084, the novel, came decades later, as world pop tops eight billion. My financial advisor is Republican. We joust. He says I don't want to outlive my money. I assure him I do. He says trees don't grow to the sky. I remind him of Jack's magic beans and the stalk to the clouds, just out back.

We agree on the Grand Old Party of Eisenhower, Rockefeller, Dirksen and Reagan; it became drastic. We disagree on the cause and the consequence. We share humor to transcend the ridiculous and profane. We laugh, thinking each other ridiculous and profane.

We agree that Earth might endure, if more people don't breed.

Also by Robert Wintner

Fiction: *In a Sweet Magnolia Time*
Lizard Blue
Whirlaway
The Modern Outlaws
Touch of the Unknown Rider
Reefdog
Was Is
Solomon Kursh
A California Closing
Homunculus
The Prophet Pasqual
Wintner's Reserve (stories)
Crux (stories)
Lonely Hearts, Changing Worlds (stories)
Hagan's Trial & Other Stories

Memoir: *1969 and Then Some*
Brainstorm
The Ice King

Reef Politic in narrative and photo/video:
Dragon Walk
Neptune Speaks
Reef Libre, An In-Depth Look at Cuban Exceptionalism & the Last, Best Reefs in the World
Every Fish Tells a Story
Some Fishes I Have Known

Prologue

As It Is

In the Year of Hard Luck, 2084, faith and war yield balance. Discouraging words are seldom heard. The truth sets us free for the best year yet.

The High Republican is a decent, Christian man who modified his personal behaviors to seem more appropriate. His vision is clear. He isn't afraid of those who make fun or hate him. It's all they can do. He could poke fun at himself, but for what? He's terrific. The truth counts, if the many can be made to see it.

By the Grace of Hard Luck, Who giveth this day our daily bread, we approach Campaign '84. The Republican Mandate is secure. The Powers that Be are confident that the Party of the First Part will retain.

Why the heck not?

Who would relinquish power to a bunch of do-nothing crooks, a dull, squandering crowd that hunts witches and blows hoaxes in the face of great works?

I

HumanSport

Belly up, boys and girls. People are telling me this hot buffet will be the best ever. I learned today that I'm number one on Warp Retrieval. I didn't know that. I think it's nice. I won't forgive the rest of you, but I won't lock you up yet. Ha!

The future looks tremendous. I'm good at this. People are asking how I got so good. I don't sleep when I'm working. That's a terrific bargain.

So sayeth the High Republican in the Year of Hard Luck, 2084, exalting The Book and Wayne Wyoming.

Let freedom ring.

This Week on the Warp calls it heavier-handed than political foreplay ought to be. Not since the New Republican Mandate, has so much been granted so few for so little. A subnormal with unknown virtue, one Sonny Wayne Bojoli, gains sudden access to THE LIFE, and *TWW* is asking: Why now? Why here? What's up?

The High Republican gazes at the truth. *No way we can lose, unless it's rigged, and all is lost. Fear not. I know things nobody else knows, not in the Department of Justice or the shoe department, where they get their marching orders. It's a vicious circle that keeps me up at night, and that's no bargain.*

At ground level, Wayne Wyoming plays to type, rustling like sagebrush. The crusty codger and brand-new celebrity calls his anointment proof positive that fame can bless anyone who lives right and gives back to the hohum like the hohum gives to thee.

Some folks think the old prairie dog got scripted . . .

The High Republican interrupts: *Nobody on Earth—not in the subdivisions and condominia on the face of it or the cozycaves under the skin of it or the orburbs overhead, not in the Penthouse Towers or mansions on Maximillion Boulevard—nobody should doubt my plan for HumanSport. I will open the place up, because I can, and you know it. You'll get what's coming to you.*

Furthermore, the name Wayne Wyoming will be removed from the name-Q pool, available for sequel only by the heirs and assigns of © Wayne Wyoming at their sole discretion. The High One resounds: *That's a juicy tomato. I like 'em juicy.*

It's not for nothing that Heather Heatherington is the second most watched warp analyst in America. She asks Wayne Wyoming what his rise to Q-dom overnight from a wasteland substratum means to him in his heart of hearts.

Wayne Wyoming chews on it for OneEye, scanning the scrub, ready to take aim on what could be lunch. Easing his steely gaze, he says: "Well, sir, you'd have yourself a fine mess, you didn't cull the herd. It ain't nothing to do with me. It's how it is. You think you know folks. You seen 'em and heard what they got to say. You listen to some of 'em for years, like to box they head in, is what you wanna do. But you don't 'cause folks is folks. You put 'em out here for something else is what you do."

Brittle stalks and serpent tails crackle in the stillness.

"You seen it plenty in the olden days, and I'll tell you what: you'll see it again, they let OneEye in here. You think wastelands is all harmony and nature? You wait. You'll see what they do. Cannibals is what it comes to. That and sport. Some of 'em might keep up the fa fa fa with the fancy boots and levitator pads and perfeclime sleeper bubbles, all them vests and electric hats and gizzies. Must spend forty thousand, some of 'em, come out here and sleep on the ground. Hell, you keep 'em out here long enough; they'll sing a different tune. They won't leave the meat."

Heather Heatherington raises an eyebrow over Wayne's prediction and turns to OneEye. "They won't leave the meat?" Bilious dismay spells it out, and she spells it again. "Mr. Wyoming's view of HumanSport may be inevitable, and I suppose, Erika, many may see human nature helping things play out. We can pray that sanity will prevail, no matter how seedy this might seem. The Hard Luck Guy works in mysterious ways."

"Seedy? What you talkin' seedy? I know these hills, and I'll tell you what else—"

"I'm Heather Heatherington on the front lines. Erika?"

Erika Swain is the most trusted woman in America. She worked her way up the hard way, from a crime and accident beat right out of grad school, tooth-and-nailing to major outrage anchor. "Thank you, Heather. The High Republican walks a fine line on this one. He's facing peril on the Clean Air Reconstitution Act, the Rivers and Streams Rebeautification Act and the Urban Effluent Removal Systems Rebuild Act. Let's face it: the war has seen better times, too. If this scheme backfires, it's curtains. He's banking on the many's love of nature and sporting action. He knows we're sick and tired of sitting in traffic. He'll storm the warp with shade and spin.

He'll need the base on this, and he's aiming for OneEye, or I'm a truth hound who can't catch a scent."

"Spot on, Erika. He needs to poll in the high thirties and pronto."

"Thank you, Heather. Here's the High Republican making his case." Erika Swain, profile right, effuses confidence, connections and appropriate values that got her where she is . . .

Cut to the High Republican:

We need this. I'm telling you: things are bad. You know who's to blame. It's a terrible situation. We can't take another disaster. HumanSport moves us forward. Hard Luck and I can fix this.

Fade . . . and back to Erika Swain:

"Should contact sport go to blood sport? Do we need the money so badly? Are we really so crowded? Is ultimate sport better than the rhythm method? Tough questions buzz in the top Republican ear. I'm Erika Swain, and this is *USS*. For more on this fascinating story, we go now to Jade Boren, live at the Capitol. Jade?"

"Thank you, Erika. You've been there, Erika. Waiting in line, waiting in traffic, waiting for the bathroom, waiting till you want to scream. I've been there, Erika. But is the First Commandment really so different than the Second Amendment? The High Republican's friend and spiritual counselor, Jimmy Grimm, is now proposing an amendment of the first commandment to include a self-defense and/or sport caveat. He says he'll deal with the Second Amendment in due time, on a compulsory fire-at-will clause. No matter what, this should work well for the High Republican, given Reverend Grimm's campaign track record. The High Republican is making very few moves since the big move, but we have word from sources in the White House that the HR will double or even triple the dependent children tax credit in the next two weeks, depending on entitlement savings projections from the OMB. What do they think this new sporting park might do? They'll run the stats up to see who salutes. The Administration is calling HumanSport another great experiment, but insiders say they're on pins and needles over the payout. I'm Jade Boren. Back to you, Erika."

"Thank you, Jade. We'll follow the play and see you on the other side of the DMZ. The High Republican is betting another term on this one. The Office of Management and Budgets projection is ninety-two trillion in annual savings from HumanSport. Gate revenues, hauling fees, fines and entitlement-savings factor most. The rules are still in committee, but *USS News* has learned that senior citizens will receive a seventy-percent discount on admission and a drop-dead double refund on . . . Oh, Hard Luck."

Erika Swain falters. Dropping her steel-rod relationship with OneEye, she lowers her gaze. Touching a temple with elegant fingers, she says, "I'm sorry." Composure compromised, she looks up. "It says, 'double refund on any three-bag session.' Those are not my words. I'm Erika Swain. This is *USS*."

Erika Swain often hints her own Republican leanings, asking how anyone could lean otherwise appropriately. She keeps them guessing. With seasoned mystique, she can infuse real meaning at will. She personifies appropriateness and can change the course of mighty meanings or stop meaning in its tracks. Viewers speculate that analysis analysis will question her lukewarm reception to the Great Experiment. Speculation historians will track back to this moment, when the HR took a nosedive from on high. Nobody delivers uncertainty with nuance like Erika Swain, her silky spritz of innuendo turning a little nothing to a hard news lead on any product or politician.

Warpanal calls her La Generalissima and speculates on her candidacy. She denies it with a laugh! Warpanal notes that it's the first laugh of her broadcast career and calls it the race of the century. Hard Luck knows that Erika Swain on the ballot would pump primary ratings higher than the Rimball Superfinals. Denying candidacy puts a glow on Erika, election-cycle blush. Her Mauve Magma lip-gloss and matching nails glisten from her fingertips, talk hole and toes. Is this the setup? Does she see an opening? Could this hard news propel her to candidacy on the first splatter, especially if the first to fall is a kinder, gentler face from a solid Republican subdivision? Death will not be proud in the HumanSport sector, and it will not be retrievable too.

Erika Swain in signature resignation fades to commercial break.

The many rise to freshen their colas, perf their pizzas, pee and murmur consensus. Two-point-two percent of viewers will file a mental note on Mucoslic J, the nongreasy ointment most doctors recommend to relieve stubborn, lumpy stool, if you want to live forever. If one in a million follow through each week for only twelve weeks on a Mucoslic J buy, the thirty-second spot will generate six million dollars per airing, which is productive, if a sponsor buys the thirty-second 12-Pak Special at forty-two million dollars, yielding black ink hardly into the first squeeze. Nobody with appropriate thoughts reflects for too long on the Mucoslic nozzle squirting that stuff up a butthole, but the global economy gets pumped on every spot, ever since the Administration outlawed digital video recording.

The High One explained: *DVR is not good for the economy. These commercials generate taxable revenue, and they're fun to watch, so we will.*

After Mucoslic J, sixteen spots allow time for bodily and economic function. Consensus on the stories *USS* will follow this hour will be in Erika's hands before the commercials end in twelve to twenty minutes. Opinion flows from insta-read as the many votes with its feelings. Insta-read feels what is felt. Data forwarded to *USS* makes the pulse of the electorate Erika Swain's to massage.

This is tricky tundra, where life-and-death variables can change in a blink; so the most trusted woman in America opts for sidebar color on another breaking wave of Breaking News, to gain another minute to better assess conditions.

Sonny Wayne Bojoli had his name changed to Wayne Wyoming, adjunctive to anointment and Executive Order that also changed a Wyoming high-scrub plateau to HumanSport. Designated long ago as a refuge for misfits and bums, this hardpan goes from dismal to dramatic on a nod. A no-count, six-exit stretch is now a game changer, and Erika Swain wants to know why.

Misfits will go away, said the High Republican. *Just you watch. They'll go away. Believe me. They're gone.*

Unwritten Law made misfits fair game to anyone seeking wasteland sport, back in the olden days. Unlike other game, however, misfits outshot and outscored normal sportspersons until '48, when the Republic gave the many a fair advantage through lend/lease artillery. (*We got the weaponry. Why not use it? We'll take Democracy into Wyoming. Why not? We're #1!*) Deep penetration over two years of lend/lease fairly decimated game in the Wyoming wasteland. If you see a wayward misfit with an RPG, he'll be deader 'n the rock he got melted onto, thanks to laser light anti-RPG detection, developed for the Pentagon for forty-two billion after the lend-lease recoup and sell off. Quoth the High One: *If you don't think that was a good deal, then you don't love Wyoming.*

The many do love Wyoming, but hunting interest will wane every time, with nothing left to shoot. A few bums still hide out in caves and burrows, scared and drunk, some still wearing berets and headbands. Most died out or went deeper. Some drifted back into the hohum, assimilating as best a bum can. A shooter could still bag a bum basking on a rock or bathing in a puddle. But that was luck, and such easy pickings could not attract real sportspersons with equipment and know-how. Wyoming soon became the safest of all wasteland sectors.

With its vast plains quelled, Wyoming yawned east to west, north to south, then shut its mouth in dumbstruck awe at its own perfection. With its beauty rendered nonthreatening, Wyoming gave witness to the word. *Subdue Wyoming and prosper*, sayeth the Republican. Then came stillness on a hot breeze. Silence wanted an ear to fall into. Silence displaced the insects once humming, the bears once scratching, the leaves once rustling. All those itchy, scary sounds were gone, giving way to security.

"And now this?" Mooja Slovac brings the backstory into the moment with urgency and need. "All's quiet here at Sonny Wayne Bojoli's RV Graveyard. RV ruins line the ridge in poetic emptiness, as if sheet metal and shag carpet could hum the sad, sweet lyric of journey's end. A few overstuffed sofas sit out front for the refrain on millions of happy miles. Down below is Sonny Wayne's humble shack, where he's lived since . . . How long have you lived here, Sonny Wayne?"

"Since the cows went home. I been here that long."

"A cow has huge mammaries, once milked for human consumption. Everyone liked to eat cows. Some high mucky-mucks still do, but that's State dinner at the White House. Mmm . . . Good with ketchup and onions. With four legs, a cow needs twenty-four square feet for grazing. Cows had to go, consuming so much and expelling methane. Your average bovine could blow fifty cubic yards of stinko a day. Now we get protein from more sustainable products without the mess or grazing room, and no gas! Can you imagine? Cows everywhere? Oh, Hard Luck. And pigs! Talk about inappropriate whiffies!"

Sonny Wayne tolerates Mooja Slovac gratuities. These media types: who never heard of a cow? A man can be happy he doesn't live near those people. She can yak with the worst of them, this Mooja. "Oh, it was wild! They had cow boys!"

Kind of sounds like a cow. Mmmoooja.

"They'd rope and lasso and bulldog, but it wasn't a dog, it was a way of getting the cows to lay down, so they could . . ."

Glazed in heat ripples, Sonny Wayne lets his chin tick to his chest, eyes easing shut. Only two days ago, the High Republican, Heather Heatherington and Erika Swain said his name on the warp, and already the follow-up has begun. He drifts. He dreams of himself talking, maybe in a new shirt, light starch. OneEye'll watch and listen, attentive to the man of the high plateau, his words infused with merit. His opinion will be worthy, possibly necessary. His birthday will be included when they say whose birthday is today. His wisdom will be sage. He'll get respect and fervent viewing, as a man will do, once he's on the warp. He won't worry about deep ignernce on topics of the world and such. A feller won't need to know so much. Ignernce is natural in that crowd, specially them politicos, nobody having yet read nor seen nor heard whatever the fuck they's talking about anyways. He snores.

Mooja says, "It all changes on this historical anointment. Wyoming is now this." She beholds Wayne Wyoming, napping.

"HumanSport is now this." Her arms open to embrace the sector and cut to the voice-over drone. "The High Republican rules."

Cut to the High Republican: *One herd left for culling. It's up to us. We can do it. Unbelievable. It's gonna be terrific.*

Cut to promo: Rimball, A Special Report: *Season Openers and You.* Rimball isn't going away, and neither are you. Stay tuned. Coming right up . . .

Cut to the High Republican, frontal contentment: *We are. You know I can. Fantastic.*

Hold and . . . Fade to space music and . . .

Back to Mooja Slovac: "This is the High Republican's proven technique, the factual message. He knows values, Christian ethic and biblical reference, chapter and verse. Detractors call him a buffoon, a nitwit, a chump. They call him a petroleum apologist, a climate warmer, an NRA pawn. They called him a liar and say he never read the bible and doesn't love Hard Luck. They call him a donor stooge. He says, *Sore losers! Losers. Who's raking it in? Who wins? Who's smart?* The High Republican reroutes logic, scoring at will and taking out experts with credentials on any subject you got. How does he do that? He just does. I'm not predicting anything, but! Some analysts speculate he'll draw a bead and pronto on some facts and figures. The HR can pull good times and prosperity out of thin air by saying it's so. Sportspersons love that action, and they want the skinny right now on what, when and where they can get in on the gloryfest shaping up here in the Hubbub! Administration insiders say pent-up demand will run pretty darn high on game in unlimited supply. Are you a sportsperson? You miss the action? Let's find out. Punch Xtrastrong on your insta-read overrides and really feel it. It's fifty years since the last of the wild four-leggers bit the dust. Fifty years since we scratched this itch. Let's see what you're feeling."

Mooja gazes off, profile right, with grace and charm.

Sonny Wayne Wyoming slumps deeper, sawing logs. Shots like this keep a woman on the fast track, imprinting payloads and . . .

Hold. Pan and zoom close on Sonny Wayne Wyoming pooling a drool, letting it roll and . . .

Cut to *Geddidon with Summelcome II, the ingredient most doctors recommend if you're approaching triple digits and still want to you-know-what. Want to get it on? Get Geddidon, now with Summelcome II.*

Cut to *Peckerup with PU1, the ingredient known by doctors to get it up and keep it up, not just in the morning but way late at night too. Peckerup, for years of performance satisfaction.*

Cut to *The Gimbal & Proctor family-value medley, featuring Petersweet, Jambegone, Dandrudead, Runistop, Dukalot with EZSLY D, 905 with HQL and Vaginoll with VJ1 for your home vaginal needs.*

Cut to *The All-New USS Missouri, for ultimate family luxury from General Cubes, where the skies are always open and the hohum hums for you.*

Cut to *Pudmizer* and . . .

Hold on George Longley profile with voice-over: We'll be right back to Mooja Slovac Live after these important messages. And . . .

Cut to *Blast for whiter whites, Roachdeath for roaches that stay dead and Suppositron Portowarps, if you want the megahertz but not the pain, now with ANALINK™—warp-speed access without the runs. Want three hundred frequencies closer than your hip pocket without the usual itch, no sluggishness and removal as easy as, 'Hey, pull my finger, wouldja?' Get Suppositron Portowarps with ANALINK™. CAUTION: Regular use of ANALINK™ may result in the uncontrollable need to defecate. Users may experience headache, high blood pressure and soreness.*

ANALINK ™ is best used close to home.

Cut to the medley wrap on feeling good, staying young, living forever and getting the most out of THE LIFE.

These important messages give Mooja time to digest insta-read data. She knows Erika tossed her a hot potato to check the smoldering spud for residual BTUs. An up-and-comer takes the heat for the dowager anchor and gives it right back as a hard news lead: THIS JUST IN! Fluctuating less than a point on the geo-sentimental matrix, the Slovac rating looks rock-solid to the next commercial break. Reinspired, she beams anew and . . .

Now back to Mooja Slovac Live. Mooja, profile left, turns to OneEye and . . .

"We remember frontier glory. Now the many can reclaim a heritage." Mooja plucks a spec from her own eye. Or is it a tear? "In the Administration's program, virtue will accrue to those who serve The New Natural Order. The High One predicts astronomical savings. His words. We'll feed you data the instant they come in. Meanwhile, this ultimate sport is not for shallow pockets. Gee whiz. Sixteen hundred dollars a day, but you can't get a day. You get two days for thirty-two hundred. The High One says he's good at this sort of thing, and we'll see for ourselves, how a two-day ticket goes ch ching ch ching. What if a loser buys the farm on day one? The HR says, *Nothing personal, just business. That's how the system works. I know how to use the system to advantage. That's what makes America great again.* The ticket includes tarcaff and donuts. You pack in the rest. Gee whiz. So close to Pudland and The Trees, this looks to me, Mooja Slovac, like the vacation I could use. You can win your money back and a bundle to boot. Vegas and Disneyland, look out. This looks like fun!"

Cut to the High Republican: *You wanna feel the action? Two birds. One stone. Sport makes you feel great again. Amazing. Some great sportsperson friends of mine are telling me how it feels to conquer a challenge. Winners do that. Let's get ready to rumble! Forget the hoops and nets and nasty goal posts with crushed glass and daggers. No more slamicades or jugublades and no pads or helmets. Clean and simple. We can do this.*

Back to Mooja Slovac, eyes in shadow with sparkling purple highlights under perfect lashes, lids heavy in absorption mode.

Sonny Wayne Wyoming wakes up to Mooja's emotive profile but can't give a rat's patootie about her ratings or image or any of that hogwash. "I heard what you said, Moja. Now, I ain't never been nowhere. Never been to Vegas or Disneyland neither one, but I ain't dumb. I tell you a name like Wyoming shouldn't go to waste. Besides, plenty more Bojolis where I come from. I tell you what else, Moojo. I ain't Bojo and I ain't Bojoli. Not no more. It'd be one thing if they knew me. They don't. They figure it's Bojo and I 'spect they'll still holler, Hey, Bojo, and want me to wave back. But I won't, 'cause I ain't. Back to you, Mojo."

"I ain't Mojo, Bojo." Mooja preempts the crusty geezer with a step across OneEye, knowing thirty-five percent of the viewing audience will forget what's-his-name by the time she splays those freshly plumped lips across her dazzling teeth. Chalked off her follow-up potential list because he's a hambone who won't pay attention, Sonny Wayne Wyoming can try to do better on his next once-in-a-lifetime. Ha. Sonny Wayne Wyoming who?

Mooja does not see herself as mean, but if a gal doesn't watch out, a wasteland bumpkin can do her in. Are you kidding? The late-night jokers pick this up; it's all over: Mojo, to kingdom come. Who needs it, after a career of building Q the hard way, brick by brick? Sure, oddball names are all over the warp, but Mooja Slovac stands out and sticks with the proven trust of a double o and the intrigue of a vac. Should a woman invest forty thou on right-name research and spend twelve years busting her balls to get ahead and then forget about it? Maybe half the world doesn't know Slovac from Cube Vac; the other half does. Mooja Slovac is the one with the eyes and unique phrase: "Gee whiz!" You call that casual? And for what? So this boob can ding a monster recog in a syllable? Not on your LIFE.

Mooja will confirm her instincts on the readout before deleting Bojo from the follow-up file, but her instinct to date is bankable. Tracking six zigahertz of self-esteem, she bats lashes to semi-charm. Maxi-charm gets dicey, looking like compensation or worse: ambition.

Settling serene as a wasteland, she holds one . . . and two . . . She sighs and says "Wayne Wyoming's front porch is the front line. For years, he wouldn't move, sat here like deadwood since way before blood sport broke into polite conversation. He's crusty. The High Republican calls him a beacon in the wilderness and says he might get the Congressional Medal of Freedom. We'll hear no more of Sonny Wayne Bojoli, the curmudgeon who scraped hardpan for a living, farther from church, schools and shopping than anybody wants to be. No more o' that hooey. It'll be Wayne Wyoming from here on out. Huh?"

She pauses, eye to Eye, giving them time to forget, letting him wither like a disposable Summer's Eve. "We'll be seeing Wayne for years." Mooja dangles the follow-up carrot till she can cross-check the readout, bring the boob back or shoot him to oblivion. Follow-up would give him Q. She might, if the readout warrants, but she's not about to gift-wrap the glory for this hick without exponential accrual for herself. Not a chance.

"Nobody's laughing now, gee, not with Corollary 8 front and center in your alpha lobes: Good Q gets good seats, and don't you forget it. A nasty old fart in the wasteland this morning is staring down Q.335 for lunch. Let's take a look at the man on the skyrocket. Will the electropulse stabilize? Who is Wayne Wyoming?"

Mooja hunches in, chummy like, wincing, whispering, "This is no walk in the basil." And asking out loud, "Mm. You had reptile for breakfast, didn't you, Wayne?"

"Yup. Same as . . ."

"Tell us, Wayne." Mooja backs an inch with a subtle turn and a wink so fast you can't be sure it's you and Mooja in a private laugh over a dirt clod with forked tongue on his breath. Sonny Wayne saw it. "What kind of reptile did you eat?"

"Now looka here. Don't go makin' me for some durn fool."

Mooja shrugs. "I guess it's personal."

"No, it ain't personal. It's lizard chunks 'n peas. But don't make like it's scrub plains white trash eatin' this stuff. Why, it's made in Japan. They eat it. Everybody eats it, 'cept maybe for you. You wanna talk survival and blood and the game, I'll tell you what—"

"Lizard chunks and peas. What are the other choices, Wayne, if you're up for reptile?"

Sonny Wayne grumbles. He double checks for a leg pull and says, "They ain't no choices. It says right there on the bag, 'Reptile and Peas.' If you cain't tell chunk lizard from snake steak, well sir, you chowed down on a rat's ass one too many, Mooja. You eat burgers now, don't you? How you tell what's—"

"You recognize the lizard? Do you catch your own lizards?"

"Used to be. Not anymore. Lizards all hunted out since the Jappos come over 'n took the breeders. Now they sell us the chunks, keep the tails for theirself. You won't see no more snake steaks neither, not unless you make the kind of money comes from pokin' your nose in people's face and makin' fun."

Mooja smiles benignly at Wayne Wyoming, then turns to OneEye on a blend of pity and victory. "Tell us, Wayne. When will you get your tickets? Gee whiz." She steps back from the acrid epicenter, shooing a stink.

Sonny Wayne reflects, "I'll get my tickets soon enough. I want to see the playoffs. I never been, live. I'll get 'em."

"One more thing, Wayne. Is there a Mrs. Wyoming?"

"Nope."

"Juicy. Who will you take?"

Sonny Wayne squints up. "You wanna?"

"You old prairie dog!" She steps in front again to remind OneEye that she is Mooja Slovac, and it's back to you, Erika.

Sonny Wayne pushes her aside to give notice: "I'll show 'em in all right. What I think I'm gonna do is keep it Sonny Wayne Wyoming. The way I caramelize it, you cain't fuck with a man's name without he don't have a say in a thing."

Mooja Slovac steps back across, blushing and gushing, "Soon enough, he says. Gee whiz! Can you believe it? Third row minimum! And he says soon enough! Ha! I'm Mooja Slovac Live on Warp 13. Stay tuned. We'll be right back."

Sonny Wayne thinks he made his point with country color and wasteland wit. That's good because color means follow-up. He contemplates greatness and THE LIFE with Q. He'll be friends with Mooja and them fancy people who might appreciate him, once they know him. Maybe he'll have a chat with Erika Swain, who might want his opinion on one thing and another.

He considers a series of his own, a sitcom about a guy with a junkyard who hits pay dirt. He could be on a talk panel, or how 'bout *Sonny Wayne Live*, where he talks to fancy folks about what they're thinking. Wait! How about some private time with Sonny Wayne, sharing thoughts on Hard Luck and the High Republican? Fuckin' bingo! He laughs. Nah. Come fifty years, he'll be sitting on the same front porch, this dream like the rest, faded duller'n a dead RV. He'll show 'em in. That's enough, if they ever get the dang thing squared away.

Sonny Wayne Wyoming watches Mooja Slovac and the Live Action News Team buzz up and away. That's how they are, them warp types, all smiles and glad hands for old OneEye. Then it's Who-the-hell are you? Pack up and skedaddle without a single adios, motherfucker. Get 'em out here; you'll see a different set of manners. By Hard Luck you'll see some skin under them claws.

It's tough to figure what comes next with a whole dang world watching one minute and all by his lonesome self the next. Sonny Wayne ponders options and settles in to watch the Ad Hoc Rules Committee hammer HumanSport, End Game, into Appropriate Language. What a headache those Ad Hocs turn out to be. Then again, it's the very stuff THE LIFE will be made of.

Sonny Wayne Wyoming is, by anointment, Resource Manager and Game Warden, Sector HS. "I'll show 'em in," he murmurs, reliving the moment of a whole world listening. When will he get his tickets? Shoot. Sonny Wayne Wyoming got the catbird seat already. There ain't no closer to the action than this without risking a few leaks. Third row? Why, a man could bag his fill from this porch, potshottin' any one of 'em steppin' over the line.

A dirt clod kicked down the road picks up more smarts than a lump in a ditch. Scrimp and scratch is how it is, and a potshot on a fat Q'll do a fellow in easy as do him up. Damn NaySayers whining over a little spec o' blood. Left to them, the creeps and psychos would have got catered brunch instead of the death sentence that meant staying dead forever, like it oughta.

Then again, a man in the catbird seat on a great new theme park might pick his targets and score a winner. You bag a humdinger with iffy Q, who's to simmer? Like that fat bastard poking boys in the Congressional sit-down. Them bungholers come to HumanSport, Sonny Wayne'll know where to aim quicker'n a neutron drift. 'Course now, he cain't very well how-do-you-do 'em, see 'em in and pump 'em full o' dead, he don't think.

No use worrying about it now. Sonny Wayne Bojoli felt old this morning, but that old Bojoli fellow is gone. It's Sonny Wayne Wyoming now, sittin' pretty for pay dirt. That's how it works. Your time comes; you get the money. A man oughta live a couple hundred years anyway, if he has the means.

Sonny Wayne Wyoming isn't so old, but a lifetime of biscuits and baco feels heavy. Never mind, he's young enough to rejuvenate his third prime on a single splice, maybe a 20 or a 50 with the money coming in easy as trout at the Boat Show.

A man wonders how he'll make it. Sonny Wayne never could see the way but believed in the Book and the Republican Platform. Who would've predicted a name Q anointment from the HR? Erika Swain and Mooja Slovac saying his name hardly two days from waking up lumpy as last week's groats? And here he is, on his way to cream gravy. To think, she stood here where he can reach out and touch, Mooja Slovac, highest daytime Q for a talk woman since forever. She'll be around a few lifetimes yet.

Sonny Wayne shakes his head. At last, he's a cog in the wheel. He could have a warp series, easy as not, what with his sagebrush outlook and speech patterns. He'll enjoy the easy money, the smart people and the you-know-what that crowd is always getting into. He might get tired of it after a while and take a break from show biz. He'll jump that ditch when it comes. Meanwhile, he'll have better manners than some. He sighs, wondering why the Ad Hocs are holding up the whole dang show.

The Wenk Administration first presented the Wyoming solution as Mansport, a plan to restore recreational heritage with huuuge economic benefits on revenue and savings for a win, win, win like nobody's business. The place would create twenty-four thousand jobs and peripheral services. Jobs for the many in a wasteland, untillable, unbuildable and unusable since it got drilled, fractured and pumped down to ridges, ravines and cave-ins. All that crumbled crust will be a family theme park displacing so much nothing. Progress will be natural. A little pocket moolah for the home team won't hurt.

Some say the Wenkers knew Mansport wouldn't fly but sent it up as a straw dog. The ad hocs wear out after a few windy go-rounds, so best work 'em up front and get down to the nitty gristle.

Right on cue, Clitoris Amarato, titular head of Women of the NaySay, went along, saying Mansport would fill the needs of fewer than half the many. "The Great Experiment called Mansport would be poetic in a sinister sense, naming a vile concept for its vile progenitor." Like a seasoned operative, Ms. Amarato conceded the floor to Doreen Bunyan, not your typical house frau.

Doreen proclaimed that fewer than half the specific-gendered plurality had dominated too much for too long. "We want to play, too." Doreen's late wife, Carlotta, had been counselor to the Echelon and among the Precious Few before dying irretrievably in '76 when foreign matter in a bad burger clogged her larynx. That agony dragged for hours, threatening yet another FDA scandal.

Nothing could capture OneEye like freak asphyxiation. Ratings soared on heroic retrieval technology. Old OneEye bulged on that scene, going intimate on Doreen grasping her honey from behind for a round of Heimlich-humping, but the slag held firm, four inches of rattail hanging out the gob. OneEye got Carlotta's dimples and chin whiskers in the purple haze: apoplexy. Doreen pinched that slippery bugger twixt thumb and forefinger but got no grip. Carlotta went deep, died and stayed dead through hyperbaric helixical modulation and cellular matrix adjustments. Doreen hung her head. "My kingdom for a pair of tweezers."

A distinguished team of white robes insisted on autopic rebuild, but alas, misplaced parts and a waste-bottle/feeder-bottle mix-up contaminated too many cells. With the rebuild delayed time and again, time ran out. OneEye stayed with the action, Carlotta's first gag to deep purple to chalky pallor to doornail dead. The living record became the riveting miniseries based on a true story—Doreen's story, with political potential in mind, after all.

THE LIFE *and Times of Doreen Bunyan* kept Doreen's anguish in prime time two seasons, spiking the ratings melee and the moolah meter more than any miniseries, follow-up series or anguish-family-franchise in natural disaster, terminal disease and personal dysfunction categories. The many were made to feel prouder still of who they were and what they'd stand up and fight for.

Doreen's valor shone in her eulogy on love, the Republic and stateswomanship. The soft-spoken domestic recluse catapulted out of nowhere to Q.4. Doreen Bunyan, homespun widow and national heroine, speaks for over half the non-specific-gendered multitudes when she says, "The draft rules can stand, but we're not all men. Some of us are only human. As the most revered species on Earth, we should revere all of our own selves."

The High Republican shakes his head. The olden days were so simple, when Republican zeal and nonspecific gender were as mutually exclusive as fecal plaque and fruit punch. *You ever see that stuff? Disgusting!* The High One gazes at the good old days, when men were men, and women weren't. This is what we've come to: nonspecifics demand power, and a homey dominatrix leads the charge, ruthless as any Republican. The leader of the free world looks back with longing. He'll get even with this bunch, too. He won't argue. He'll give a few nicknames to lather the base. A reckoning draws nigh. The ad hocs are tired already.

Mission Statement HumanSport, Another Great Experiment, spells out new insight and benefits to fulfill sporting instinct. Firepower and stealth will not make sport clean and honorable, but goodness and grace shall thrive at HumanSport. Park entry and behaviors therein will be voluntary, except for blown-to-smithereens or shot-full-o'-dead, either one ending the show and THE LIFE as well. No shame on sudden death; every game needs a loser, a victim to superior sporting skills. That's how we roll.

So rolled the message across the land, the High Republican interrupting as necessary: *Let me tell you about the Chinese. Nobody loves Chinese like I do. What do they use for money now? Yen? Doesn't matter. They'll change to dollars at Immigration Checkpoints anyway. Isn't that a beautiful word? Immigration Checkpoints. I love that word. Bring on the Chinese. By Hard Luck, they deserve a fighting chance. Too many of them. We can help. They should have started eating Chinese a long time ago, if you get my meaning. I think you do. They got money. We'll take it.*

HS entry will not be voluntary for convicted misfits, going in with little or no ammo, wearing pastels of varying garish hues, according to depravity. Further savings will accrue in A) elimination of penal overhead and B) misfit bagging shall be recreational only with no payouts. Some analysis analysts argue that misfit bagging should pay, because misfits are a drain on the many. The High One scoffed, *Give me a break! Shoot the bastards. Have some fun!*

Real opportunity will be in bagging fair game. Cash payments to sportspersons will be forty percent of savings to the Republic, based on remaining average LIFE span, with Social Security payouts weighted in projected death-dollar value. Peripheral entitlements of bagged game shall include Medicare, Medimeds, Medimore and Medimoreplus plus Medimax and Maximedimax, Parts A, B, BB, C and G. One analysis analyst asked why Urgent Wenkare was absent from payout factors. That analyst vanished.

Those persons who eat the big one in Sector HS shall bear no onus; payouts will not reflect sporting skills. The New Natural Order will yield superior visual, auditory and extrasensory acuities for the many. With not so many, and a stronger populace, THE LIFE may be achievable to more of the many. Non-players will maintain current standards. If you don't play, you can't win.

Ground rules for HumanSport, the game, are:

1) Roads in shall be named for truly great Republicans.
2) Billboard frequency in HS shall double in re: Corollary 20: *Billboards are art. Art has merit and creates jobs for the many.*
3) Safety first. Each billboard or cluster shall enjoy a twenty-yard DMZ buffer. No firing on pinkos—pink jumpsuit crews who refresh billboards and clear foul kills.
4) ONLY the Game Warden can call Time-Out in Sector HS.

5) Nobody wears pink, except the pinkos.
6) Every hunter must have a ticket or pay the price: Mandatory yellow vest in the Open Zone, one hour for each infraction.
7) Bag limits shall be set by each hunter's ability to carry game from the sector. Bag your limit and flee.
8) All kills carried out by cube, rack or tow. Foul kills on ledges or in ravines for pinko pick-up must be tagged (tagging darts okay). Foul kill fees will appear on next month's statement.
9) Sector HS Game Warden Sonny Wayne Wyoming reserves the right to refuse admittance. No flak jacket, no service.
10) Nature is sacred. Untagged foul kill, an expired ticket or real-death experience will cancel all entitlements divvy.
11) Death shall be final in the sector with no exceptions, except by special dispensation from the High Republican.
12) The High Republican, himself, shall enjoy the great outdoors and the thrill of sport on a very special Executive Holiday Weekend at HS. Time and date to be announced.

Catch and release would be pointless and inappropriate.

There you have it.

Let the game begin.

II

Damage Control

With opening day set for Tuesday, the Ad Hocs argue to the wee hours on appropriate points for right thinking. Republican leaders thank Hard Luck for Divine Guidance.

HumanSport may slow the SD (Swelling Deficit) on a future of not so many. But if costs outpace revenues, as birthrate exceeds Collective Bag Limit, what about that? Pundits peruse and project, agreeing that the Republic must prevail. Murmuring fades on agreement that failure cannot happen.

What could go wrong?

Who the heck is asking?

The Ad Hocs get stuck on twisted logic and agree that it's time for a break. Can opposing viewpoints be so right and wrong? Can two sides claim the most appropriate values? Accusation and infighting ebb and flow, until dominance and submission are one. Backflows and eddies ripple the shallows on both banks, but out in the middle, the river of LIFE flows tranquil. Will still water peter out or head over the falls?

The resistance has the votes to defeat the measure—if a spokesperson will risk speaking the unspeakable: that the Senate of the United Sectors of America has outgrown its britches. Are you crazy? We're talking diehard constituents shooting each other dead! This HumanSport thing will boil down the base!

Party stalwarts sense another hoax to threaten party unity. They will not cower, not now or ever. That so-called logic wastes time and confuses the many. Any Republican legislator who dares to oppose the High One will lose Republican National Committee campaign funding and face a primary challenge. Capiche?

Hush their mouths, until Senator Dusty Dwayne "Hop Along" Cassidy of Salt Lick Sector steps up to throw down for the truth we hold dear. "I am the only Republican against this harebrain scheme," Dusty Dwayne goes from soft spoken to oratorical for the key question: "Save the Republic? The Republic is greater every day! Lines and traffic are a small price to pay for THE LIFE, liberty and chasing what we love. We fought and died for the freedom to shop till you drop, which isn't free. Any old errand out and about, you see a jerk change altitude—no signal! A psycho neutralizes your chargers. Pile-up makes you fightin' mad!"

Dusty Dwayne resets, downshifting again. "Golldarnit, it's folks, with hopes and dreams and home teams to root for. Every hour is rush hour. Hard Luck knows we got retrieval systems on overload. So what? The crush motivates new tech. I'm hearing that many will soon stay dead, backlogged to expiration. Isn't that better than blown away in a family theme park?"

On rhetorical pause, Senator Cassidy scans the poker-face gallery for feedback or kickback. Only murmurs roll from the aye side to the NaySay. A political future can hang on a single quote. Just so, the sage senator bellows, "My fellow Americans!" But no sooner does United Sectors Senator Hop Along Cassidy kick into a gallop than he blinks at a dry rattle nearby.

Ray Rogers, nine-termer from Western Heritage Sector, looks like a High Republican. Silver sidewalls frame the granite face, sculpted from Republican wisdom. In epic existence, he grants a moment for absorption: stern smile, perfect teeth, bright eyes and bronze skin. Interrupting Hop Along Cassidy at full stride, Ray Rogers rises to extoll the virtues of values and vice versa verily trumping any doubt or claim on who'll be the next High Republican. Verging on candidacy for decades, Ray Rogers has declined to challenge the High Republican. Would he? "Too many is the problem. The sporting solution seems harsh to a few lily-livered, liberal-leaning leftists, but the many just might swallow hard for National Defense, Security and Freedom to keep the Homeland free! Like the High Republican says: Reality calls for real rules."

Murmurs level on consensus. With no further discussion, the vote is taken. Senate Bill 2084 establishes the National Recreation Park HumanSport, where the many may enjoy ultimate sport to enhance THE LIFE we hold dear.

Just that suddenly, it's done! Or rather it begins. On a collective gulp the many takes comfort in the redeeming character of sport, and that's how warpanal plays it.

Senator Rogers submits more daring rhetoric on a taxidermy clause. "Now, a lawn all tore up ain't much worse than half tore up. Two loads o' protein ain't much harder to swallow than one. When you get down to it, pain and suffering ain't no different from suffering and pain. We ought to go ahead and get the gall bladder, too, long as we're in there." The Rogers Addendum calls for optional taxidermy with ten percent off and a Virtue Boost of .085 to those pledging busts before entering. This meander spins positive on jobs, revenue, growth and much, much more.

Freeze-dried busts will be a lasting tribute to sport and America. High-Q busts—Q-4.5 or better—will be honored in plastic replica in twelve-, twenty- and thirty-six-inch models, or special-order custom sizes from the sector gift shop. All remains can be beautifully rendered and shipped to family, friends or admirers for three easy payments from one ninety-nine ninety-nine plus S&H, which is affordable. Net revenue on taxidermy and plastic replicas will be split fifty-fifty between the Republic and the heirs and/or assigns. The plastic replica offer holds for any body of no Q, middling Q or a high mucky-muck. "This too shall generate," Rogers proclaims.

Bickering seems unavoidable these days, and the NaySayers cry out that special discounts on park admission exceed a hundred percent, calling the Rogers scheme insolvent from the get-go.

Daryl Dale Dalrimple says it's the same kind of turnip squeeze that got us in this pickle in the first place.

Never mind; Rogers finagles the votes on his taxidermy addendum on a compromise caveat. To wit: celebrities in HS shall donate busts by law and receive no discount. Celebrity status shall be any Q over .001. Celebrity busts shall sell at a market-rate ratio of average-bust price over Q times the Cost-of-Living Index for valuation in direct alignment with overhead and THE LIFE.

Daryl Dale Dalrimple shouts down this so-called revenue potential and makes his move. That is, the distinguished Senator from Cracker Sector jumps in, as only a five-term Republican stalwart can do. "Now why in heck would a Q-ed-up mucky-muck with plenty of money go risk getting his head shot off in the first place?" Daryl Dale's doubts meet silence. With uncanny instinct for change in momentum, he bellows the follow-up: "Well, why would he? Or she? Or whatever?" Resolute as a lone tackler in the red zone, he dares a challenge.

Wait. What's that sound? It's Ray Rogers, coming on like a sharpshooter at full gallop on the high plateau. He fires back, "Q goes up. Q comes down! Q-down is what'll bring the high mucky-mucks. Chalk up the score! Nobody wants to be a nobody!"

Senator D^3 chuckles, "Well, Sir. I expect most folks in Cracker Sector want to set crosshairs on a joker or two."

What the . . .

Senator D^3 raises his trademark wry eyebrow, and the point is won. Oh, Hard Luck! Those boys from Western Heritage and Cracker Sectors did it again, tag teaming on a smoke out and flush to blow the NaySay to smithereens, proving yet again that Republican wit and charm beat NaySayer browbeating every time.

Sources disclose to *USS News* that remaining differences will be resolved in recess; the United Sectors Senate is loaded for bear!

"I believe the many appreciate this extraordinary effort so far," says Senator Lester Phug, eight-term Republican from Southeast Hominy Sector. Phug is the only U.S. Senator ever elected from Southeast Hominy with solid support in the red hills *and* the low coastal regions. He's also the only U.S. Senator with a wife younger than the youngest wife of Hop Along Cassidy, distinguished Senator from Salt Lick Sector. The distinguished Senator from Southeast Hominy praises the distinguished Senator from Salt Lick Sector for years of public service, and the gavel bangs for recess.

It won't be long now.

"This is a trying time, a time for leadership in uncharted territory. We must fight the good fight, on land, on the sea, in the air. We have nothing to fear but fear itself," says Senator Rogers from Western Heritage, in a statement widely analyzed as supporting the recess and therein the spirit of compromise.

The High Republican's prepared statement in re: the Ray Rogers Taxidermy Addendum hits the monitors for subliminal ingestion during the recess. The High Republican takes the vague road, insulting one subculture or another along the way. The many love his wit! Warpanal calls him incisive: *Giving Q to the many would be like giving wine to grapes. We can't do that, unless we can. We can give them something. I don't drink. You know that. Or drugs. Cocaine. I tell the truth. It's unbelievable. Fantastic.*

Sector delineation and anointment of Wayne Wyoming followed by sudden recess and rules resolution lead painlessly to the next phase: Rules in Appropriate Language.

Meanwhile, insta-read data shows the many anticipating HS Opening Day more than any regular-season opener in memory.

Rumor abounds. Could rimball season be postponed? Speculation solidifies when unsolicited electropulse on random topics in peak VU hits 20-25. That's double minimum for perceived truth to equal true truth. Warpanalyst Fuzzy Bollinger says, "Postpone rimball? What, are you nuts? It'll never happen!"

It happens, but only for a week and only because Wanda Ann McGunty, aging fitness queen and staunch Republican provocateur, greases her old AK 91 slow and easy. Stroking the long, blue barrel, she winks at OneEye like they have an understanding all their own, which they do. It was love at first sight from the moment Wanda Ann turned home liposuction to gold on a major market share of the diet/surgery segment with her amazing fitness program: *Freedom from Body Fat Isn't Free.*

Deliberate and sanguine as a founding father, she hikes her weapon over her shoulder and strides from her stretch cube to Sonny Wayne Wyoming's registration desk, where she casually intones the monumental truth that every man, woman, child and everybody else on Earth knows already and loves hearing again. “I’m Wanda Ann McGunty. I’m here to make a few bucks and have some fun.”

Turning to OneEye, she winks again, not like a Warpanal woman playing one-up with a hapless guest, but like a woman who can win the west one more time. “I’m here to do my part for the Republic and the many. I’ll bank on the Hard Luck Guy any day, see your thirty-two hundred and raise you another thirty-two.” She grins the old, familiar grin, effusing warmth and humor, a pillar of Republicanism in any subdivision or condo living room. Turning back to Sonny Wayne Wyoming, she says, “Give me four days, sodbuster. You heard me. I said four!” Warpanal whispers that Wanda Ann is taking four days to set a standard, to prime the pump and get things rolling. Leave it to Wanda Ann to prove that patriotism is as ramrod rigid on a Q-up as it is on the way down, easy as you please. Confiding again to OneEye with that sunrise grin of hers, she says, “If two days is good, four days must be better. Ain’t that right?”

Sonny Wayne ain’t no sodbuster. Any durn fool knows there ain’t no sod in Wyoming, and he doesn’t appreciate the levity at his expense, but Wanda Ann McGunty is bigger in LIFE than anything he’s seen on or off the warp. Shrinking under her massive shadow, he inks her receipt and mutters a humble welcome.

Wanda Ann is first Q in and far from .001. OneEye follows her every move, panning each ridge and crackling crease of her chiseled face, practically mining the deep vein for more humor, more warmth, more love. Wanda Ann makes you glad to have her on your side—not to mention having your back. A farm girl from MidSector who grew up to full potential, she evokes reverence and gratitude for a great Republic. Slinging gear on her own broad shoulders, never you mind, thank you, she moves out from Sonny Wayne’s desk, stops and looks back to OneEye. “Look out, children,” she says. “Wanda Ann and ol’ Blue Lightnin’ are goin’ in to put some meat on the table.”

Wanda Ann approaches the line with a Q.672 but every frequency on the warp shows the Quelator box in the corner soaring in a dozen paces to .675, 689, 693, 708 (!), 726, on up to Q.766. Warpanal agrees: never has Q risen so far so fast. They analyze through the night, giving HumanSport the kind of coverage you can only pray for. The Hard Luck Guy in heaven must be smiling on the New Great Experiment, they say, speculating to the wee hours on Qs across this great land of ours. What other high muckaroos will be drawn in to avoid the sheer negativity potential of staying out? Why, this could be better for GNP than another war!

Meanwhile, sundown on HS is still and serene as a distant planet, except for nineteen billion fans, give or take a half bill, who watch this sea of tranquility through OneEye. They share the tension fans live for; this is pre-game. Stretching his neck like never before for nuance and emotion in each minuscule movement, OneEye catches it all, from the spark in Wanda Ann’s eye for the sheer happiness of another great day waiting over the horizon. It’ll begin right after some shut-eye. Many imagine the same spark arcing amino acids and electrons on a similar moment aeons ago, when Adam gave a rib, so he could have an Eve.

At Wanda Ann’s level of greatness, camping out with OneEye seems natural as wearing sox to bed in a wasteland. With no pads, no ready warmers or perfeclime sleeper bubble, she alone camps in a clearing under the stars. “Why wouldn’t I soak up a little fresh air and starlight?” She grins, turning in, as cozy with the nineteen billion as if making room right there beside her. Slightly more than half watch her magnificent slumber through the night.

She rolls out at sunrise to a viewing audience that swells like a time-lapse pregnancy and quickly exceeds ratings for any playoff in history. With trademark gumption, she tells OneEye and home viewers that all she ever asked of the Republic or the Hard Luck Guy was a sporting chance. She moves directly to the two-minute stretch and *Wanda's Wake Up*, known by heart around the world. Speaking softly, she leads ten billion devotees with, "And a one. A two. You can do it." Ad-libbing with her signature good cheer, she asks, "Oh, Hard Luck, is this a beautiful day for sport or what?"

OneEye drifts over Wanda's warm-up and cool-down routines. Firing up her campercaffer, she regreases Blue Lightning till he glistens in the morning sun. A single droplet of oil dangles from the barrel like the first dewdrop at the beginning of time.

Whispering excitedly, Erika Swain calls it one of the great moments in sport anticipation.

Warpanal worldwide disagrees on the approach Wanda might take. Some say she'll keen on oldies to minimize loss of LIFE in terms of years remaining and to demonstrate the consequence of advancing age with no speed or alacrity, resulting from insufficient aerobic input. She stands for sufficient input and more.

Some say she'll take the greater challenge, young'uns with speed, quickness and rapidity, thereby proving the value of her *Full Freedom From Fat Program*, which happened to go on sale this week. Wanda Ann McGunty is a pillar of Republicanism. Filial duty, paternal reverence and a right lively market share are the building blocks of the Wanda Ann franchise.

Some say she'll simply play the game fair and square, because that is who she is.

OneEye doesn't miss a lick, morphing macro on a shrub, then going in till leaves delineate, and among them trembles a timid visage behind a barrel, humble pate bowed in obeisance to Hard Luck. Wanda Ann's risk inside HS is a touchy subject. Perceived as nearly risk free, she can't generate a line in Vegas and mere mention of probability lights the squeamish VU brighter than coverage of the great sewage treatment failure of '66.

Speculation on Wanda's possible demise seems incidental to who'll be the hapless sportsperson She'll bag first. Erika Swain assesses insta-readouts and intuition; the numbers don't lie but can miss the truth of a thing. Erika Swain won't miss.

Erika profiles those sportspersons most likely to end this opening day of Sector HumanSport in Wanda Ann's bag. She eases tension with calmness and a dash of deliberation. "It's simple. If you have tenants, you want a woman or a nonspecific with womanly bias. Your nightmare tenant is usually a young man in hormonal crisis. I'm not being chauvinistic. Anybody wants to end a nightmare. Look out, boys. Besides, those fellows have natural athletic ability, which is the more sporting target. Nobody wants to see Wanda overpower anyone. We all want good, clean sport."

OneEye finds the prey, the likely and the not so likely, hunkered in. Some cower as Wanda carries her tarcaff and Blue Lightning boldly from her campsite to the near precipice. "Who in their right mind would want to be in there now?" Erika whispers. "I guess you need heroic odds, if you want to be a hero."

Wanda takes her time, sipping and sighing, "Barkwell Tarcaff gives me rich aroma and fine flavor." You can't blame her for making a few bucks on the side. Wouldn't you? She glances and nods yonder at Sonny Wayne Wyoming sitting on his porch like a man worried he might not get it right. All he has to do is fire his starting pistol at six a.m. on the button and divide history into two parts, before and after HumanSport.

OneEye follows her glance at Sonny Wayne and comes back for her good-natured quip, "Q.3 He *better* get it right." How the many love her. Not a care in the world but a good cup of tarcaff on a beautiful morning and a joke about a gamma normal thrust to greatness. "Hey. You got to see this view for yourself. It's so darn beautiful. It lets me know in a Sector 00 minute what I'm playing for." OneEye peers with her across the ravine as the sun rises.

Sonny Wayne fires his pistol.

Wanda Ann looks up, looks over, finishes her tarcaff and says, "It's showtime." Close-up on warmth, reverence and love, she turns, takes a step and . . . *BLAM! BLAM!*

Wanda is hit! Wanda goes down.

A small, round figure, covered head to foot in camo-fatigues, zigzags, somersaults, dodges and dives to the edge of the cliff, then rolls Wanda sideways and takes cover behind the body as the fusillade pummels Wanda Ann.

She twitches like a rag doll on a live wire.

OneEye zooms close.

The figure plays it safe, by the book, pulling a rag and bottle from its pockets. The contents of the bottle go onto the rag. The hand reaches over. The rag covers the face of Wanda Ann McGunty.

A collective gasp fills the airwaves. Wanda Ann is bagged six seconds into the official opening of Sector HS. With a ruddy tarcaff blush emblazoned on her rock-hard face, she's dragged by the heels, foot by firefighting foot, out of the skirmish.

Back in scrub cover, the bagger rises to reveal nothing—full fatigues, ski mask and sunglasses. Wanda gets hoisted onto a hood rack and driven out. She gets bled, dressed out and stuffed quicker than Tut, and for want of prior directive on the status, disposition and display of high mucky-mucks, she goes on display at the HS Warm-Up Burgers joint, of all places.

Who's hungry? The frikkin' stitches are dripping. The holes are showing! Hard Luck . . . But entry and exit wounds really ring the bell on the reality aspect of the thing, and consensus murmurs: Cool!

Maybe some fries and a Baco Double Cheezy Thang'll hit the spot after all. What the hey. We're here!

Janitor Jock Jacoby scrutinizes a few wounds and says, "Ain't none o' my business, the right and wrong of it, but *somebody* ought to enjoy Wanda Ann, after all she give. Why the heck not?"

That's a tough question the many is often willing to ponder. But this feels stranger than reality ought to feel. Everyone wants to be free of the over-pop nightmare, but this hardly feels refreshing. A Jumbo Cola Slush might help, but still . . .

The world watches the dream. Wanda Ann has brought home the long and short of ultimate sport in America. Numbing loss makes time stand still. Realization will take forever, or so it seems with the analysis, subanalysis, analysis analysis and continuing speculation on meaning in every tense.

Benefit to the many is conjectural, as the gristle is chewed for predigestion. Praise for Wanda Ann and shock over her demise jolt the airwaves. Bios, parental bios, film credits, aerobic contributions, political influence and daily routine are listed, relisted, scrutinized, assessed and praised again. Warpanal speculates on misfits in the Park. That'll darn sure lead to double whammy loss for the HR. Misfits are soon discounted. Security is too tight.

This is not a war, unless it's war they want. We can give them a war. I'm a wartime Republican. We can show them destruction, the likes of which the world has never seen. By Hard Luck, we can show them! But, really, it's a game. If Wanda Ann's Ultimate Sacrifice can make her country great again, we've done very well. Sport is like war. We feel no personal hatred for our opponent or Muslims or Jews in general. Mexicans. Black people. I never said that. We want to protect our great country from threats. You think that's wrong? We want to win. What makes sport great is that the home team can lose. This loss is different. This giant among women, Wanda Ann McGunty, will enjoy eternal greatness, free at last from a busy schedule. It's really something. She was fabulous and still is.

Warpanal is nonstop for days and nights. Early morning talk and daytime talk flow seamlessly to primetime and late-night talk.

They talk and talk from Wanda Ann's adorable youth through her rise to greatness to her last curtain call. From the messy aftermath of a quick bleed and stuffing, she taxis out full torso, with muscle tone and skeletal balance to inspire the many. Neck tendons to sinews, veins to washboard abs, Wanda Ann is a role model rotating on Lazy Susan. HS management moves her up the road from Warm-Up Burgers to the Main Reception Center.

Some want a frequency dedicated to Wanda Ann so she can rotate across this great land of ours 24/7. It won't pencil out, but thirty days of nonstop tribute on the 24/7 fitness channels—with some amazing additional discounts on her latest workouts—demonstrate Wanda Ann's massive contribution. She is soon perceived as a pilgrimage destination. This nuanced move may be a commercial plug for the Main Reception Center, a money loser since opening. Who cares? The news cycle begins on tentative talks of a Pudland negotiation. Woohoo! Pudland! At HS!

"Wanda Ann proves that hard work pays off infinitum," says Erika Swain. "It's a shame Wanda can't be around to enjoy this. She's dead and worse yet: taking thirty-six shots with two to the kneecaps and toxic brain trauma, she'll remain retrievable for another month. The many agonize. *USS News* is a wholly owned subsidiary of Bunghauser Deuche."

Some want her back. Some vow revenge on the sportsperson who didn't have the decency to pass on Wanda Ann, especially in the opening moments when nobody knew if the game was on. Casting a shadow over the land, the foul mood seeps like effluent from a wore-out drain field.

The High Republican asks, *What's new? It's a game. People tell me it was fair and square. That's how Wanda played! I loved Wanda more than anyone. She was terrific. Fantastic. Still is!*

A guy in the third row of the briefing room cries, "Come on!"

You're nasty, says the High One. *You're a terrible reporter!*

The guy calls back, "Hooey! You're nasty and terrible!"

A High Republican, who many of the many see as Hard Luck's emissary on Earth, doesn't need that noise, and responds with a huff, *I'm outa here!* He's outa there.

Some demand immediate shutdown of HumanSport.

Administration pollsters point out that most complainers are card-carrying NaySayers. Who listens to that? Demands for Wanda Ann's retrieval fade to Naysay whimpers. Wanda Ann hated the NaySay; "They're so durn negative!" The many soon agrees that she rests easy on Lazy Susan and in history, still terrific.

As the collective gasp fades to acceptance, her LIFE is scripted for a Major Motion Picture Event starring Charleton Heston. The High One praises brilliant casting. *Your Federal tax dollars working hard, like you do. It's going to be beautiful.*

That is, Charleton Heston may be past one-sixty but thawed, fluffed and revived with the miracle of Extreme Retrieval (severe shelf-life may apply), he's ready to go. Heston challenges fairness among the many, who grouse and grumble that he gets to come back from dead, but what about them? Changing the ad hominem undercurrent from ebb to flow, the crumbling thespian asks, "Fair? I'm decomposing. Is that fair? You decide. While you're at it, stay clear of my cold, dead hands, or I'll shoot you quicker than Wanda Ann would have done!"

He doesn't look all that bad and still has the old magic, masterfully redirecting with, "Wanda was a real game gal who wouldn't want it any other way. She was a credit to the Republic. She loved the Republican. We love her, and I'm proud to get the part. I pray I can play it well." Heston laughs when asked if aerobic scenes will require a stunt double. "Heck, yes," he scoffs. "This bag of bones can't even fool Spandex. With production costs running twenty-eight million dollars a minute, you bet we'll use a double. I want to show the real Wanda Ann." Nobody doubts the miracles of simulacron electroputty or facial duplication. "She'll be back in your living rooms all right."

Wanda settles into permanent exhibit with OneEye on every move. Home viewers follow the action for a month. The next month brings confusion over death and expiration dates—and a new bill in Congress: *WHEREAS* human LIFE delineates on sperm launch and vaginal ingress on the one hand, it should not be squandered on a retrieval caveat because of a stupid game on the other.

Let's face it: they brought Charleton back long after the so-called deadline, and LIFE is a sacrament of the Hard Luck Guy. Wanda Ann shouldn't get short shrift on a crowd-thinning policy, huge as she is.

But the Ad Hocs emerge from closed session with a special ruling that dead is dead in Sector HumanSport, and that's no caveat; it's a fundamental ground rule as stated right off the bat.

But so is special dispensation by the High Republican, who is besieged with special-case retrieval requests on this one—just this once! It's Wanda Ann!

Often calling for a get-even approach to trade, treaties, tariffs and the tar brush, the High Republican draws a line: *Wanda Ann is a hero. She died for the Republic. She did more for HumanSport than any other Republican. She stepped up for four days and paid the price. You did not. Who are you? You want to mess it up? Give me a break! Besides that, Charleton Heston has about as much time on the clock as a bag 'o fertilizer in April.*

Warpanal agrees; the High Republican had no clean path on this one. Political blood is let, and with blood-and-guts exposure, nonstop praise and a Major Motion Picture Event, retrieval could be catastrophic, shattering hopes for HumanSport.

Wanda Ann turns, steady as Earth. A produce mister keeps her in a light sweat. Hard-driving aerobic music with heavy breathing make her real. With a willing mind and an open heart, the many can jump, swing and twist along, hearing her call: "You can do it! Come on. And one! A two! All the way. Looking good. And five!" Viewers can pump the jam, give a hundred ten percent and feel that special feeling.

Erika Swain tears up. "Wanda must still enjoy the show."

The one who bagged Wanda Ann, a huge fan, remains anonymous, granting only shadow interview with voice modulation. "I knew it was Wanda, pretty as a buck woman ever was, looking across those plains, proud as you please. She heard the starting gun. Don't think for a minute she didn't know what was up. She was loaded for bear, her and old Blue Lightning. You think it would have gone different with me in Blue Lightning's crosshairs and her in the bush? Heck, she savored the sweetest moment of THE LIFE.

She didn't care about danger. Now she's immortal, living free forever in the wasteland of our minds. You think it was easy, holding her on the cross and squeezing off gentle? I was so excited. I took her at the knees, two shots, quick as double skeet. You don't think I was scared? Could she have rolled and recoiled to put me dead center on two quick shots of her own? I wanted her unspoiled for the taxi and dress out and display? Shoot. She had a shot. She coulda toppled over the edge for all that foul-kill fuss. She didn't. She crumpled right there, like she knew. She knew. I finished her with chloroform. She deserved the soft kill. Imagine how I felt, all those yahoos pumping her full o' lead. Shameful. Then tooling into Reverie with Wanda Ann laid across the hood, chest up? Jeeminy Christmas."

Reverie, first exit out of Sector HS, was a sleepy burg in the foothills last week. This week, after Sector HS reclamation, it still is. The difference now is volume. The economic base of recharging, burgers and colas remains unchanged, but now it booms. No longer a grease spot on the high plateau, Reverie is now a quaint example of how THE LIFE can find room for growth. Heavy traffic by-passed Reverie for years, even with The Trees and miniature golf only minutes away. Traffic veers to Reverie now, thanks to Sector HS. Prosperity is on Reverie like grit on growth. Developers stroll the main drag with clipboards and vision. Word has it: Four electron domes will go up quick. This is only the beginning.

The sportsperson who bagged Wanda Ann is a native Reveriean, born and raised. The no-count burg of hardly half a million will not divulge identity; no background profile, no parental or teacher bio, no former classmates or neighbor opinions, no nothing but speculation. Warpanal sleuths track a cold lead on a Reveriean who says "Jeeminy Christmas?" The cold lead turns to permafrost when half the homefolk spew the same creepy phrase on every eye-opener. Then they scratch the old brainpan.

On the bright side: the Wanda Ann exhibit is a shot in the arm to Reverie. Just off Exit 1293, Reverie pulls them in for the same burgers, colas, Cola Slushes, Cola Slush Supremes with or without fries, tourist info, recharging and sit-downs with the same convenience. Now the place has drama and impact like Late Breaking News and This Just In. Reverie thrives.

The High Republican murmurs: *Reverie is fantastic. Amazing.*

The one who bagged Wanda Ann remains in shadow and audio warble in fear of reprisal and outrage. A no-count nobody made global news with an interview and speculation out the wazoo, all at Q.00? Wha? That can't be! But it is.

The heavily wrapped assassin in silhouette speaks through a modulator. Q won't stay low for long, or will it? Resentment surges on Emotion VU, as the bagger discloses diagnosis of dissinoma, a degenerative condition indicated by nagging misanthropia with bouts of acute loathing, aimless aggression, hostility, claustrophobia and episodic eczema. Since bagging Wanda Ann in Sector HS, the bagger's symptoms vanished.

Glued to every word, the many wonders. Who the heck is this?

Resentment VU softens on disclosure and again on symptoms clearing. Rambling fast but sure-footed over youth in the wasteland, the bagger glances at the VU panel as Curiosity and Possible Interest glimmer. Reflecting on the High Republican and Corollary 1: *Attitude is all we have*, the bagger says, "It's so true." Closing with confidence, the bagger promises to disclose gender and degree of specificity and to cancel voice mod in follow-ups. If perceptions improve, says the bagger humbly, actual identity will be next.

Curiosity and Certain Interest VU flash and darken, flash and darken, and the first interview is over. Now, this:

Warpanality Tonight hostess Whispy Fendlemin calls it a very, very effective foundation for Q. The bagger disappears from the airwaves, from the hohum and memory. The bagger had risen to why, where, when and how follow-up and extraordinary Q-in.25 on a single interview. Like a nine-ball perched on a lip, the bagger had only to drop in the pocket from Q-in. to the real McCoy. At .25, Warpanalysts and talent scouts lend an ear—with endorsements just around the corner. Breakfast cereal? Plastic shoes? Polyflak jackets? It isn't for nothing when Whispy Fendlemin goes very, very. A single appearance and kerplunk, the bagger is guaranteed talk along with worthy opinion, good seats and the works.

But does the bagger resurface? Nada. What happens? Q-in .43.

Some call it a ruse. Q-in levels at .35. Some say the bagger strains the issue. Q-in fades. It surges on a rumor but sinks like a stone instead of a nine ball, over and out. Some say a studio staffer working the first interview bagged the bagger. Wanda fans are legion. Sector HS and ultimate glory are one thing, but Wanda Ann embodied ultimate hope, showing the world that a woman can walk like a man and still look terrific.

A nonrenewable resource like Wanda Ann McGunty going extinct is not good for the many. Who can replace her rare magnificence? "I don't know about you," says Fuzzy Bollinger, "but I can tell real sweat from glycerin mist. This torso exhibit is fine for saps who didn't love Wanda like we did. Like the little mole with the two hairs at the top of her thigh. Where is it? Are we supposed to forget the mole? Come on. I'm not knocking ultimate sport, but let's get with it!" Fuzzy underscores collective sadness. In a prepared statement, the Echelon calls Wanda Ann a pioneer hero. Her torso raised standards for all high-Q taxidermy. The statement doesn't mention the mole but announces a taxidermy extension to the knees. The mole and small hairs growing out of it show predominantly in sketches leaked to the warpanal news corps. Pervs will see the crotch and buttocks covered tastefully, with no butt crack or bush hairs, except for the two in question.

The Pudland negotiation ends when Bunghauser Deuche buys the torso and moves it to the Pudland Theme Park three exits out.

Reverie goes back to sleep.

Now the many can view Wanda Ann in person, absolutely free, once inside the park, with better access to rides and refreshments including Pudmizer, the beer that doesn't make you pee. *We're proud to squeeze your pud.*

Cut to Pudmizer ad: three frogs guzzling to full bloat. One belches, *Pud* . . . The second belches *My* . . . The third belches *I don't have to pee. Do you?*

Fade to Pudmizer logo: a winged bladder shaped as a swollen P, in flight.

Fade to George Longley profile, hold, and fade out.

III

Billy Moline

Now and then, while stretching, Billy Moline gains insight to the hohum. It's a brief glimpse, and he's grateful. Who wouldn't be, stretching at odd intervals, vegging out on a gurney with snacks, colas and Pudmizer?

The hohum is more. Immersed in alpha saturates on a lazy afternoon, fifth rush hour winding down, Billy can open a window and know nothing. Feeling that wholesome anesthesia, free of stress, distraction and coordinates, his pond shimmers, ripple-free. This is essential hohum. The steady buzz of traffic headed home signals all's well. And he's at that point in every hour, where the story he's watching will soon resolve, or he'll change the channel.

Why would a monk spend years in deprivation, seeking light, when he can get it on a plush gurney with a cold cola and a world-record pee coming right up? Let's face it; a man has to pee sooner or later, even drinking Pudmizer. World records are falling like never before, and Billy feels a player's chance coming on.

He feels THE LIFE in carefree splendor, a blip here, a synapse there, a line or a gag sliding off his nonskid brainpan like hot links off Scrofulon. Billy M feels no friction. In an hour, the Thursday night line-up begins. Next week hovers like a great adventure about to cast off from the dock: the playoffs.

Could he improve a perfect moment? What more could a man want? Come on, Billy, sky's the limit. He laughs, knowing the answer. It doesn't take a world record to feel pretty darn good about a pee, and he has a great pee queued up, along with a reconstituted pizza and the playoffs. So? The answer is nothing. It gets no better. The toilet is flushing like a precision machine, a Big Family Box O' Pizzas waits in the drybox; Thursday night coming on. THE LIFE looks good, like the sum of the parts and then some. A stray worry buzzes. He laughs again. Cracking his BF Box O' Pizzas'll leave him short for the playoffs. Heck, he can get through on eleven pizzas; he's done it. With the box open, the pizzas vanish. Next thing, it's an hour to tip-off, deep in personal profiles, childhood pals, assault charges, old coaches, nasty girlfriends and their outrageous claims, off-site betting, lingering indictments, aunts and uncles and stuff. It's nitty-gritty good, but he's gotta make a pizza run, and bam, traffic is maximum rush, like everybody cracked their stash early. It's second quarter by the time he gets back, and he missed the opening flavor of the whole darn thing. Sure, he could d-load, if d-loading was legal. Even then, he'd be watching history instead of history in the making. Worse yet, everyfrikkinbody has the game on, spoiling any spoiler alert. Are you kidding? It's play-by-play in the air, want it or not.

Still, a man ought to have a pizza if he wants one. Scientific fact: THE LIFE approaches perfection, beyond that, nowhere to go. It's a vital stat. Reach and be happy. You want more? Have a Coke, a *Pepsi* or a Pud. Better yet, have two BF Boxes O' Pizza on hand.

He doesn't want another Pud and has four minutes to pick Coke or *Pepsi*. He can tell the difference, each a specific feeling. He won't insist like a *Pepsi* fanatic or a Coke fiend and can make do in a pinch. Heck, you drink enough Pud, sooner or later you need to pee. Billy Moline knows these things, as he rises to go pee.

In position, flopped and dangling, he checks his timer: 3:00 p.m. straight up! What a break! Go! 1, 2, 3, 4, 5 . . .

Who but George Longley could come up with a self-absorbing enzyme? Hard Luck, what if George Longley never was? What if everybody never was? Some people think beer tastes sour. The HR said, *Some people think sour grapes taste sour.* What a joker. It doesn't taste sour. Little bit. Sour grapes taste sour. That's funny.

3:01 and 1, 2, 3, 4, 5, ah . . . Not too bad. Anything over a minute is definitely worth the trip.

He hits the gurney refreshed. Keeping with Healthful Watching Habits, he switches ends, changing one buttock to the other and fluffing his pillow for the show everyone's talking about, a rerun of George Longley's second interview ever. It's old, but Billy's into it for personal reasons, if he could get the darn gurney adjusted. Someone should invent a gurney on a big Lazy Susan that would turn one-eighty on a rollover without getting up. They got self-fluffing pillows, drink holders and foldout trays, so why not? Roll and rotate. Billy makes a mental note but tears it up. They tried it, had to. It didn't work, or we'd know. Should he call George Longley on the rotating-gurney idea? Getting George on a talk wave has gotta be way longley. Ha! That's funny. People like to laugh. Hey, why not suggest that they change the name of Pudmizer to America? Nah. Too stupid, but funny. Did they do that already?

They were friends, he and George. They met anyway. Maybe Hector could get through to George. Billy stares up, tired of lying on his side. What he could do with thirty-three billion smackeroos.

George Longley got thirty-three billion from Bunghauser Deuche for the self-absorbing enzyme. He didn't need the money. A zillionaire with Q.8 and only two interviews on the warp, ever, George can gene splice to infinity. He lives for his work, he said, so Whispy Fendlemin pressed him. "Define your work, George. Can I call you George?" She touched his knee.

He flinched; everyone saw it. "You just did."

She grinned, maximum charm. "Define your work, George. In your heart of hearts, what really turns you on?" He flinched again, end of session; George was done. That interview was non-viz by stipulation; OneEye on Whispy while she watched George. Panning was okay to George's knees, so she could touch for drama. She described the action and how it felt, with a melancholy smile, like George, going in-depth on what his knee really felt like.

Billy Moline feels the melancholy. They shared the limelight and OneEye as equals, neck and neck with old Mo. Billy reached Q.28 late in '48, the highest-scoring high-schooler ever, twenty-two points a game at rimball, with a razor-sharp rim at thirteen feet and lethally jagged goal posts. A few superstars of olden times would still be scoreless. Critics called him a one-trick pony, scoring at will from the five-line, bumbling to zero on rebounds. Billy smiled and frowned. "I'm no pony. It's a good trick. I do other things, too."

Fuzzy Bollinger let it be known: "The kid is terrific!"

High scorer of the All-Sector Championship Rimball team gets a call from the High Republican each year in the locker room while the sweat still rolls. Billy got one, electron retrieval generation, but still. It played on local warp, back and forth, Billy and the HR talking rimball, sporting action, right living and values. It seemed natural, like the High Republican was on the other end! It was easy, with so much to agree on.

With Q.28 and a future like no tomorrow, NRA teams bid big for Billy M. The Underdogs, North Northwest offered four mil to sign and twenty-six more over four years. He could have done quadruple that, but the U-Dogs, young and spirited, gave him a feeling, going in.

Thirty-six years later Billy Moline has a different feeling, gazing in sweet sadness. Next week, the finals: Vengeful Warriors of the North versus Bloodsuck Scourge of the East Southeast. Billy's career ended on a head whack. White Robes might have kept him in the game to fifty or fifty-five with bone regeneration and painkillers, pumping his speed and quickness to keep five-pointers launching for years.

The U-Dogs could be on top right now with Billy M dinking fivers, if it was meant to be. It wasn't. Billy denies himself the satisfaction of knowing. Going retro, reverberating event data to the elbow smash on the ocular cortex, is there for input, but he won't punch in. What if glory was meant to be but never was? What if he'd missed it on a random freakish intersect?

The injury caused double vision with dots. "Never mind the dots or doubles, just play," Coach Wyant pleaded. "You see two rims? Shoot left. Gimme 'leb'm points a game; I'm happy. Go under 'leb'm; we shift right."

Billy lives THE LIFE with inner meaning. Maybe shooting left would average eleven points, but he can't shoot left without weighing right, and the critical pause let a defense smother him every time.

"No! No! No!" Coach W echoes down the years.

Billy flinches. Tough love is part of great coaching but could not convert potential greatness to real. A lovely afternoon turns inward and gray. With good intention, all he got was blocked. "I can't . . . I mean . . ." Billy couldn't shoot on time. At nineteen with a waning Q.18 (Q down), he held faith in Hard Luck. Human interest tracked well on his recovery from surgical realignment, reshaping and electroscopic sizzles. The U-Dogs paid that bill, so why the heck not?

One White Robe said the procedure went well. Another predicted double vision in six months. A third predicted death in three months, retrievability uncertain. The fourth said ocular duplicity is better than dead. All counseled thoughts and prayers.

Billy waited years to see single, but destiny faked him out. He lost the ballgame on a bad break. Fading fast as a fall-away jumper to 00.00 by twenty-four, a has-been down to rent and groceries by thirty, an alpha junkie by forty and one more melancholy baby at the big five-oh, he hit the stretch at fifty-four. At least Billy M didn't foul out, and a guy can still dream.

Billy Moline stays in shape, working the aerobic side and hand/eye synch with one goal in mind. He moves—fake, duck and shoot; fake, fake and shoot; fake, fake and fake; fake, fall away and shoot. Billy has it after thirty years of living right and staying fit. Every day is a playoff for Billy M, pitting his best against what might be better yet. A man driven to play both sides of one-on-one found his mark again at forty-five and didn't look back. He wouldn't transmog on a reverb, because mighta been is the same as never was, with regrets. Those buggers never did anybody any good.

Billy M shoots to score. If the rim doubles, he'll split the diff on instinct. The past is gone. Like a record pee goes to another flush, so, too, goes potential. The present is now, not then. THE LIFE, like the game, doesn't tell you who'll win or lose. Billy's a winner with time on the clock; no gut, no handles, no sag, good tone, good heart; let's get it on. More fit at fifty-four than most persons half his age and still good for a fiver in the clutch, he keeps up with Wanda Ann.

The workouts keep him pumped. Too bad about her. Hard Luck works in mysterious ways.

Billy M and George Longley got Q in the same season. *Sports & THE LIFE Illustrated* called them players to watch, shy point guards for technology and sport. Billy's twenty-two-point average got viewed from every angle. When the S&LI guy asked for his secret, Billy said, "Uh . . ." Fans roared and slammed seats, until Billy M said, "I guess . . . I don't know." They romped and howled.

The interviewer turned to George Longley. "Can you genetically duplicate a five-point deadeye?"

George sat across from Billy, mere boys dabbling in brilliance and natural skills far beyond their worldliness. S&LI loved that in an interview. George said, "No. I can't do that."

Fans went mum.

Billy perked up on that note, a one-off, unclonable. He liked George Longley for that. George had recently invented *the chair*, his first breakthrough. He didn't generate sporting excitement but came on strong with logic as yet unimagined. *Getting the chair* took on new meaning with unavoidable truth. Special Reports got the many murmuring to consensus: At last, the guilty could burn.

Nobody wants a murderer getting off, even a perp with Hollywood credits and box office returns. NaySayers spewed their usual tripe, calling the chair a totalitarian tool and George Longley a pawn, a puppet and a pig. The Echelon bought all rights to the chair, paying George Longley with wealth. The chair gained acceptance on the shy smile of the brilliant young man on billboards, bumper stickers and warp bytes. George's mug as background to the message: *The Chair Knows* didn't seem all that totalitarian.

The chair embraced the seated one with truth and measured degrees of untruth like an antique polygraph. Unlike the polygraph, the chair corrected the matrix. Just for fun, the prodigal youth went analog on a numbered dial with a pointer, to amuse history buffs and show that he could. With artful flourish, the pointer showed morphic convergence, un to truth. George Longley said the chair merely measured RNA replication of cells shaded with untruth.

The High Republican surmised. *What a terrific example. Youth working for a better tomorrow. That dial. I watch and see lies, lies, lies. Doohickeys go bonkers. Fantastic! I was a blue-collar-type working guy in those days. Fantastic!*

Old hat now, back then, the chair was hot stuff. The HR called for broad application for the best interests of the United Sectors of America, with Executive Pardon as necessary. Why not?

The chair could supplement lobotomodulation, an effective cure for behaviors deemed inappropriate. Inpatient insertion could modify eighty behaviors with less pain or expense than hard time in the sector hoosegow. It hurt, but you forgot! It was better than dying, which hurt, and you forgot and were dead! Lobotomods activated as necessary, jaywalking to pederasty or any nasty.

The fake lobo scar undermined the hohum. Illegal and immoral, the fake scar seemed as low rent as any scar or tattoo—until the lobotomod look caught on, got chic and ultrachic with festers and loose stitches, oozing blood or yellow goo for occasions.

The chair could out the fakes.

In a scathing exposé, *90 Minutes* outrage sleuth Mike Magnon revealed the alarming spread of fake scars and the chair's ferreting role. Lobotomodule dodgers ran rampant. Hardened criminals as well as the fashion-conscious had false scars, some laughably crooked with peeling rubber edges in garish pastels. The anti-lobotomod movement promoted fake scars, opposing compulsory implant. The echelon wanted insertion at birth as the path to appropriate values with added value: lobotomods could process utility payments on the warp! No more late fees! You're as good as paid up from Day 1!

Fake scars sprang like spore growth, as a style statement and for fun and protest. With his brow brutally gashed by the end of the show, Mike laughed, "I got this for parking tickets. All paid! I don't do that anymore. I'm Mike Magnon. This is *90 Minutes*."

The Echelon issued a statement: Rumors are unfounded. All reports are based on bad data. We will find out what's going on.

The High Republican wondered in prime time: *Can anyone kill the fake scar? Must happen. George Longley's chair will get the truth. I know more about truth than anybody ever knew. Why spend money on anything else? Wasting money is wasteful. It's like my money. Good for you.* The High Republican faded over four billion flickering Doubts and Murmurs.

The Questionable Association VU spelled: George Longley.

George Longley didn't care; The High Republican could get snippy at any golden youth surging with Q.

Besides, Billy Moline was the brighter star then and loved the action. The High Republican said, *Billy Moline will be a credit to any race, creed or color. Five-pointers. A white boy. You think that's racist? I call you a NaySayer. Okay?*

The many chuckled in that long-ago season.

George Longley got follow-up interviews when the HR said mandatory lobotomodule implantation would save a bundle on census, surveillance and wasteful expenditure like the world has never seen. *You want America fantastic again?* Warpanal asked if foreign interests were bearing down, but the HR said no. *I asked. They say no. Why would they lie?*

Erika Swain asked George Longley if he would help the High Republican with government control.

George Longley lowered his eyes. "No, I can't do that."

Erika Swain asked, "Do you mean you can't? Or you won't?"

Poor George hung his head.

"There you have it. I'm Erika Swain with the outrage you need to feel." News buzz on The Chair moved over for newer buzz on the lobotomodule and over-buzz on compulsory implantation and other outrage in short order, until all talk of truth and untruth settled to hohum. The many knew many truths anyway from the outrage, no matter who denied what.

George Longley retained decent Q, showing up on billboards, bumper stickers and mini-bytes to age twenty-eight. Billy M shrank to 00.00 that year, when George unveiled his *Random Event Sampler*, taking him from fade to surge (Q down to Q soaring), to Q.5 in days and worthy opinion when the *RES Home Use Model* came out. The home box gave probability quotients, mini to maxi mightabeens. Assessment mode with easy access and upgrade options made alternate realities knowable on a daily basis, easy as toast and tarcaff. *The Road Not Taken,* sold six billion copies.

Billy Moline did not subscribe.

Decades later, belly up on a vintage gurney, he stares up, at meaning in knotty poly. Can alpha saturation max out?

Whispy Fendlemin prattles over George Longley's latest triumph; Georgie this and Georgie that. Will they ever tire of George Longley's latest triumph?

Who would tire of Billy M dinking fives?

By thirty-five, when most young folk still fumble with career options or more grad school, George Longley brought voice-print genetics to the warp, in the year the Republic achieved 25-inch viewing radius per household, minimum.

George Longley didn't call 25-inch radii maximally short sighted but thought it. His thoughts showed up, putting egg on a few high faces. When he apologized, the High Republican scoffed, *Longley. Virtue and merit. What about manners? My kid? Military school.* Anything over Q.6 meant punditry, rendering opinions worthy and necessary. George hit Q.7 in days.

Then came backlink configuration, readjusting electrons and protons. Tumblers tumbled, and the big door groaned again.

Warpanal concurred; primitive components of holographic electronscan combined with the modified gene splice let George Longley trace recombinants to the source.

3-Hole Magazine went down overnight. Why pay for porn when you can down-tune any celebrity anywhere. Mix in a few associates—known, unknown, who cares? Mix in yourself, if you want to. Choose any kink from the menu or transcribe the code for any of the many from time immemorial, engaged in living 3D. If the many isn't enough, transcribe the Precious Few or the Echelon.

Murmurs abounded. Where would it end? Who would prevent sick minds from transcribing *You-Know-Who* in acts of decadence, indiscretion or worse, perversion? Pornographers rejoiced at celebs doing the nasty in the privacy of anybody's home at popular prices. Any scene imaginable could be punched up! A serving of that pudding made legal minds reel; carnality could be used as proof! Warpanalysts agreed: with traceable events, who needs investigation or analysis? Tail spinning madly, Warpanal assessed the critical need for analysis; must the many know what it's looking at when it's looking at it?

Archivists swooned; in days, George Longley's backlink configuration made any event in time accessible on Lazy Susan with audio and speed control, including pause, reverse angle, slo-mo, close-up and scent-around on a single electron from that event.

Sports & THE LIFE *Illustrated* still offered the complete set: *Violence in Nature, Eruptive Moments of the Past, Friction in Sport* AND *How to Build a Cubeport*, yours in a single electron cap for only three easy payments of ninety-nine ninety-five plus forty-five clams S&H. That market went stone cold-dead overnight. No takers!

The many passed on the past to opt for now, down tuning unregulated transcriptions of the highest Q-ed celebrities of modern times. Billions watched Whispy Fendlemin engage in nonspecific gender play, Wanda Ann getting bagged in HS, George Longley on the toilet—back-linked from a dingleberry! Some hailed George as the most playfully honest Q.74 around.

George shrugged. "Back-link electron manipulation can be foolish and negative in the wrong hands."

Warpanal noted his constraint, but analysis analysis said *anyone* on the pot with billions watching would suffer constraint.

Some thought the Echelon would ease content guidelines in light of new technology.

Some thought the best was yet to come.

Most watched the past unfold in their living rooms, back to Erika Swain, working her way up, back to Fuzzy Bollinger cheating at golf, all the way back to O.J. mincing meat, George W tooting up a fat 'n fluffy Hooverville snoot, the High One, himself, pleading with a contestant, *Come on! Ya gotta help me out here!* Or going raw dog on a porn star and shouting, *Fake backlink! It was shaved!* Quickies were good for a few laughs and groans, but . . . Ho, boy!

In a few days, it was back to the hohum. What could you see that you hadn't seen already? What could you possibly not imagine?

But the very nature of the hohum changed as the many tuned to high-Qs making deals, sniffing iffy places, struggling.

Whispy Fendlemin railed against images of herself sniffing her index finger, swearing she never did and never would, not now or ever, and she hates any smells from below the waist.

Erika Swain said she never used narcotics, not by inhalation *or* intravenously, nor has she worked a casting couch, ever, not once, ever, any more than Herbert Hoover sniffed his index finger. Denouncing this sniveling, heinous prank, she thought disembowelment might be appropriate for the culprit.

The Republic quelled the chaos, licensing ET&T to buy total backlink modulator rights for two point nine trillion. Subscription service hit the market for only nineteen ninety-five per month plus nominal surcharges for color rounders, audio filters and incoming sequencer detectors to filter filth and secure personal stray electrons. Less than six hundred bucks a month for access and security felt like chump change. The many signed up. Why the heck not?

Nobody was surprised when electron piracy surged. The many cried out: the beginning of the end; a challenge to humanity; something more or less. Soon enough, criers faded in the din and watched, easing back to the hohum.

George Longley tweaked the hohum in his first prime.

The High Republican made small ado over electron backlink and its ambitious inventor. In a brief statement he said, *Electron backlink is bad. People are telling me. Terrified the living daylights, showing private lives. Terrible. Nobody wants it. The fool. You won't want it. Not nice. She was nice. She had a daughter. Grew up to be a schoolteacher.* The HR sniffed his finger.

Some said nuts; filter glitch.

The rest gasped, shushed and watched more intently.

Billy remembers and laughs but is drawn sadly inward.

Whispy Fendlemin senses a drifting mind and reaches out to touch his shoulder. "Pay attention, Billy."

Billy laughs again, amused and . . . touched. He likes to nearly feel Whispy's fingers and personal contact.

She calls out, "Hey. Wake up. Let's graft a fun one. Let's see Georgie and the High One, one on One in Sector HS. I'll punch it in. Let's see . . . The High Republican calls Georgie out? Let's go for broke: All's fair. Wait! How about the High Republican wears pink in HumanSport? I mean, shouldn't he? Come on. Let's see what you're thinking. Punch up. Who'll win this one? A buck a vote. Vote ten times. You get paid tomorrow. Don't be so tight, wouldja? And hey, don't go away. We'll be right back with a thriller YOU won't wanna miss after these important messages."

One on One? George Longley and the High Republican? That'll be a humdinger. Billy isn't clear on who to vote for or how many times. Sadder still is the reminder, coming down to one-on-one again, and Billy M is neither one. Heck, it's not so bad. Wiping his eyes, he remembers once upon a time, when Peony Lu Hardaway, U-dog cheerleader, visited in his dreams. She brought the winning spirit to practice sessions those days, loving the game and THE LIFE, leading cheers, ten points down with a minute left no problem.

Peony Lu Hardaway married Danny Blanda, a coach with bedrock fundamentals. Coach Danny had a string of losing seasons but matched Peony Lu's spunk and attitude. She met Danny on the road, away game. Danny's team lost; the U-Dogs won. She went out with him like a good sport and stayed out till Tuesday. Quick betrothal relieved the morality aspect of the situation for both teams.

Billy savors the bittersweet memory and the gap that once separated him from his beloved. It could have been him showing excellent attitude from Friday night to Tuesday afternoon. He only had to ask her. He couldn't—too shy.

He rolls again across that bed of nails. Painful memories remind him that winners don't give up.

IV

The Replay

Peony Lu married Coach Danny Blanda but stayed on to cheer the U-Dogs, commuting three sectors that season. That was attitude with a full pump, beyond mere lip service. Where is meaning without team spirit? Uh huh.

Reduced to injured reserve by then, Billy could only watch his fellow U-Dogs on the practice court or games, offering long-ball tips as necessary. If anybody sensed ulterior motivation on the Peony Lu issue, nobody said boo. He watched and wanted but never whined. She showed up in ocular rehab too, indelible as scar tissue. Like strangers in the night, they passed casually on hello, what a game. U-Dogs united, they cheered, in the bond.

Three babies in six years did not dilute his hopes. At each child, he told her, “Nice play,” faking casual, as his heart throbbed, his chest ached, and he flashed hot and cold.

Peony Lu Hardaway divorced Danny Blanda fifteen seasons in. Danny scored more cheerleaders than winners. She said he had the sexual discretion of a paint mixer. “One of those big bangers who doesn’t care if it’s a pint or five gallons.” She moved back to the North Northwest the year Danny’s contract ended.

Like a dreamer in a bog, Billy feared calling the woman he’d loved, feared that a call could end the dream. A woman might love a five-point deadeye, but who needs a has-been? Better to savor a fantasy than state his love and . . . air ball! What if she laughed in his face? Her? Love him?

Billy still dreamed of poise, timing, altitude and sweet release. He came down smiling in his dream. Forget about it; nothing but net. But call his dream angel? Dream on.

He joined *Electrochem Dating Service—Electrochem*, for optimal matches, because stats don't lie. He met women who could whither confidence in a blink. He'd wanted company and conversation and filled the little vials with sweat, blood, urine and a spermatozoa dribble extracted with indecent imagery as necessary. He answered the questions on psychometric parameters.

Electrosensors churned with hormonal wisdom and Hard Lucky confidence to find his perfect dates. She profiled big, a strapping woman, good for hoops, camping in the yard or drinking Coke or *Pepsi*, regular or diet either one, no biggy. She would like him. She might love him. She would know who he'd been and his former potential. He dated.

She asked about the signing bonus.

That was ages ago.

How much was left?

He came up short: "Uh . . ." Missing easy lay-ups, he shriveled when women viewed him as a sports object. Electrochem shrunk his shorts. Women lusting for a lean, clean, money machine could take their needs elsewhere. Billy loved who he'd been but could neither open up or deliver on base, tawdry needs. What was a man of former greatness and continuing virtue to do?

Two years after Peony Lu's divorce, he thought, *Two years*. He pondered missed openings. No attitude is better than a bad attitude but not by much. It felt nonaggressive, like an iffy biorhythm, until they passed by chance. He saw it coming, like a point guard reading a shift. He could cross over, blur out. Every player tries to read the fake, shot, pass or dribble. *Freeze up*, the phantom whispered. *Why not put it off?* Hopelessly afraid, he looked down, opting to pass. Eye contact would make him weak and end his dream.

She blocked, held firm and waited for the charging foul.

Peony Lu at five foot two profiled perfect as a cheerleader, cute as a pixie with a pixie smile, pixie eyes, a pixie nose and pixie ears, a pixie do and oh, those melons. Billy M thought she populated many dreams, some off-color. But the smut fell away, toe to toe, as she led his favorite cheer without saying a word. She led him home to show him a new cheer.

Some people scoff at a woman focused on kitchen and bedroom. Not Billy. She simmered, looking and smelling better than pig-likes and potatoes alongside two over easy to please, please, please. It seemed like only yesterday that he couldn't imagine Peony Lu taking her shirt off. But there she was, realizing that she'd always loved him, too. Who knew? Slipping buttons, gyrating slo-mo in a cheer of blinding beauty, she looked like a butterfly squirming free of her chrysalis, spreading her wings.

Billy heard a capacity crowd yelling for joy.

Mo was back, the stadium on its feet, the offense pumped.

Sloughing her blouse like a seasoned pro, slipping straps from shoulders, she murmured, "Come and get it, honey. I'm all yours."

He froze.

She smiled at the timorous jock. Billy's shyness was known and lovable. He could give a gal some breathing room without banging her on the head with his you-know-what. Best not get a gal started on that issue. Better to thank her lucky stars on the new issue.

Unhooking the harness, she peeled one side and paused, as if waiting for the crowd to yell, *More!* Peeling the other side, she felt her heft and firmness, leading by example, smiling anew.

He trembled, staring at two of the face he'd loved and two dazzling racks. He wanted the moment to last, but time marches on. The voltage between them recalled a high-school playoff, down by three with less than a minute, plenty of time, but still. A five-pointer made it up by two with twenty seconds left. An interception sealed the deal with a feed to Moline, who looked down, stepped *back* across the five line, let her fly and . . . *Swish!* Twelve seconds to go, up by seven, no way José, the All-Sector Championship in the bag. And there it was again, that eternal moment Billy M lived for, victory secure but not yet booked, because the game was still on.

Gazing on Peony Lu Blanda in their first round of skins and shirts, he wondered which face to kiss, which rack to grasp.

Coach Wyant whispered the face and pair on the left.

Billy leaned in, puckered, opened his hands, closed his eyes, waited and . . . *Swish!* It was nothing but net on Peony Lu. One score led to another and Mo moved in. Showering out at last, he welcomed a post-game wrap-up, marriage and scoring at will on a heady bid for happily ever after.

She got on at Montclair's, utilizing her lingerie skills and rising to lingerie manager. The money helped, with the four-million signing bonus down to chump change twenty years later. Peony Lu's bonus felt natural, in helping women maximize potential.

Billy replays his score daily, even when Peony Lu is tired after work. He says it's okay. "Who showers before a workout?"

She tolerates the replay. He's cute, with his sound effects for the crowd cheering and gasping. A few minutes don't matter and give her time to plan dinner. Sometimes she worries about the kids and the bills, but Billy brings her back with what she knows is a blessing for any woman. He can't get enough. Like a kid with an Erector Set and a learning disorder, he insists on parts fitting where they won't. Peony Lu likes most of it, till she likes some of it. Some days she likes none of it, but browsing a *Cosmo* reminds her that millions of women yearn for her thumping bill of fare. He calls it *the moment* but takes up to ten minutes. He calls her the best quarter of his career and more fun than double-bracket elimination.

She worries: late in the game, no time-outs or money.

"How can you worry about money at a time like this?"

"Lick that ice cream cone till it melts. We'll still be broke."

"Don't worry. I got plenty."

"Yeah, you and George Longley put together are rich." Peony Lu makes that joke with everyone.

Billy doesn't mind her kidding. They're not so broke, and hey, what's this?

Getting along with her daughters is easy. By the time Billy moved in, Rozomon was grown and moved out to her own apartment to everyone's relief. She and her companion planned a small business, a tarcaff stand or burger stop. Success seemed likely for Rozomon, after seventeen years of getting her way.

Marya lives at home but wishes she didn't. She knows she can be hailed as a most startling display of talent this season, working and thinking, scribbling notes, sending files and waiting for word from 00. Confident, she knows the literary greatness waiting in Sector 00 is for those willing to live and lunch there.

As for little Alysyn, who can complain? She wakes the household, cavorting in the driveway in sunrise cheers when Danny shoots a few on his way out to look for a new job. She cheers for Billy, too, during afternoon practice. She loves the game and understands former potential, cheering for *coulda been* and *ever was*. Little Alysyn has team spirit to share.

Danny Blanda is solid as an ex-husband. His coaching career fell short, but he's still a great guy. Danny and Billy get along like seasoned athletes, with a feint, bounce pass or back dribble.

Billy makes small loans to Danny, because a slump needs support, and Danny's got the spirit, with a "go for it" here, a "nice hustle" there, or out of thin air, "that's attitude." It's easy to see how he and Peony Lu got together.

Rozomon broke up and will move back in.

Danny lost his security job, so he's behind on the old cash flow and needs to hang a while longer.

Billy says Danny is slow but solid on the rudiments, and that counts. Besides, Danny makes the little women happy.

Peony Lu calls Danny stupid and wants to know how long this hang will be? And why can't she and Billy do the replay after dinner, like normal people? Why can't Billy get a job, so they won't need to scrape every month? She hates his alpha soaking. Worst of all, why hasn't anybody yet written a cheer for a woman of forty-nine who can't take it anymore?

Billy says Danny is sure to play out of his slump. The replay is best before dinner, when it's more like half-time entertainment and doesn't mess up the primetime lineup. Earlier is better. They're not so tired. He thought she liked it, and he'll look for a job, something athletic, like in a sporting goods department or sports broadcasting. He could open a rimball clinic or give private lessons or be a rafting guide. New rivers open all the time. With a job, alpha soaking would cut back. "Hey, here's a cheer. Peony Lu! What a scr . . . Uh . . ." He'll work it out, he says, and she can help bring Mo back too. "You got to believe, Peony Lu."

Shedding a tear, she hugs him and wishes to Hard Luck that they'll get through this together.

With his nose in her cleavage, he asks, "Get through this?"

That was fun, but that was yesterday. Belly up on a gurney and gazing at lost potential, Billy sees a flash as fractious to the hohum as a five-point shot with two seconds left, four points down.

He sits up.

Whispy Fendlemin is gone, never to be seen or heard from again. Whispy Fendlemin! Q.what? 5.5? 5.7? Gone forever?

Warpanal will recall her fondly as more lipstick than lips and too thin to profile. Expedience is best in correcting the hohum. But Whispy F gone in a blink?

Never mind! It's Bony Meadrikes on Warpage Tonight. Bony is another shrill split in the rouge, just like Whispy but different. Not too different is best. "Hi! I'm Bony Meadrikes, and I'm back! Okay, here's some fun! I got Hunk Grogan on the line. He's up against Zombie Zoomba for the title and raring to go. Hunk?"

Hunk is plenty upset. Some see him sniff his index finger.

Some think he copies the High Republican.

Some think it's a hoax.

Some stare.

None go away. They stay tuned.

Little Alysyn begins her hunger cheer. "Gimme an S!"

Rozomon at the door yells, "I'm home! Anybody even thinks about a snivel, I'll break yer frikkin' neck! Hey, Billy," she says in passings. "What can you do? Can't live with 'um . . . You know?"

"Gimme an N!"

Marya yells for quiet so she can lose her block. "How can I flow with no supportive atmosphere? I can't . . . I mean . . . Every time, I just . . . need you all to . . ."

"Gimme an A!"

Danny yells that these are not his shorts.

Peony Lu yells from the driveway that she's going full speed, darn it, so hold your horses.

"Gimme an X!"

Sitting face to face with Bony Meadrikes, Billy sees the picture; Whispy was inappropriate, suggesting that George and the HR go one-on-One. The Blanda starting five are back together, as if he, Billy, never happened. But something happened, and a man with double vision is virtually surrounded. What a day.

"What's it spell?"

He's a houseguest who can stay forever with his disability stipend if he wants to, a houseguest with special access to the head cheerleader once a day.

"SNAX!"

Houseguest status isn't bad, unless he thinks of the playoffs and George Longley's success. Then it's bad.

"I can't hear you!"

He stands, pivots and makes the door in three strides.

"SSNNAAXX!"

He slips down the back steps to the practice court between buildings for a few hoops, to offset a niggling curiosity.

"One more time!" The little pixie could blow his rhythm in the low post. "I WANT SSNNAAXX!" Flipping switches for the brook, birds and a mild spring breeze, he freezes, clarifying the commercial he's seen twenty times today. The seed cracks. Faking left and going right on a turn-around jumper with a fallaway from twice five he keeps on falling—and laughing over the resounding swish on two tenths left and the crowd going gaga.

Belly up for the second time in three minutes, Billy M knows: he's going in. He doesn't have thirty-two hundred but can borrow and pay back pretty darn quick with bankable odds on a five-point genius. He can borrow on his half-cube. He can . . .

Heck, he'll earn thirty-two hundred in a morning—in an hour! If he stays, it'll be like overtime, where he never lost a game. Sure, it's been a few years, but athletic prowess is like riding a bicycle. You don't forget. He's going in for the Republic, for the money, for Peony Lu, the girls and the gaga crowd.

"Louder!"

But first he'll go to Hector's, to float a little loan.

V

Getting Out of the House

Corollary 1: We are. Attitude is key. The many fights to the end. It is written and shall be.

So sayeth the High Republican. *We defend the Republic without and within, Under One Roof, for which it stands, with liberty and justice for all who deserve it, against bums and misfits who undermine the hohum we hold dear.*

Misfits got decimated in Wyoming three decades ago, pursuant to the lend/lease conflagration. They went deeper with their canned foods and camo-clothing, in baggy pants and bandoliers, grease and grime, like Rambo. Knitted caps and ratty hair are common. High caliber weaponry is a mark of status. Few bathe. None vote or alpha-soak, go Under One Roof or support the hohum. Civic pride is sparse. Misfits and bums don't go shopping or chat with neighbors.

Bums avow nothing. Most were NaySayers and Democrats, until those affiliations proved worthless. Called Liberal until woke, they rail at the hohum and demand the oh, no. The High Republican makes loose reference: *My opponent, that bum!*

Fans call out, "Ya bum! or "Throw the bums out!"

The High One also calls: *Kill the bums!*

Bummism is frequent fodder for programming defaulting to more of the same, if a first go-round generated appropriately for sponsors. Stable revenue keeps content constant.

Republican Comedienne Binky Stardust does an incredible standup shtick in a Special Presentation. "Take the bums," she opens. "Go ahead. Somebody. Please. Take 'um." Laughter is light. "Hey, how can you tell if a bum's been soaking your warp?" Pause. "Because of fingerprints on the scent-around!" Laughter fills in. "Hey, how can you tell if a bum's on the warp?" Pause. "The resolution VU inverts to plaid!" Tumultuous laughter!

"Okay, I'm walking down the street, and this guy says to me, strange guy, shabby, you know the type, denim, drools, polyfoam cup with coins, guy says to me, 'Hey, lady,' calls me lady. 'Spare twenty-three cents so a bum can get a cup o' tarcaff?' So I stop. You know Binky; always an open mind. I ask the guy, 'You can get a cup o' tarcaff for twenty-three cents?' He says, 'You can if it's already spleened!' Ha!" Binky beams in outrageous tumult and keeps it going, fading to commercials over a zinger: "Hey! How do you make a Bumatov cocktail? Two farts in a bag with a pull-string dipped in thinner! Ha!" And fade over Binky's final yodel; "We got a tuhrific show lined up. So . . . siddown 'n shaddup! No! Go pee! Get your colas. Ha! We'll be right back . . ." And . . . cut to commercials and promo for *Bums in the Basement VI*, coming up, right after *Binky's Night Out—Catch a Falling Stardust.*

What a show! Binky hammers the bums with more laughs than an 8-pak of Pudmizer can hold onto, and it's straight to the bathroom, quick to the kitchen and back to the gurney for another Special Presentation after these important messages.

Cut to commercials. What the hey, you just peed and *Commercials are art*: 21. Production costs are higher than the average signing bonus, and airtime is more than that. So why not? They're good! A hot pizza is steaming up the nose holes—Mm . . . pepperoni and grizzard with red relish! The nuclear antacid is ready to drop down the gob hole to save your sorry guts—two tabs of *Soft Landing with Burnostat*, the gastro-suppresser most doctors recommend if YOU want to eat out of a stadium dumpster and live to laugh about it. THE LIFE gets no better. Why not?

Cut to *Dukeysoft with EZTR D!*, the ingredient most doctors recommend for soft stool.

Cut to the HR, voice-over, profile left, delivering Corollaries with breaks for ad lib. Off the cuff! His fave! So clever!

A pliant Republic airs its humor, until topical fatigue settles on bummism like mildew on day-old donuts in Hurricane Sector. The many see bummism as a joke. But the Special Six-Part Presentation of *Bums in the Basement* on *Republican Playhouse* examines the shadowy margins. The *National Endowment for the Warp* loves substantive mentality and real human meaning in a storyline. But what gives? Why the long face?

Reviews are mixed. A thriller needs sinister sound effects with shrieking and cello. Can an aging couple pose beta normal in daytime, then meet in the basement at night with friends from the subdivision? Does that threaten the hohum? Add liquor, narcotics, smut, railing against the Republic, disavowing weaponry, absorbing no warp and wallowing in moral subterfuge. Now you got some bummism. Some scenes are graphic! Where did these bums come from and how? The many wants to know.

Erika Swain says the Echelon deemed *Bums in the Basement* fair and balanced. "Short on special effects, it captures the hazard of inappropriateness as a gateway to vulgarity. We know what nasty thoughts lead to, and it's good to see the consequence. Oh!" She shimmy-scrunches. "I get the willies thinking about it. That music!"

Millions of women will scrunch and shimmy in the privacy of their own mirrors. Most will chill with the willies, taking a cultural trend from embryonic to fetal by bedtime. Erika lingers in hearts and minds, briefly disgusted before moving beautifully to The News. This just in from the Oval Office:

Cut to the Republican, dreamy profile, hair buffeting in the breeze with voice-over: Corollary 31: *If threatened, we respond.*

Some say yeah, yeah, yeah.

Billy Moline gets dizzy on the spin, either from ocular disparity or too many thoughts bouncing off the backboard. How can people think one thing with the opposite thing on the warp?

"SSNNAAXX!"

He goes back in for his visor, shin guards and polyujac, not that he'd drift under a nitwit's tail wash, but a high-mileage half-cuber plays it safe. He thinks the bum special is thirty-eight minutes of primetime warpage and a terrific dose of entertainment.

"I! WANT! SOME . . ."

He tosses two bags, Dingle Dingies and Cheery Loops, into the gurney room to shut Alysyn up, asking aloud if everyone else is deaf. Sitting to buckle his boots, he hopes she won't need a pizza and ponders Mooja's advice to rethink certain individuals in his own subdivision. Gamma normal by day and bum by night may be more common than meets the eye. Beta normals can be suspect. He tells Rozomon, "I bet I know a bum."

"Billy, I think you're a bum."

Billy can do without the sarcasm, thank you very much. Rozomon digs a toe into his thigh and laughs, "Only kidding. You didn't have a pizza."

How does she know? Lucky guess, or Alysyn made everyone hungry. It's not easy keeping pizza around. A man responsible for the hohum at home goes into the kitchen for two pizzas, make it three. Oh, heck, make it six. That way nobody'll want one. They'll get cold and lumpy, and tomorrow Peony Lu will gripe and eat two so they won't go to waste. It never fails. He puts three back but pulls one back out, then the other two; attitude goes to giving, too.

He'll get more tomorrow. What the heck. He lays out six to eat and split but not on an empty stomach. How can that be, when most people get pukey out there?

Erika Swain preempts: "We interrupt this program for a Special News Bulletin. This just in from our Sector One Bureau: A 7117 Jumbubble has crashed in South Hurricane. Experts on the scene tell Warp 1 that all nine hundred sixteen passengers and crew are known dead. Two thousand people on the ground are feared dead with over three hundred irretrievably dead from disemboweling or decapitation. No known Q on board. We'll keep you informed as we're informed. Now this from the Oval Office . . ."

Billy laughs when Erika Swain sniffs her index finger. Didn't she? He shags disks, jams the perfecooker, punches up diameter by crust gauge and fills tumblers. Moving with alacrity shows well on a player, but a guy wouldn't mind a little help once in a while.

"Hey! Quiet! Special Bulletin," Rozomon yells, as if she cares what the High One has to say. Maybe she does, or the juicy plane crash got her attention; three hundred irretrievable. She does love the gristle. Hey, let her microfoc her own red sauce 'n cheezies.

Billy feels the surge, as OneEye goes in low and personal to scan eyeholes, scooped torsos and some parts is parts. Sponsors pay extra for preemption over blood and guts with ticker tape product promos. The gory stuff gets watched.

Billy wonders how they do that with the tickle surge into the kitchen, ten feet off the radius.

Rozomon giggles.

Billy plucks disks from the perfecooker, hot and floppy, oozing and smelling better than samples at Valueco. He works fast with the colas and paper towels and makes the gurney as the High One fades in on ghostly profile with sincerity, reminding us to . . .

Consider your future and children, grand. The unborn trust they put in you. The Republic. Sporting skills. Opportunity in HS. You wanna be rich, like me? A LIFE *is a terrible thing to waste. Don't be a loser. You can win. So much money. I did. Fantastic returns. Fun, bagging oldies. Ha. I'm joking. Oldies have the time of their lives. Live forever? Bag the youngsters. Good for the Republic. Bring your Jupiter Card. HumanSport won't take Union Express.*

Billy stuffs his gob. Could he invent a perfecooker that could do up a pizza without burning his mouth? He still loves the sizzle of that first sip of Coke. Or *Pepsi*. "Sss."

Rozomon shushes, jamming her own gob. With *Doctors in Love* coming on, she gets pissy on peripheral talk.

"It's the credits," Billy says.

"Sh!"

So much Sector HS promo is bound to pump the turnout. More targets, very few at Billy M's skill level. Are you kidding? The guy was a global all-star. A crowd limits mobility, and Billy M moves fast. Too many targets get tricky. He needs elbowroom in the brush, any rock backed with a target. It'll be fat pickin's all right. Then again, Sector HS is pretty darn big. What if some jerk sprays automatic fire all over the place? He licks his fingers. Some jerk just might, but anyone spraying fire will draw return fire. Jerk tries to cover three sixty; he'll make more fun for everyone else. Jerk'll be leaking worse than the drain field behind the mall.

The HS game looks good. The Rules Committee took forever and was more boring than a book. Rules will be tight, all concerns and what-ifs preprocessed by experts. *Attitude is all we have.* 1.

Downing his cola, he comes up for a laugh. Doctor Sandy Loam, Chief Cardiac Specialist, carrying on with both nurses in nonspecific gender foreplay suddenly sniffs his index finger. "He sniffed his finger."

"Did not," Rozomon says. "Now, sh! I'm trying to watch."

But he did. Billy thinks the whole show is a joke. He watches another minute, but Rozomon won't say thank you for pizza and cola service. She's too old for reprimand, and if he says you're welcome, she'll know he's baiting her.

Alysyn yells, "I want more Coke!"

Billy asks Rozomon, "Can I get you more cola, too?"

"Nah," Rozomon says, holding the last pizza wedge aloft, unhinging, engorging to a half-gag, "Mm. Nguh huh, noh Coh. I wah *Pehsi*."

She can get her own *Pepsi*. Polyujac exchangers overheat every time. It's the price he pays for fatec, and Billy M thinks it a fair deal. Rozomon will have to get her own cola. He steps into the cubeport to uncover his old maxicap. Slippery Bullet shines like new. Squeezing the handles, he checks mach linkage and cross-arcing diodes. He reflects on skill and attitude and tenses the main plates. Few people know his reflective side. Peony Lu knows him inside out, painful shyness to lunacy, but anyone at the pro level has two sides. He's a fan now, world-class with stats down cold, bios memorized. Billy M is a screamer for all seasons, and a blood-curdling shriek can make a difference, like in the championship finals of '72, going out on a stretcher frothing go, go, go. His seat number will be retired to the Team Spirit Hall of Fame.

Billy reveres farther, faster, higher, wider, longer and more, more, more. It's the recipe for greatness. Greatness is why Hard Luck made people in the first place. Fans want home-team greatness to compensate, and Billy M follows attitudinal corollaries. Some people scoff. Not Billy. He feels growth potential.

Sport can be a tease, like any romance. Then comes the hunger for more. Billy doesn't think a threepeat too much to ask. Or a fourpeat. Calling for five in a row might be loony. He knows the players by name, date and place of birth, rap sheet, signing bonus, vital stats and free agency odds. He knows nuance and idiosyncrasy. Who runs the back office? Who fears headlines? Who's leveraged? Who's promotable and who's whistling Dixie? Billy M knows the diff between three years/thirty million and a supernova open-ender starting at three bil and going Mach IX on points, rebounds, feeds, blocks, off-court color and outrageous antics. Like that guy who clocked his girlfriend on the elevator—BAM!—knocked her frikkin' lights out. Or the guy who beat his kid for bad manners. Talk about bad manners! Or the guy with a dog-fight ring on the side. Boy oh boy. It gets rough and cruel down to the wire. Sport and THE LIFE need action and ratings to make moolah. The High One says, *It's all about the money*. He didn't need to say it, but it's good to hear.

Deliver what they crave; fans cough up the dough. Your agent squeezes the turnip just right: Bingo! You're immortal. Go ahead and change your name to Salasar Snopes while you're at it.

Billy M can genuflect in perfect sync with Salasar Snopes and feel pride in three hundred mil a pop for four seasons with doublers for playoff wins and half-again overrides for championships.

The guy next to Billy said that was too much money to play rimball. “Sheesh, it’s only a game.”

“Only a game?” The second guy down asked why Salasar shouldn’t get the dough, if the game brought the dough in. “What? The owners should get it all?”

“Heck no,” the first guy said. “We should get it. Cheaper tickets.”

“Yeah, right,” said the second guy. “You been down at the NaySay Hall?”

“It’s not right,” said the first guy. “Frikkin’ Snopes making that kind of dough while I bust my brackets every darn day to make a frikkin’ game once a month. Sheesh. Twenty-eight bucks for a burger that’s all gristle and tails. It ain’t right.”

Billy held fire till leaning in to set the record straight. “Salasar says, ‘A world championship team is nine guys out of nineteen billion. What’s that worth?’” That shut the first guy up. Some people. The guy blamed players like Salasar for six-hundred-dollar tickets. Hey. Ticket purchase is not required. It’s optional! “Besides,” Billy said, “What do you think attitude is? What’s a championship? When we win, that’s a we. Some players cost more. We spend more on tickets to get the best free agents. We hump our hinges so’s we can be champions. Complain all you want. We made the sacrifice so we can be champions and wear the rings with the big rocks. I mean, they can’t give rings to everybody, but you know what I mean. Pricey tickets mean more power in free agency. That’s where a championship begins. You want to save a few bucks and sit here watching a bunch of losers?”

Both guys hung their heads and took a lesson. “You drop six bills on a seat, two more on parking and a Coke or *Pepsi*, a few Pudmizers, sportsburger and a piglike; it’s tough to keep the spirit stoked. You got that faint pounding sensation right in the old keesteroo, and you're gonna be a shut-in two weekends running, just you and the alpha and a Hard Luckless load o' Tater Balls & Gravy. Attitude maintenance. Game time is now! Drink up and holler for blood. We earned it."

Would these two ask where he worked? "Besides," he added with jocular levity. "The rim got razor sharp. Nails and glass on the goal posts. Six hundred bucks a ticket? These guys can get slashed to slithereens. Snopesy could bleed to death on a slam dunk!" Both guys nodded and half-laughed at the comical ring of gruesome truth. "You forget why tickets cost so much, unless you're out there."

"You're right," said the second guy. "Six hundred clams is small coinage to make the playoffs. First time in twelve years, thanks to Snopes. I watched *Sport* LIFE last night. They're talking about *us* for a change. I took a chance and burned it, so's I can watch anytime. I get feeling low; I punch up some *Sport* LIFE from *our* season. Snopes did that. The heck with the money."

The three fans waited, pumped on Corollary 10: *An open mind is a healthy mind.* Billy knew he could open these two minds on sport as the essence of survival, from the caves to the suburbs. Sport teaches teamwork. Then comes grit, when it's only you and your own self. So what? That's what. Billy flagged the Pudmizer guy for a threefer instead of running the old pie hole on what ought to be obvious. Better to pull together on a Pud, enough talk. Just that quick, the first guy stood to whoop and holler as the Dogs took the court. Sport can bring fans together on so many levels.

Billy loves bringing fans into the fold, making it more than just a game. Sitting on a lactose crate in the garage while the hotshot hums, he gains perspective. He thinks bums must be real, with undercurrent and subterfuge everywhere. He suspects a few bums, having inappropriate thoughts. But he can't go around pointing the finger. What do people think of him, dinking fives in the driveway? Then again, a Category 1 exhilarist is darn near off the hook anyway. A bum wouldn't crave speed and danger. Would he? Bums are depressed. They don't get wired on altitude and speed. Do they?

The hotshot flashes: Full.

Category 1 exhilarist? Boy, the stuff they come up with. Billy's a rush junkie, jonesing for a brink, a g-force, a thump, a sear, a pressure slam, a walk down Memory Lane. Does heavy action compensate for lost glory? What if he never lost the steam? Tears streaming, he'll hang on by the hairs of his chinny chin chin, what a purebred athlete, Cat 1 with all new potential wants to do.

Slipping into pre-game, he clears the cobwebs. Winning comes into focus like second nature, no big deal. Snake-eyed on domination, he steps over and oozes on out, no questions asked. Billy M is no rebel. He loves fair play and that for which we stand. He can block, shoot, swing, slide, cleat or goose boosters with anyone. Pumped up, he pumps voltage to glow hum and amps it up to let 'em know. Backing down the ramp, he twists his levitators and swings into the alley. Wheelied up, he hovers.

Boy, he doesn't mind if Danny uses his maxi now and then, but a houseguest ought to learn to back it in. Well, Danny was probably in a hurry. Billy doesn't mind the neighbor kids using his rim. Corollary 18: *You have to share*, puts it straight, plenty for everybody. Seven-man teams, or women, or eight? What's the diff from five-point range? But boy, they could take a break and let him out the driveway. He waits with a chuckle, his rim sharpened to NRA regulation—kids banging rim shots won't jam the driveway for long. He can't help grinning as the ball arcs off the mark and . . .

POOSH! Game over or at least delayed while someone scrounges a new ball or a patch while the rest grouse.

Billy eases out. "Excuse me. Excuse me." At the end of the drive, he calls back, "That's why they call it rimball!"

"Hey, you owe me a ball," a kid yells.

"Yeah, me too," yells another.

Stone-cold focused on the go, go, go, Billy hits the power curve and holds it. High speed is incidental, once he sears the stratohaze internal. Sweat trickles but dries in a blink. Bones roll. It's time for one-on-one, nose to nose, Hard Luck and Billy M. Let's see what you got. Let's go for the upset with a legacy on the line, loving every minute. Tall heroes come from long odds, and Billy is out to prove merit at six-six in his socks. Even at 00.00, he can sense the stares and whispers. They know who and what and how close he came. Even his Mach IX bow thrusters with chrome pegs can't keep his knees under the dash panel. They know.

"Hey," the first kid says. "That's Billy M."

Billy half-nods, or was that a lurch? The electrocket shoots him to future tense. The kids shrink in his rearviews, staring in awe at a five-point legend, or what could have been.

VI

Mindset and Attitude for Floating a Loan

Down to man and machine under brilliant gray skies with humidity stabilized at ninety percent, it's an afternoon made for a turbo half-cube and weather to put cares and woe in electreverse.

Ah, THE LIFE is good, cruising the subdivision on low voltage. Kids playing, getting into trouble, Moms screeching over no money, too much laundry, wait till your father gets home.

Billy has to laugh at the human comedy, dads pulling in from work looking way too tired to take on the kids, always feisty, ready to challenge dad or anyone. They'll have to wait. Retrieval is right inside with some Pudmizer and alpha saturates. Not that dad'll be a contender by six, but he'll decompress. The kids'll hit their twilight games by then, moving into the shadows.

He can set his watch by homing dads. Foxwoodburrough Hills Estates may be bum free. Bums don't work. They hang out, ignoring the need for growth. Billy enjoys a good think, cruising low. He hovers, feeling good, like injured reserve is about to end. He thinks again about sportscasting and laughs, shy as he is. He's got the stats down cold, but what good are numbers and bios if he chokes for OneEye? Heck, he'd choke for EarHole too. What a laugh.

Easing inertialators to drift over Foxwoodburrough Hills Lane, he feels like times are changing. Maybe he should write a song. Nah.

He's a jock, headed for the finals with no tryouts, no politics or deals. He's walking on, a global pro. Ultimate sport cuts to highlights. Every subdivision has its coulda- woulda- shoulda-beens. Forget it. No need to chew old bones if you got a fresh fillet. Let's see who's been and gone and who's back.

Billy M was ultimate and gosh darn it still is. Seriously, a guy works out every day for twenty-seven years, soaks alpha and makes the replay; he's ready. With some cash coming in, Danny can get his own place and Marya can be a competitive writer in Sector 00. Rozomon can get counseling or sedatives to keep her companions around. If anyone profiles first string, it's Billy M. He wants to work, not wallow in the sauce or go mental or get stuck on pizza or one more twin bag or another 8-pack of Coke or *Pepsi*. That stuff is not his lobotoproblem. Not anymore.

Billy waves to folks in their yards, arranging yard chairs, unloading their cubes or relaxing, yelling at the kids. Most folks see the man on a half-cube waving. They wave back. No attitude malfunction here. This place hohums!

Picking up Mo, Billy tweaks for a climb, feeling good about prospects. The subdivision is growing. He loves how mall zones and rechargers blend from Foxwoodburrough Hills Estates to Silverdale Haven Glenn. Heck, it goes five horizons, which ain't 00 but darn bigger than it used to be. Swooping low to scan rooflines and check some new quick stops, he sees one of those new osmolizers that can pump a recharge *and* a hotdog and a Coke or a *Pepsi*, no guzzle, chew or swallow required. Call him old-fashioned: he likes to grind. What the heck, he might try it.

They look clean and new, but Billy might wait. He'll let these osmolizer recharge & snacks machines shakedown for side effects. Too many folks got twitchy on foodstuff tech since the Burgerfest fiasco, when they extruded burger like a hotdog but skipped the red protector. The meatstuff went green. Pshaw! Who can't taste camel dukey without red protector to clean it up? Boy. Some people.

He could stop in for a real burger or maybe a Redrat™ and a Choc-o-Pop. That combo makes him pay twice, but a guy likes variation from the pizza/*Pepsi*/Coke/Pudmizer routine. Maybe he'll give up a replay to see how an afternoon feels without it. Peony Lu needs a day off, though she loves the attention. Is he killing time, putting off the inevitable? Give up a replay? Just thinking of Peony Lu jams his shifter. Maybe they'll spice it up later. She always wants to wait till later. Why not?

Pulling into familiar hazes over Silk Daisy Lane, he gooses it, arcs a hidden speed-buzzer and crunches boosters to head up near vertical to the stratohaze. What a prankster. The new patrol cruisers might have plush seats and air filters the cops deserve for putting their lives on the line with nothing but donuts in return, but can they soar? Billy soars, looping, careening, dodging tracers and showing his stuff. He won't hit anybody, if they stay calm. Just over pressure max, he climbs on a peel, north-northeast, toward Hector's place, way yonder. Dumb speed tracers can't even follow a half-over pressure max, much less a peel on obtuse angulation. What do they think, everybody gave up maxis for skysofes? Guess again. Stupid skysofes look like creampuffs.

Hector lives in Boxville, not exactly Memory Lane, but only Hector lives there by choice. He's rich but tighter than a gnat's anus. Billy doesn't care how Hector spends or doesn't spend his money. Billy likes to hang out with a bona fide old guy. Besides, the route to Hector's goes past the roller coaster that rolls over the giant Coke can. A much younger Billy and his little pals raced the roller coaster as kids, cruising up innocently, then jamming to pressure max till the roller coaster riders shrieked mayhem. Those were the days, when crossing the line felt like money in the bank, when splices were a laugh, and you could get up next to sudden mortality three times a day, if you wanted to.

What Lucky days they were, with a theme park in convenient access to the subdivision. Kids today can't know that side of nature. Billy is grateful to Bunghauser Deuche for endless benefits to the many, but he hates seeing Nine Flags go forty percent condo and sixty percent timeshare. Then again, heck, some kid might be up in the giant Coke can right now thinking how neat it is. Attitude.

The old coaster tracks stayed up for a while like sculpture, but now it's only the can, split up into living units inside. It's neat, with old-time fire escapes and clotheslines. Somebody ought to pick up the trash. How do they wax that thing? Do they light the sign at night? How many people know that sign is where Corollary 24a: *Drink Coca Cola* was born? Billy doesn't mind the taste of *Pepsi* but wants an ice-cold Coke when he cruises past the giant can. He used to think he could drink a giant can all by himself. What a kid.

Three! Two! The shot is up, and—Billy M peels and drops like a rock; the shot is him, a game winner at the buzzer. Like a Z-ray shooting a gap and out through a hole in the yellow dog: *Swish!* On plays like this, he should have audio, really.

Down to fifty feet, he tweaks inertialators near the old Coke can tree in the ads, the one they saved because of the Coca Cola Co.'s love of trees. Years ago, the tree had Mama and Daddy songbirds and baby songbirds that sang regular, to show the Coca Cola Co.'s love of songbirds. That was something. They broke or got stolen. Sometimes a cold Coke helps him remember how it was.

Taking Peony Lu and the girls to see The Trees at Subsector Arbordale is a great idea and not too far from Sector HS. Seeing The

Trees in person might show the kids the importance of saving them. Heck, Danny can come too, especially if he hasn't seen them. They're on the warp with a huggable hologram and green sense. It's okay but not real like the hurricanes. The hurricanes get so crowded with outragers, aftermath assessment and meaning; they blow hard as the storm. The Trees are better. Some are huge, over fifty feet, and little creepy things crawl up the trunks. Billy has seen the trees three times. Pudland Theme Park might be a good stop too. It's close, and with extra money on hand for a better LIFE after Billy finishes at HS . . .

Wait . . . He loses the last minute and laughs when a spook chills his spine. Not to worry. Ditching spooks is easy. Billy learned how on the downside of a twelve-point spread against Cavewank of the West in a division opener. That spook came on stinky, but the final buzzer smelled like roses on five points of perfect dink with seven-hundredths left. Those were the days. Billy savors the moment, with six hundredths to spare.

In pungent recollection, eyes closed, he fakes left, goosing boosters, cupping ailerons. Goodbye, Mr. Fearbags. Look at you, on thin air all alone.

Billy M can't really look, shooting out from under. Up in a banshee screech, capacitors burning protons like they were cheap! He laughs on a war cry, "Who the heck cares?"

VII

Uncle Hector

The children giggled behind Old Prunehead's back. To his face, they hailed Our Papa. Money lust lasted decades, giving way to need and then desperation. Immortality ain't cheap. Hector Moline had the dough, so they sang his praise, hoping he'd show mercy on kith and kin, shoring up the bloodline, paying so that they might dodge mean old Mr. Dead.

Fifty-two years ago, a floor baby squirmed over to climb Uncle Hector's shin, leaking yellow stuff from nose and groin poly. Old as Methuselah by then, Hector groaned: "Oh, fu . . ."

The little snotrag reached up for a beard pull and shrieked.

The heirs and assigns watched, aghast. The father said this baby adored his Uncle Hector.

Hector grasped the gooey, poopy one and got another shriek.

Others on hand cried "*Eeww*!" With millions on the table, they jumped to rescue the old poltroon—make that our patron.

"Get it off me," Hector also screeched, going blue, as those in triple digits may do.

The baby puked and blew reveille, crying its little eyes out, as if knowing his doom: average LIFE span. Tsk tsking and shaking their heads, the relatives murmured: poor baby.

"Too many," said Hector. They closed in, hovering, waiting.

In a far corner, another toddler sorted trash. Indifferent to favor or derision, this infant wadded things into clumps. "Look at Billy," called an heir. "Cute. Recycling again, and he can't even talk. He'll be a garbage man. Ha!"

Billy had nothing to say. Focused on the far trashcan, his childish skyhook and fallaway jumper amused the heirs.

Uncle Hector thought a baby destined to work garbage more useful than most. That was long ago, when Uncle Hector was old.

The neighbors still talk when a ninety-year-old woman stays over. Hector doesn't care; he says it's good for her and good for him. With Q.40 ranging to .655, he's a shoo-in for QFA with afterglow. Hector and Billy don't care. Hector's door is open when Billy comes around between seasons or in the evening for some one-on-one with a guy who knows everything.

Hector was never athletic. He thinks attitude, spirit, quickness, rapidity and speed are incidental. He doesn't care who wins.

Billy might cut to the fast break for a slam dunk on population control. Hector hates people but likes a few persons. Negative outlook in dynamic format will be key. It's a challenge for Billy, who believes. He can open on a pileup and a sewage spill and go straight to trophy game. That should do it. Hector hates high Qs. Billy could talk about bagging a few to taxi out for hanging in Hector's den. Oo! Nice. He and Hector could split the dough on a high-Q taxidermy deal with Pudland. There's potential.

He'll open on Wanda Ann.

No.

He'll come in flustered over traffic jams that had him stuck two hours, a problem crying for a solution. Old Mo will take over from there. It's tough, sudden death on the whole season in a clutch game against himself. It boils down to a sports hack looking for funding.

Hey! Watch it! Attitude.

Descending over Hector's yard, he puts down easy in the weeds and junk. Maybe he'll start cleaning up. Or not. Hector likes the cover. Flipping his kill and recharger, he steps off. What a place. He can't stay long without missing the hohum. But Hector's is great for modulation and rethinking.

Everybody knows it; HS will make heroes, once the Wanda Ann thing turns around. An all-season sporting event with big money, warp, winners and losers? Throw in the latest camping gear and sport utility cubes, some premium gore; it'll get the big share. The extreme guys won't hang back, firing out windows, vaulting gullies and cheating death. Mostly young and broke, they'll be humping! With no bag limit, they'll load up. OneEye watching spells endorsements. Billy doesn't need fame, but a little appreciation might be nice. He does need dough. Heavy artillery is no substitute for skill, but he's ahead of the curve on skill. Hector oughta see the light. HS is gonna frenzy like Moonlight Madness at Montclair's, with unlimited inventory and social contribution.

It'll get crowded, and Billy M could go to Billy 0 if he's not cool in the clutch. He needs room to move, and that's okay; adversity makes for champions. A finesse player flows, and who has better odds than a long-baller? Jam him tight; he'll slip and spin, dink and run, double dink, hook dink, slam dink, and don't forget the dink de maison or the dink du jour. The long dink, sky dink, low dink or high dink; they all dink five. Billy M! *Haraaah* . . .

He'll lay the cards on the table. Hector likes that, sometimes.

The blinds open on two dewy raisins in a stiff leather mask slumped onto a skull.

Billy sloughs the jitters and leans his maxi on some junk.

Hector's hovel is a wooden relic from the hard time, when wood tyrannized construction with mildew, bugs, rot and sags. Wood cost more than polystyrene and didn't last; just look. Hector hates poly. He says a house on fire ought to burn, not melt.

Billy knocks. Could more trees come from polystyrene, like the Coke can tree but smaller, with nests and songbirds and all? They wouldn't take much room if the bushy part was over the roofs. Why not? Billy makes a mental note and pushes on in. "Hector!" A hero to some, Hector is a great-great-great-great-grandfather to Billy, who hopes a little duct tape here and there might hold things together another month. Every mummy needs a wrap. "Hey, Hector."

"Bill . . ." The talk hole opens. In a bit, ". . .y." Hector gets going once his voice box warms up, which isn't often; it's only Billy coming by now. "Sit." Billy sits. Hector's bony hands squeeze a digitizer to help the vocal cords: "Hey. How . . . 'bout a love . . . scene . . . with Wanda Ann . . . and Char . . . Charleton Heston? Charlie . . . plays both parts." He coughs on a laugh.

"Yeah!" Billy laughs too.

"Nah! It's a scent the . . . dogs . . . won't track."

"It's a great idea. Don't you love Charleton Heston?"

"Why would I?" Stick-skinny from the front and paper-thin sideways, Hector shrugs. Billy doubts he takes his clothes off anymore, or that they'll come off. His face squeezes like an empty boda bag. "You don't . . . remember. Used to be an actor, Jimmy . . . Jimmy . . . something. Made a movie . . . *Stupid.* Made millions. Made another . . . movie . . . *Stupider* . . . *Than That.* Made more . . . millions. Made one more . . . *Stupider* . . . *Than You* . . . *Could* . . . *Imagine*. More millions. Then . . . *Ugly*. *Ugly II*. Jimmy got whacked, one shot . . . to the head." Hector ticks. "I thought . . . something . . . bad happened. Then I thought: What a . . . relief."

Billy doesn't get it but nods.

Hector gazes, fading like sandstone in a breeze, cracking a smile. Billy might be slow, but he comes around to chew the fat, not for handouts. Billy wants to know what to think about Wanda Ann or the weather or the taste of peanut butter. He's easy—and he can reach things. Besides, Hector likes to mess with a wholesome young Republican at six-six and two-fifty. Billy drinks the Kool-Aid and might ask: "Why do they pour the plastivat of Taterade over the winning coach when the losing coach needs the dousing?"

Hector is less patient on another potential. Billy knows the sector Capitols and corollaries by heart. He said thinking is the best way to travel, but most people ride the bus. Hector senses spring-fed curiosity, a shallow spring that bubbles prerational—a source of underground thinking! Hard-pressed to pass the baton, Hector wonders. Can Billy can take the handoff, or is he stuck? Hector needs to know, with death as a roommate and the ghastly hangover from each retrieval. "Billy. Stuff is the measure of success."

"I know that," Billy says. "I have some stuff."

"Yes," Hector says. "More . . . than me. I'm a hundred . . . hundred fifty-six. You know what that cost?"

"Plenty," Billy says.

"Yes. Plenty. Everyone wants to . . . get there, but . . . nobody wants to . . . be here. You wouldn't trade, would you?"

Billy loses a nervous laugh. "No."

Hector pours a whiskey. "You want to get here but maybe not for a while, but you hit a hundred . . . hundred ten, hundred twenty, you think about a splice or two. Takes . . . money." Billy senses dangling bait. Hector drinks. "You drinking?"

"No. I'm in training."

"When does . . . training . . . end?"

"After the playoffs."

"You're not in the playoffs. You know that … don't you?"

Billy looks down. "I have my own."

"Your own . . . playoffs? I suppose everyone . . . should." Hector slumps like a man in a wax museum. Billy is deluded, thinks he has his own playoffs. "You still . . . banging that . . . cheerleader?"

Billy smiles. "Every day."

Hector squints. "I got to . . . bang a . . . bang a . . . cheerleader once, about a . . . a hundred . . . hundred . . . hundred thirty years ago. Ha! I wonder where she . . . where she is now. Haahgg!" He sputters, swigs himself dizzy, drools and pants, watching the dots drift. He waits on death, or at least a lengthy coma.

Billy waits, too, timing his soft pitch. Billy saw the dots for years and mentions them in the way of men bonding on common experience. The dots might ease them into talk of sporting ailments, ultimate sport and big money. "Hector. I saw the dots. I don't mean these dots. But I saw some. For years."

Hector dry heaves.

Billy lets it go. If Hector wrote the Corollaries, #1 would be: *Keep your big mouth shut.* When he dry heaves again, Billy wonders if Binky Stardust would ever do an impersonation of Hector. She's done men before; she has the moves and would only need the leather, the sauce and the dots. Binky's the best.

When the dots drift out, Hector says. "At a huh . . . huggh . . . hugghyuh . . ."

"I know, Hector. At a hundred fifty-six, you start to feel tired. But you're not a hundred fifty-six, not for three months."

"Uhggh uh huhg."

Billy stands and drifts with the last dots, past the awards and diplomas, past the crumbling birth certificate. Hector Moline, born May 13, 1928. On the wall hang goose feathers, bark strips, pressed leaves and original bird nests that can't hold up like the new poly nests. Even the old beads and trinkets seem unstable. At the picture of Billy's great-great-great-great-grandmother as a girl, Billy says, "Great-great-great-great-grandmother."

She stayed dead at a hundred ten when Hector wouldn't cough up the coin for another splice. Hector whispers, "A nice enough woman. But a hundred ten is no spring chicken." He tops off and pours one for Billy. Billy shrugs and takes it, because ball handling can be integral to a play. "I know what you're thinking, Billy."

"You do?"

"No. I don't. Nobody knows what you're thinking. Some people doubt you think at all. You keep them guessing."

"I'm not as good as you, Hector."

"Oh. You're good. Go ahead. What do you want?"

Time out! The coach internal jumps into the fray. Better to burn one than lose the ball. Billy shrugs. "I don't want anything."

"Yes, you do. Everybody wants something."

Billy signs, "I want to show you something, Hector."

"I'll show *you* something." Hector moves in small thrusts of bone surging in leather. Dragging his load across the floor to a plastic box, he rummages. "It's a machine." He slips a plastic disk into the box. "The blues. Music for what ails you. Not that happy crapola. Moody. Sad. Erratic. Makes you feel better. Does that make sense?" He drinks more liquor, warming up in a way that seems different from pregame.

Billy fears a nostalgia plunge that will kill any chance of getting home for a replay before primetime. But: *A man has to do what he doesn't want to do*: 26, so he sits back.

Hector turns. "Say what you think."

"I like it, Hector. I . . ."

"I haven't played it yet." Hector pushes a button, and his bones rattle to twangy guitar and plaintive lament over muddy water, loneliness and whiskey, no money or love. "The blues suits me."

Billy sits up, uncertain.

"Go on," Hector says.

"It's like grits, huh?"

"Like grits? You think it sounds southern?"

"No. You can have a grit, but nobody does. They have grits. You can have a blue, I think, but then if . . ."

"Billy. You're fooling around, aren't you?"

Billy blushes and rubs his jittery thigh, looking up and blurting, "Peony Lu says you have fifty-two million dollars."

"Who's . . . Peony Lu?"

"The cheerleader. Hector, I know fifty-two million isn't what it was, but it's good for a 20-seg. But you got deposits on a bunch of 20 futures. Everybody knows it, and . . ."

"You do want something. Don't you?"

Flushed from the low post with no time for doubt and nowhere to go but up, Billy glances one way and releases to the other with the blind skyhook. "I want to go to HumanSport, Hector. I can kill a lot of people there. You'd like that, on account of you hate people so much. I can pay you back and get out of my slump."

"You need money for some immortality? Billy, I shoulda croaked thirty years ago. I got every disease in the book. I die every Monday; get retrieved on Tuesday, *if* they read my meter. I've seen

Demolition Derby cubes less dented. I can splice a 10 in two minutes on a down-tune and a credit blip! They got these mini-segs now. Twenty-eight days. Time for one more look around before you croak flat broke. I've seen what there is to see. Billy, it's not so good. I'm tired. You can't imagine when you're young, that taking a nap forever makes sense. You don't want to kill people for money. Remember: in every crowd of people, you're gonna have some persons. You don't want people shooting at you. That's not for us. Here . . . I got a hundred dollars here, somewhere. Take it. Piss it down a rat hole. Go on. Get some panties for your cheerleader." Hector takes a drink and plucks bills from the debris on his desk.

"She works in lingerie, so she gets a discount already. Besides, I need six grand."

"HumanSport is only thirty-two hundred."

Billy feels the court opening up, like Hector knows the score and this is one more test. Billy eases in for the easy three. "Thirty-two hundred for the ticket. I won't go in there with .22 shorts and a popgun. Hector, I got agility, speed, quickness and court wisdom. All I need is . . ."

"It's not a court, Billy. It's a war zone. It's ultimate human all right. You live long enough; you'll see what we used to call insanity. Now they call it appropriate, if you have the right attitude. It's not a sport. Billy, it's not nice to kill anything, even humans."

"You hate people."

"No. I hate what they do. They kill everything. My spirit, too. Killing people won't solve the problem. Plenty more people where they came from. I don't care if they kill each other. But you . . ."

"What?"

"I thought if anybody knew my secret thoughts, I'd be arrested. Now I think you're one of them. You scare me."

"Hector, I want to take a weekend with nature. Me and the great outdoors. I need a Supralight 909 smallbore automatic with a telefinder and laser marker. I don't care about spray fire. Give me accuracy and range every time. Hector, I care about finesse and style. You know who I am. That and a 64-magnum sidearm, just in case, and a bayonet and a calf dagger. A few death disks I'll never need anyway, but forearmed is, well, conservative."

Hector's face sags. "Nobody knows who you are. We only know who you could have been."

"Hector, you're famous. You have Q. Everybody knows Uncle Hector." Billy cocks his head, trying to see if Hector is smiling or grimacing or merely stretching leather.

"You're a turnip, Billy. I think you'd score big in Wyoming." Billy sits up. "But tell me two things."

"Okay."

"How will you feel, if you kill somebody?"

"It's voluntary, Hector. You go in there knowing you might not come out. It's like war used to be but better—you don't have to go unless you want to. You can make money and come out in two days. It's good for everybody. Every game has a loser. I lost plenty. It's, you know, quick and mostly painless. It's not like people torturing each other. Heck, you still have community spirit and a chance to meet new friends. You got to use a little attitude, Hector. How tough could it be to take out a few oldies? No offense, but they feel guilty about the entitlements and the drain on the many. That's why they're in there, to help the Republic or make a few bucks. Boy, if you don't use some attitude, you could say everything is negative."

"You'll find a nice, decrepit line-up waiting to be blown away for the good of the Republic and some extra cash for you?"

"They're not gonna line up, Hector. They . . ."

"The place could be crawling with washed-up athletes looking for lost breaks, some of them thirty years old. No offense."

But offense is taken. Humility comes naturally to Billy M, who doesn't give a snit if anyone thinks him a tad thick. Who cares? Yet he wonders if Hector might not know who he's talking to. Billy blinks at the blinding truth and let's fly: "There's only one Billy M. I'll take my chances."

Hector stands, chair legs screeching. Slow as a sweep hand, he shuffles to his shelves for another disk and puts it on.

Billy reads the case. "Miles Davis. Looks like high-mileage Davis."

"That's good, Billy. You made a joke. It was funny. It was stupid but funny. Maybe you're a turnip with potential."

"I've always had potential," Billy blushes.

"I know that. Now calm yourself and listen to what Miles Davis left behind." Hector pushes buttons.

Billy asks, "Did he leave it so we could have it?"

"Okay, Billy. Who pays me back, if you get blown away?"

Billy hems and haws. "It's only six grand, and I . . ."

"You got six grand? You eat the big one in HS, and I lose. I can't spend potential. No retrievals in HS. You're not worth six grand alive. You don't have a job."

Billy hangs his head. "This'll be my job, Hector. I'm an athlete. Lotsa guys have risky jobs."

"Sit back and listen, Billy."

Billy sighs again and listens, wondering where to go for money. Hector didn't say no, but it doesn't look good. Patience is key when a game looks bleak with time on the clock. Let it play. Wait for it. Hey, they played these tones on *Bums in the Basement.* Awash with symptoms, a bum will mesmerize over tones instead of alpha.

Nearly anyone can sense erratic rhythm, so nearly anyone can turn into a bum, if he's not careful. What if everyone listened to jazzy blues and thought the world gloomy?

Avowal is the bedrock of the hohum. Is this another test? On *Bums in the Basement*, the bums gaze and mutter. "Crazy, man." It's crazy all right, and what a waste. What else can happen with no radius to focalize? Lay around on a voltage drop with no alpha zone messaging? Billy feels creepy on mere contemplation; the bums in the basement fell into paralysis and addiction.

Hector must like it. Then again, Hector can't very well uptune the boom shakalaka with a hormonal youth chorus in this hovel. The baseline alone could delam the trusses. Elysian Fields Elevator music would be appropriate, but these tones go away and come back at you. Maybe that's the test. Billy tries to feel what Hector is getting at.

"Listen, Billy. Just listen." Billy sits still. "Nothing wrong with the hit, if you go with old tones and have an heir."

"The hit? Who's checking out?"

"Listen."

Billy listens. Hector won't check out, but if he does . . . Billy tries another joke: "He oughta be Kilometers Davis."

"Just listen."

Billy humors the old guy and calms to mild fidgets. A guy on waivers can't help a case of nerves. When he's a hundred fifty-six, hobbling out for some one-on-one, he'll need some attitude, and it better be good. Billy likes Hector in spite of letting the family die off. Hector's eulogy every time: "So much for the future." Money-grubbing tightwad is the profile Billy grew up on; old Mr. Don't Get Your Hopes Up. He'll let you croak before your third prime. Wait and see. Billy sometimes doubts what he'll see after croaking.

Billy was twenty-nine when Hector bought him a half-cube with maxcapacitors. Hector asked out of the blue who'd want to cruise an inversion layer in a half-cube that cost more than a whole cube. Who'd take such risk on so much discomfort and no gain?

Billy confided his need to get over the line.

Hector asked what line.

Billy shrugged.

Hector punched a voucher in Billy's name.

Billy chirps, "I can get over the line in HS, blowing the bastards away." It's a long shot, but Hector *does* hate the bastards.

Hector says, "Billy, you're fixated on this line fantasy. Fifty-four years old and you don't have two nickels to rub together."

Billy hangs his head.

"Billy, what's Corollary 9?"

"*When it's time, don't go. Death to negativity.*"

"That's right. And what's 3a?"

"*Buy One Moon for the good of the many.*"

"One Moon. Twenty-eight days. They want you gone, but they want your money first. One Moon. Available at street level. Constant demand finds constant supply. I got money, Billy. I got enough for a 20 and a 50 and then some. I got sags on my sags. My pulse is buried under so many wrinkles they can't find it. They're talking bi-cents by the turn of the century, tri-cents soon after. I'll take dead. I've had a long life. It could have been different, if some talk-show woman hadn't cinched ten seconds on a guy named Uncle Hector. I caught on. I didn't do anything. I got old. I got Q. You should have it but got a whack in the head. I got Lucky. I got rich. Did you know Erika Swain is going to tell me happy birthday?"

"What? Hector, that's incredible!"

"That's not incredible. What did she ever do but read a prompter deadpan? Wake up, boy. She'll lean on the eyeliner and flap her lashes and say, 'Happy Birthday, Uncle Hector.' With nineteen billion people watching, I'll skyrocket for a minute when thirty-five percent of them will say my name, which isn't even my name. Twenty-eight percent'll laugh, and ninety-nine percent will emote the feel-good. Forty-two percent will make an impulse buy within two weeks of any item under the sun under twenty bucks that says Uncle Hector. The day after Erika tells me happy birthday, I'll get thirty-five calls for endorsements, and I'll make more money. For what? People like the feel-good but don't have the brains to feel it on their own."

Billy ponders the stats.

Hector pours a long one. "Billy, I got another script in mind. I won't get as many laughs, but I'll get a better grade of laughter." The sardonic smile breaks through the sedimentary crust.

Billy thinks: *Hard Luck! He can't be rude to Erika Swain with so many impressionable minds tuned in.* Billy shifts, smiling and frowning, no longer comfortable with his quest for financing. Hector stares, reliving a moment from twenty or fifty years ago. Or a hundred, until Billy says, "Hector, uh, I . . ."

"Billy." Hector raises his index finger for a savory sniff.

Startled, Billy sees and wonders what the heck it is.

VIII

Tired of Living

Uncle Hector Moline has recog he can't shake. He could hide under a hat, behind shades and stubble when he was younger. He can't cover a hundred fifty-six any more than Tut can blush. He ventures only on the inside of the inside, what the many call the great indoors. That's on QFA, the hypercyber of known space. Uncle Hector, ethereal swashbuckler, buccaneer of the airwaves, sails the bounding main for mischief. He might leave the inside of the inside but never goes outside.

It's just as well. Q is a nuisance. Q can kill. The many jones for Q like vampires; water won't do. Five hundred hostages can't get the warpage of a middling Q. Plenty more 00.00s where unknown hostages came from. Who cares? Qs with decent recog are getting rare, and many low-to-middling Qs seek hostage situations in keeping with Corollary 22: *Q generates Q with proper coverage.* A calculated risk with some inconvenience, unsavory company and possibly permanent death can catapult marginal Q to worthy opinion on world events and minor sporting events, on surviving a single hostage situation. If the hostage gambit fails to generate, a waning or iffy Q can put a porno seg on the airwaves. Alas, that doesn't work like it used to, with bj transmog among whomever. Paydirt seemed certain on vanilla terrorism, until airbus crowds got thick with familiar faces, character actors mostly, with a few politicos and sector weatherpersons mixed in. Ratings now wane on hostages in the .1-.3 range; obtuse, plentiful and predictable. Hohum.

If a big Q gets smoked, on the other hand, it's guaranteed: "We interrupt this program!" Bloodletting on a Q.5 or better is bankable, good for preemption primetime, except of course in playoff finals with mere minutes to go, unless the score is too lopsided for a comeback, in which case preemption is appropriate.

Some upper-Q warpunditry suggest Q is not what it used to be. Good seats, instarecog, preferred access and follow-up potential pale beside risk. "If that don't beat all, then I don't know what," says Tucker Ramses, "The Prophylactic Republican" who speaks with impunity, which is different than disregard. Pundit consensus on the Ramses comment: hohum.

Hector Moline wants Q to cough and die like a gas engine. It won't. OneEye engorges on upstarts, charlatans, young persons with rippling abs, surging testost, posh lips, a three-finger gap, floppy tas, huge buttocks and numbing speech patterns. Nonspecifics with deep sensitivity are nice. He feeds at the Q trough, as new Qs rise like lumps in the gruel.

Hector once felt secure; funky recog is not primetime, less exposed. Who would harm an amusing irritant? The many is who. Fans want a Q touch, a Q shred of flesh. And blood.

Collectible Q-tifacts spawned an industry with the EZ DNA ID home-proof kit. Shroud of Turin threads and Elvis hairs vanished. A collector put a genuine item up for bidding: Harlo-Killdeer's chin whisker plucked on his ride to irretrievable death doing Mach VII in a cabriocube up a gray hole. The authentic speck sold on QBAY in moments for a million times its weight in gold. *Reality is real*: 26.

Hector fears collector value on an artifact named Hector, decades past shelf life and worthless on the hoof but tallying a tidy sum, steaked out—make that cured, tanned and stripped out, great for lanyards, wrist or biceps bands, headbands or dick constrictors.

Most Qs go incognito, avoiding the bus and its contagion, cramped seating, hostile stewards and ghastly feed: perfecooked pastaglop or a dough-ball sub for forty bucks, rodent bits or extra cheesefood a few bucks more. What a deal after two hours on the tarmac, waiting for repairs while some goose promises all done in a moment or two. Thank you for your patience, but patience wanes. Who needs to take the darn bus anyway, with EDZ?

Expansion-Density Zoning in '63 required new subdivisions to share a border with existing subdivisions (existence rendered at the point of conception). Likewise on new condominia (existence clause applicable). E-D Zoning meant maximum yield and minimum waste on remaining spaces. Memory Lanes became avoidable with bridgeable spans. Once bridged, THE LIFE flowed in the comfort and security of the great indoors. The many could eat, work, shop, score a pizza and a Pud within a few bridges and floors without going to street level, much less down to Memory Lane.

Resulting density exceeded projections. Cohesion brings economic stability on an internal base. Commerce flows like blood in veins, as little corpuscles strive for more. Nature buffs can air out by cube for a day or six, always an exit from snacks, comfort stations and shopping.

Or they can cube offshore to see the fisherpersons drinking, sunburned. Delusional fisherpersons wait for something, anything to take the bait, so they can work that sumbitch to gaffing range and put the motherfucker in the boat! It won't happen, but drifting along drunk and dazed is perfect for them and their boisterous good cheer.

Fisherpersons, lines and nets span the seas like kudzu in Bubba Sector. They squabble when they tangle or run out of beer. Armed conflagration spices the briny life with bilge talk and rowdy behaviors that compensate other failures.

Ocean liners plow through, folks jammed at the rail, green in the gills and agreeing, “Must have been something I ate!” Wipe-downs discourage viral onset, and the big wakes settle, as fisherpersons fill in, cussin’n screamin’ in their colorful way.

Fisherpersons soak up sauce, stare at glare and seem unhinged. Real-LIFE drama and/or sitcom stabilize the many, who can shag fishlike sticks or put anchoviekins on a pizza. With no programming, fishers endure sunstroke and cirrhosis in a hohum of their own. Removed from network ratings, they drift. The more appropriate of the many condemn fisherpersons as marine misfits.

Softer voices say the hohum is impervious, and besides, Echelon policy renders misfits nonexistent. With no coverage, they can’t exist, not really. Let the fisherpersons be! They hurt only themselves, which may be the solution.

Sadly, it was too much slack for fisherpersons that allowed the COVID Chaos of ’20 and Quick Death of ’27. A few million of the many perished, which wasn’t major, but still. The High Republican said, *It’s the Chinese. The Chinese and fish people.*

On the bright side, the C-Chaos and Quick Death, a 1-2 combo with a hohum interval, paved the way for hohum ever after. The Living Republican Platform blamed CC20, QD27 and all that woe on the Chinese and misfits, including the moist segment.

Emergency funding shored up banks and corporations along with park and mall renovations. With trillions on the one hand and two hundred thousand on the other, the many enjoyed new benches, rimball courts and swings by '31, when QD27 officially ended. Thank Hard Luck, fisherpersons were gone, official status pending.

The Quick Death took six billion humans in four weeks. Jimmy Von Thang, king of 102.665, said another six or twelve billion wouldn't put a dent in the limo. Jimmy Von got afterglow—and tagged for indecency. Sponsors fell out. Jimmy Von stayed cool. He said, "I'm thinning out here. This could be Sayonara, folks. Hey, who's our next caller?" Jimmy Von had attitude, bad.

Pharmaceuticals could have saved the day on QD27, but at two grand per person per day, probability on a federal fix went from slim to gaunt. Then it died. Insurers fell like dominoes as the many followed suit, beginning in Memory Lane. Poor folk repopulate quick anyway, but still. One-third mortality all around and into the orburbs made a ripple on the pond. Republican stimuli boosted rebound propagation on compelling promo for some old-fashioned squisheroo. Quoth the Republican: *We can do this!*

With joyful reverence, Republican Chairwoman Margaret Meriweather proclaimed, "Corollary 12: *Human* LIFE *is sacred!* Sacred is not free! New Boom babies will earn tax credits and make a fantastic future base! We turn setback into growth! Give thanks to Hard Luck and the HR!" The Living Republican Platform added stroller paths and playgrounds to the New Civil Rights Package. "Now let's get out there and squisheroo!"

Love you, Madge! What a fantastic lady! Really fantastic!

Madge Meriweather could not procreate personally but did jump into the red, white and blue spirit of the thing. The Republican got caught on a live mike: *She's not my type*. But sources say they'd already grappled to a stalemate, with a settlement coming in the form of a State Honor. Madge Meriweather got to announce the gene splice and the Great Amendment, eliminating death and taxes in one miraculous swoop. With immortality, no tax *and* a broader base, the New Boom would generate solid potential forever. The LRP, as it came to be called, was born. Why the heck not?

Some say the Quick Death antidote derived from underground misfit laboratories. That idea lacks evidence and remains unspoken.

Meanwhile, Uncle Hector wants no Q because, because. He tells Billy that misfits are real, foreign and domestic, inside and out, in shadows and mirrors. Misfits are thin and fat, organized and chaotic. They have method and hierarchy. They activate at random, with a point or without. Misfit minions seep from the polywork. They whisper and are heard. Or felt.

If a closet misfit of Q.5-or-better croaks, a warped funeral gets the riffraff rating. Concerned Republicans sense a horrible truth and call for legislation to stop the threat. The many must fight for a future free of such and such and so on, so greatness may stay upon us as it was and shall be.

Hector has avoided croaking permanently, mostly from sheer loathing of the dog and pony to follow. With recog, his identelectrode is easy prey for warp hustlers: "Uncle Hector!"

Looking like Methuselah's shoes, he doesn't need an identelectrode. But the many gloms onto the one and only Hector Moline. The glom is an issue for Echelon stalwarts. Hector revivals can infect many segments with dark optimism and negativity. Woe unto us, lest we forget: *Attitude is all we have*: 1.

Hector Moline's acerbic wit and outlook are divergent at least and illegal at worst. The FBI suspects he took the baton from Jimmy Von Thang but have no proof. G-persons scrutinize but can't find electron prints to bring charges. They pursue. The HR scoffs at a failed federal agency that can't even pinch an ancient loser.

Hector doesn't care who thinks what. He says the many propagates more in a day than oldies die in a week, and a seven-to-one ratio is a poor bet in any book. Population growth vanished from Republican talking points, dismissed with caveat, that overload shall resolve by Republican means. Tax credits for babies abound, as death and taxes are banned, along with abortion, family planning and birth control. Take heart!

Yay, though we sleepwalk through The Valley of Death, we fear no evil, because the High Republican is making deals with Hard Luck. *Believe me, these talks are better than rubbers, coat hangers and counselors. Support our troops. They board first. The War was, is and shall be. It will end with escalation. Like pebbles on a bottom, roll this way and that . . . The playoffs. We're #1!*

Republican thinking realigns reality. Subnormals and their mischief won't go away. They jam the works, skew the corollaries and scoff at appropriateness. They lack turnout.

Subversion keeps an old man going. Ethereal engagement is a contact sport, which seems contradictory, until sparks fly.

Like when Jimmy Von Thang said QD27 was inevitable. Alas, rancor was inappropriate. Jimmy Von tampered with perception and went maximum south, vaporizing in moments.

Hector watched him transfigure.

Jimmy V did not go gently into that good night. He stormed out, figmenting mucusation on major sitcoms and variety shows, oozing casts and chorus lines in primetime—family entertainment, Rated G! Jimmy slimed monster blockbuster smash hits like *Fat Dezmun the Pig's Gang*, *The Slawbs of Eastpucker* and *The Casual Fundamentalists*! Jimmy Von rated higher than any playoff with a seven-point spread pregame. Melting down, whining like wicked witches of the west, the sitcoms flailed in goo.

"So, too late!" Jimmy sang. "So, you got *that* right!" He squealed, "I mean, absolutely!" He howled, "So, don't even think about it!" He whimpered, "So, are you okay?" He bellowed, "Moving forward, on the ground! Having said that . . ." The Friday Night Meltdown could have been a smash hit, too. Too bad it was illegal, immoral, vile and dangerous to a freedom-loving Republic!

Jimmy V's parting shot: "Next." The many regretted the muck oozing into the living room. Jimmy Von gave puddles of snot, calling gleefully, "But it's not!" Figmentation came none too soon for irate Republicans. They couldn't catch Jimmy V but locked him in the EMF with no exit code, over and out.

Reduced to synaptic animation, Jimmy Von faded fast. In a *Special Report* spanning all networks, channels, frequencies and cyber layers, the Echelon exalted baby Rocky Pimento.

Who?

Never mind. With background bio, parental bio and subdivision profile, baby Rocky was a name to know. Mama and Daddy Pimento went out on the financial limb to pay for the Pimento name Q mere moments after Jimmy V's life sentence. The Echelon set up financing (duh) to facilitate diversion, leading to Q.4 for a bawling brat with a brown boogie butt bag and Erika Swain calling him a star of tomorrow. "Oh! What a darling!"

Hold in pregnant pause three, two, nada mas . . .

Jimmy Von who?

Hector Moline only got stifled, because he was legal, so far. Some Republicans referenced "that old jokester," showing love for an icon of the gene splice. Most Republicans said they hadn't yet read the report so they couldn't comment, to the best of their knowledge. Uncle Hector, the legend, went unmentioned till he registered 00.00, elderly alpha normal.

That was then. Resurging at Q.6, give or take, Hector is a threat.

The young'uns don't know about Jimmy Von or any baton—Jimmy V arced across Hector's radius with bypass data on his way to maximum space. "Take this," he said, casual as you please. "LIFE is full o' changes," was his last blip to eternity.

Hector Moline took the baton but lacked the know-how to zing.

Hector knows how now.

The blues play on.

Billy stares.

Hector says, "Drink."

Billy drinks his liquor.

Jazz underscores their inappropriateness.

Billy senses what's up but can't see the good of Q-sniffed index fingers on the warp. "Hector? Why?"

"You ever hear of Referendal Deletion?"

"Yeah. It boosts morale by redacting the negative. You get to vote in a forty-two second window eleven minutes past midnight on the third Monday of the month. It's late night, so it won't trigger a power surge. Voting takes a second, but you get forty-two seconds, because The Republic gives you more than you need. Consensus realignment is instant, and the many is heard. Referendal Deletion gives us freedom of choice. The many delete what it doesn't like."

Hector tilts the bottle till the glug, glug, glug fills him with color. Coming up for air, he sputters, "Forty-two seconds! The vote lets you participate in keeping things good. Right? Right. But I follow my vote with a sub-binary request for personal help. In nineteen seconds, I'm in, leaving twenty-three seconds to put fingers to noses. I subvert to primary, because electrosentries are too stupid to screen help requests from sub-binary. Tell me something, Billy. Who sniffed it first?"

"High Republican."

"What did you think?"

"Think?"

"Did you laugh?"

"I thought about laughing. Maybe I laughed. Or grunted."

"You thought it was funny?"

"Not really. It's strange."

"It's my little game."

"You'll get caught."

"You have no faith."

Billy is struck by the idea of no faith. "Isn't attitude the same as faith? I have faith."

But Hector opens up on odd concepts and the reality of no reality. "I'm old, good as dead. Did you know nondurable purchases will soon accrue merit?"

Billy knows and quotes the Echelon: "The Republic thrives on nondurables, especially disposables, as long as we all recycle." But a little seed sends a filament out to see what might be fertile. "Wait a minute, Hector. I keep up with Breaking News. I never heard of *merit* for nondurables."

"Does it sound good?"

"I put a new gurney in layaway so we can relax without crowding. We got a burger press, a nice one, and now you say . . ."

"Don't worry. Nondurable purchase merit will be retroactive for six months, if you saved your receipts."

Billy looks pleased, finally able to use his receipts. "Merit qualifies for the Christlike Medal, too. I know that."

"Yeah, but you got to buy big to go Christlike."

"A burger press is big. I got the extended warranty." Billy shrugs. "You never know. I mean, you know?"

"Buying a ton of burger presses can make you Christlike."

Billy thinks it over. "That's not what they mean. You wouldn't really be Christlike for buying a ton of burger presses."

"Why not?"

"Because." Billy wonders if the Son of Hard Luck ate burgers while walking the earth. He contemplates adequate counter space for enough burger presses to be Christlike, not that he, Billy M, wants to be Christlike, but boy, if he could . . .

"Billy. Merit on a burger press? Virtuosity if you sign up for dust-to-dust? A four-pound bag of you sells for eighty bucks."

"You get the eighty dollars when you sign," Billy says.

"You surrender. Billy, it started with drive-thru espresso and a 2-splice for hardly more than a used cube. Look what they did. You think you want to shoot people. Violence can't have merit or virtue. Didn't you study the '60s in school?"

"Sure. In the '60s we got Expansion-Density Zoning."

"Not *those* '60s."

"I don't want to shoot people, Hector. It's not like that. It's like when you go to war, you have to kill some people, but you don't think about it. Everybody knows they have to shoot each other, or you can't win. This is better. Nobody gets drafted. The inactive reservists grouse. That would be your wheelies and other gimps, your convalescents and retards and really old codgers—no offense. Besides, grousing is half the fun of being in the military. Any way you look at it, your aces and war heroes get to board first. They get medals, recog and parades but not for the most kills. It's for patriotism and heroism beyond the call of duty and supreme sacrifice and everything. You can't just go out and kill people. I mean you do, but not like you're talking about. This is patriotic."

"We have met the enemy, and he is us?"

"You twist things, Hector. That's not healthy."

"Twist this, Billy boy. I want to go to HS with you, my treat."

Billy frowns. Taking Hector into a contact sportzone would be like playing rimball with double vision and leg irons. How can he move, run, dive, fake, duck, spin, pivot, rollout, feint right and fire left with a bag of bones hanging on?

"My treat, Billy. Like I say, I can't lose."

Billy shakes his head.

"You want some money, but you don't want to work for it."

"I'll work plenty for it. I don't want to be a sitting duck for it. Besides, what if they find out it's you? I'm a big enough target on my own without a bull's-eye on my flak jacket. You'd draw more fire than a summer burn off in Cosmic Sector! Hector. Q.6!"

"6 and change. But they say it's going away."

"It doesn't go away, and you know it. The sportnuts would tear you up, Hector. Anybody finds out you made everyone sniff their fingers; you're primary in no time."

"Yeah? What about you, Mr. Smarty Britches? You think a five-point genius won't draw fire? Hell, I'm your cover."

"Shoot, Hector. I had potential. Me and a billion other guys. I know what I got. I got real zeros. Heck, I can ride the bus and nobody looks twice. They don't care about me."

"They're neutralizing me, Billy. I'm as good as zero on the airwaves, same as you and every any warp addict out there. You know the score, Billy. They got me on 27, way low and inside."

Billy knows Corollary 27: *We shall maintain a worthy standard of worthiness.* What can a hapless applicant say? But he tries. "You got neutralized, but you still got—"

"Zero Q is what I got on official readouts. I made them laugh more in one zing than Erika Swain did in forty years. They censor the many, Billy. Then they say the many calls out. They're neutralizing Uncle Hector for Luck's sake. No more QFA for the old man. They postulate my worthiness as non-accruable. They call it 0. They call me 0. They call me a quirk on a chance, invalid. 'Questionable merit is subject to Binary Q Code subsection blah, blah, blah.' Billy, I'm an outlaw. You're a has-been. You need some money. You got talent, kid, real talent, and you've given me an idea. Here's what I'm gonna do: You need six grand?"

"Boy, Hector."

"You want some money?"

"Yes, sir."

"Six thousand dollars? Billy, how about fifty-two million? You'll get your Q back and get up on the QFA, where you can spin yarns about your old Uncle Hector."

Billy is all ears. The inflammatory language stings like all get out; talk about subversive. Boy! But such is the pain of the gain.

"You take me in and bring me out, you get my money. For years, I couldn't make you my heir. Now I can."

"You don't have to make me. We're related by blood."

"Blood shmud, Billy. You're a . . ."

Like a sorry pooch, Billy hangs his head for another brow beating.

Hector pulls the punch. "Such a kid. I couldn't be confident. Now I can. We're in it together, Billy."

"What makes you confident now?"

"You're going in. I'm going with you. You'll cover my ass or eat pigflavor links the rest of your LIFE."

"I like pigflavor links."

"You're undermining my confidence, Billy. Just answer me this: do you want to be rich, rich, rich?"

"Yeah. I do. But . . . what'll you live on if I get your money?"

"Won't you take care of me?"

"Yeah. I'd do that."

Hector smiles. "I'm tired. You get me out of there; I'll take the hit. Nothing wrong with the hit, if you got decent tones and a sole heir who's up to snuff. I get bagged in HS; you get nothing but the charge on next month's statement. Six thousand dollars."

"Why do I have to worry about getting you out alive, if you're gonna take the hit anyway?"

"Keeps you honest, Billy. You can see that, can't you? Easy to say you'll take care of someone till it's your own sweet ass on the line. Let's just call it a little display of affection."

"I am honest, Hector. The only way to score in HumanSport is to get over the line and stay there. You can't worry about survival. You go funky mad dog or die. Show 'em you're the meanest, craziest death machine out there. You know how I play. I foam for real. How can you keep up with that?"

"I know you're honest. This'll keep you honest. Besides, you don't need to score with fifty-two mill coming at you."

Billy shifts and scratches, seeking comfort in prospects but finding none on account of the burr in his shorts that an ornery old misfit put there. But he can't put his finger on that either. "Heck, Hector. I need to score. Why go in if we're not gonna score?"

"Why worry, with fifty-two million on the rim leaning inside? You're not gonna score. I'm gonna score. You're gonna cover. Plain and simple. I got connections, Billy. I know things. You think what I'm telling you here is something." Hector sniffs his finger. "I'm gonna blow away a big Q."

"Wha!"

"Isn't that the idea? Why not put my cannon between a pair of everRepublican eyes and see who neutrals who? Think I can get back on QFA? Think I can get re . . . rev . . .reveh . . . I'm . . . gonna . . . gonna . . ."

Uncle Hector chokes on vengeance. The satisfying words of vindication bottleneck in his own neck and turn him quickly red, flashing headlong for crimson. With mottles pulsing and creases aquiver, he sits up, straining, gagging over the biggest laugh of all. Then Uncle Hector Moline convulses, jams into reverse, leaps an inch and chokes on hurl, as deep purple falls over sleepy garden walls. Cringing sweetly into cobalt blue to match the bottles on the sill, he clutches his chest and falls over dead.

"Aw, Hector." Billy props him up, but he falls again, so Billy ties him to the chair. New retrieval technology, thanks to Georgie, can jumpstart most stiffs within ninety days of croaking *if* stored in a cool, dry place. Better make it sixty days to play it safe with this heap. Billy pours a long one. Why not? As Hector would say, training shmaining. Go into HS with Billy M potential and not score? He guzzles, feeling THE LIFE stack-up against him—one more time, as it is. The sauce, the tunes, the hovel made of wood feel like a wrong turn somewhere. Do bums ever play one-on-one or tear it up on some half-court scrimmage? Where in the heck is attitude now, when he can't win for losing?

Some guys get the feed on the easy score. Not Billy M.

Some guys rack stats easy as pie. Not Billy M.

Some guys can't dink a five wide open and all alone if a triple bracket depends on it, but Billy M can! So? Why can't he catch a break? At his age?

All Billy M ever wanted was rightful glory. Sure, money is nice, but he's not in it for the money. Hector sees Billy's simple needs but wants to hold out on the dough to fill his own needs, and those needs are not so simple. It doesn't seem fair or appropriate. What about the recog due to a gifted athlete with uncanny long balls? How can skill, spirit and drive in the face of adversity get bent over a Methuselah on a haul-in and jumpstart with his LIFE on hold? What is *that*? Billy humps the old guy outside and lays him over the half-cube. He cuts a rope into four pieces and lashes the load like saddlebags. He goes back in for some rags to wrap the head so it won't bang the air dams on peals and banks. Can he put the retrieval on Hector's Union Express if Hector is dead, or will *he* eat the tab if the retrieval doesn't take.

Doesn't take?

Billy M never cries and won't cry now, but he chokes one back at the image of fifty-two million swirling for the drain.

Scratch that image. A long odds long ball rounds the rim good as dinked, if he can get the bones home in retrievably good condition. Hector hangs over the back end like a giant wad o' putty, the kind that goes off in an hour and gets brittle. He stares at the lump while his mind juggles a load o' crossfire chaos. Can anyone survive center court in Sector HS with an old fool firing aimlessly while a young fool scurries to keep him covered?

On second thought, saddlebag style is no good; too many bumps and jolts. You can't slow the rigors, and any retrieval station will charge double on a stiff stuck in a gainer. Better to tether Hector around the chest and under the armpits for a conventional tow. A stiff in the wake can bob and weave like a . . . like a stiff in a wake. Billy ascends for a beeline back to Foxwoodburrough Hills Estates, but the return trip seems a long way from recollections of childhood. Old over-the-lines are incidental to the task at hand, and it's time to put childish things aside. How do you tell if a dead guy is still retrievable? Do the stats get worse if the stiff is one of the ten oldest guys in the world? Boy, fifty-two million. That's some money.

In the garage, Billy doubts he can get eighty bucks on a dust-to-dust voucher if a guy is already dead. But maybe. Better eighty bucks than nothing.

Peony Lu walks in to find Billy thinking on his half-cube with a dead body in tow, and she opens wide on a silent wail.

Billy hates that, but she does look funny with the fear crinkling her face like a freehydrated peach. It's only Hector. She'll recognize the old poltroon. But her scrunched peach persists, and he realizes he missed the replay, first time in three years.

She cries, "Are you okay?" Leaning over to see Hector deader than usual, she screams in the key of bloody murder, "Get that thing out of here, Billy. I mean it!"

With everything stressing at once, he tells of fortune unfolding, if they can find a cool, dry place.

They retire hours later in lingering doubts. Billy's inspiration was the Polybrick Oldestyle Pizza Oven, the white elephant darn near everyone bought when it first came out. Guaranteed to neither melt nor taint your pizza, it didn't but never baked pizzas fully, and some folks tasted polycarbs in the redglop. Yuk. Never mind; the darn contraption might just pay out after all. Hector conformed to cube shape with no audible breakage. Let 'um charge double. Billy heaved like a nose tackle to get the head and shoulders in, grunting, sweating, praying to Hard Luck in this, his hour of need.

Peony Lu chattered gleefully over money, mobility, power and immortality. She knocked polybrick with a nervous laugh, recalling Billy's crazy buy on the Polybrick Oldestyle in the first place. "Forty-eight payments on pizza forever," she said. "Forever and then some. Hey. I'm missing *Bubba Doctors*. It's okay. I can catch up. It's slow since Doctor Phylo tried to get into . . ."

And on to midnight, because you can't just jam a stiff in a box and call it done, not with fifty-two million smackeroos stampeding your dreams. No, you got to check your compaction, your pressures and, what most folks fail to realize, your scope off horizontal. With Hector curled fetal, physio-skeletal factors can go trigonometric in a blink, and it's your funeral if you don't measure and cross-check the chemistry. Chemistry? Where the heck can he find Retrieval Chemistry Guideline Testing on Saturday night? Cross-town at Emeretrieve Systems Ltd. is where, because they only sell the chemistry test at the retrieval station. Is that a subterfuge to discourage abuse or murder one, or to get you down there with your stiff and a credit card?

Never mind, just go. Of course, it's closed, but the chem tab testers are in a vending machine out front, don't you know, forty-two bucks a tab!

Many groans later, too tired for a hose down and way past hungry, Billy and Peony Lu somberly finish a freeze-dried pizza and a few Puds. Fatigued as post season, Billy hits the sack on a low approach, rolls over and breathes deep. Barely touching wheels to runway he's off again, next stop dreamland, where sugarplum fairies two-step down the aisles of incredible new stuff, like carpet and cubes, fashion apparel and appliances.

It's not just new appliances in Peony Lu's dreamscape; it's more. A woman suffering deprivation of new features for so many model years, knows the value of new stuff. She's learned the hard way. She wants a new cube, loaded, for starters, one of those eleven-seat units with furniture. She wants a propox barbecue for the deck and the new Lazy Susan with 106 arcutrons per micron that the

Molines could only dream about heretofore, because new stuff isn't affordable without a few lifetimes of EZ payments, which have not been an option because someone strong named Peony Lu drew a line in the sand on additional payments.

Scrimp 'n scratch no more.

Worries be gone with fifty-two mil lubing the dream. Yet she knows Billy M. Give that fool a five-point shot from way back, he'll back step for longer odds. He's a charmer but should have sunk one by now. Maybe this is it. She drifts on the magic of immortality and the new appliances she'll outlive, and then what? Newer appliances is what? Should she begin with the avocado or the peach? She laughs in her dream. Either color would be okay.

But a niggle ends her drift: Billy missed the replay. Should she ignore it, knowing his ga ga for the go? With pixie fingers in playful proximity to Jack in the Box, she waits in vain. Jack could be a corpse in a pizza oven—without the rigors.

He snores. Does he care? Why not replay now? Yesterday was already thirty hours ago. Is another woman draining his capacitors?

Peony Lu was everyman's dream for years, with her special brand of spirit, which did not include the you-know-what, thank you very much, except for those with right timing and cute tushes, and they weren't all that many. She sits up to a new fear, that THE LIFE anew might be sullied. She never yet met a man who couldn't spoil things. She lies back to wait and see what the morning will bring. Every Jack jumps at sunrise. Peony Lu knows. She read it in *Cosmo*.

IX

George Longley

Money goes well with youth, for wanting and then having. Envy and need are often palpable in youth.

Money is better in early prime, when want gains depth.

Better yet is third prime, to cinch wrinkles and see the world.

Best of all are triple digits, when scads o' dough can fend off mean old Mr. Dead.

George Longley knows money but hates being rich. Filthy rich is worse. Humility comes naturally to this giant among persons, and so does practicality. He knows poverty is worst of all.

Bunghauser Deuche pays sixteen million a month for the Longley profile as backdrop to Pudmizer ads. This windfall to the young scientist who developed the self-absorbing enzyme assured Q forever or until the world gives up beer, whichever comes first. Ninety-six million bucks in six months made for heady spending power. That was years before the gene splice and billions. How much can a person spend?

George Longley can splice to Kingdom Come with rehab, rebuild, renewal and no remorse. The works! Billions bring immortality and then some. George Longley's Hard Lucky presence is greater than the National Slamball League and National Rimball Association owners combined. With more money than the Hard

Luck Guy, George Longley has THE LIFE Everlasting. With his mug at the bottom of thirty-nine percent of all beer cans in the world, George's celebrity equals that of the clear gray sky. Billions see him on bottoms up, with eternal recurring thirst.

The Pudmizer contract ran two years with renewal options, according to exigency clauses of the first part, subordination of foreign rights in the second part and accelerator clauses of the third part, et al, etc & blah, blah, blah, giving George face value on every Pud guzzled on Earth. George's agent retired on a single drop of each and every dribble. That was twenty years ago.

He works on, as the many drains its Pud to see his half-smile. "Mud in your eye, Georgie," some say. Some resent him. That's how they are. All wonder what he'll think of next.

George Longley is loved as a hero, no threat or ulterior motive. Yet the many requires him to live as a shut-in. Not for a burger with fries and a cola can George venture out, without the mad monkey in pursuit. If the monkey catches up, George can lose his clothing, composure and health. The monkey can kill or worse, like with Rotten Skull Hole, the steel rocker who lost his good eye, had his eyebrow, cheek and tongue jewelry torn out, gave up both ears to ear mavens, got shaved clean by hair fetishists and suffered groin damage at the hands of zealots, proving their love. Rotten Skull Hole could have changed his name to Macaroni Casserole once the monkey fed, leaving a sadly retrieved carcass with labored breathing, iffy digestion and no rhythm. What did Rotten have in common with George? Nothing but astonishing Q.

George Longley has been a shut-in since school. Known then as tubenose, beaker brain, pinhead, four eyes and so on, he suffers no more. The cruel stories are legendary, as LIFE goes on, solitary and airless. Nothing lives in a real vacuum, not cockroaches or George's social contacts. He has none. He must work alone and die. Trouble is, he won't die soon.

Physiologically intact, he needs stimuli irrelevant to databases. He allocates two point five hours per evening for alpha soak and calls the interlude Taking a Break. This pause may provide a link to the many and quell his social shortfall. A movie can be amusing. He can watch two hours, if it has no special effects. Taking a Break isn't easy, with the lab waiting, its zygotes, polymatrices, bicarbs, antimatter, triheli and neutrino residues primed for convergence to ultimate synaptic regeneration.

The lab and its electron optics, molecular manipulators and proton ionizers don't have the stuff of cinematic dreams. But George Longley's dreams are not mouth-breathing, tongue-thrusting, slow-pan-on-rigorous-hump movies. His dreams are techno.

Years of hypothesis, experimentation and data have led to LIFE inconclusive. The lab is rife with procedure and speculation, some smocks suggesting svelte features beneath the polyfab. Some lab personnel posture receptively to the great one, yet his presence, like the Pope's, is transcendent. George Longley *is* the connective tissue, the walking tube of glue bonding humanity to the firmament, making miracles Under One Roof. Nobody calls him the Son of Hard Luck, but Central Warp VU indicates resistance factors below .0001 on perception and belief. *Kiss me, you fool,* the many whispers to George Longley. George has never been Under One Roof. George tinkers and thinks, his mind quick as a heliostyrene trap on a seemingly innocuous string. His heart stays empty as the seventh moon of Uranus, still and frozen under the very neutrino residue he struggled to discover. *Ping, zip, woh woh* go George's synapses when gender-specific females emit estrus in pheromonal proximity.

Yet the mouth stays mum, while twenty-eight times the coefficient of the tangent cosign cartwheels through his head.

George Longley never *learned* science; he merely reads a thing and knows it, sometimes knowing a bit more, playing the big board three moves in advance. He processes data like no human hitherto. Yet social nuance, the gender dance, hormonal parity and dialogue are codes he has yet to crack. With notable achievement in the Science Club came notable dismissal. Under his yearbook photo: *Our egghead, soft-spoken and kind. Not a serious threat.*

Nothing changed.

Advanced degrees brought enclave, seminar, forum, think tank and honorary degrees. A standing joke in the Academic Complex is that George Longley is his own faculty. Ha! George could speak to billions, if he wanted to; the many craves his every mutter, twitch, scratch, nibble, forethought, passing and afterthought. He is annotated, analyzed and pressed for meaning. Few persons question George Longley, except to ask why.

By middle age, with more money than a developing country, he faces a clear and present danger: social atrophy. Isolating the parallel ports of his neuron receptors, heart and mind, he seeks manipulation. The ports should be serial, but failure to find traction on distraction may reflect mutation. The challenge defined may be a last chance. He has the lab tech to self-modify on a pre-programmed procedure, precluding the element of surprise, wherein lies first blush at first sight. Moreover, last chance notwithstanding, preprogramming can turn a brain to mush.

No, the prudent course seems external, at least for now.

At forty-nine, George Longley brought in a hair restoration expert for a frontal wave, hoping to facilitate the human mating ritual. Social discourse could, in time, lead to sexual congress, perhaps with a woman. He did not presume to know the result, but his big, wavy hair with a few strands dangling over his brow seemed titillating in the mirror. The wave and dangles reflected an adaptive self. He swung the dangles back like young actors on the warp do every ten to twelve seconds.

Lab staffers glanced, which was good. No sniggers or grunts were better. Alas, when unlikely neutrons amassed in a Petri dish, George Longley grabbed a pair of scissors and cut his dangles, to better see the breaking action in the dish. He didn't look back.

Social awakening calls for timing. His second attempt to engage in society feels safer, both random and sublime. Taking a Break will expose him with lower risk, loss limited to time wasted on a bad movie. *Ah, well; that's showbiz. Warp participation will be a learning experience in any event*, he thinks. He can tolerate canned laughter and applause, joining the ha, ha, ha and applause for no reason. He strives to break through and decides to order a pizza and eat it while watching, doing as they do to gain insight, maybe.

Digesting doughy bread with red glop and oregano, as a concept, requires predigesting. George Longley is driven. He doesn't mind garlic or bacos, but childhood Gooveta trauma left gastrointestinal scars. Recalling Cheesefood Whiz and Individually Sliced American still triggers phantom heartburn. Pizza with cheesefood will be a challenge. In faith, he secures a box of *Fatchuwant Chest Relaxers*. He asks a lab tech to arrange pizza with the nearest 00 Pizzeria. 00 is the brand name and, in this case, the original locale. *00, to Taste the Sector without the Hazards.* Hazards are minimized through 00 delivery service—make that minimized to a point. The lab tech calls the 00 order line, seeking to arrange for a person "who shall remain anonymous, to stop by with pizza delivery, say, during a movie. The, shall we say, resident recipient, will suffer no anxiety over what we'll call potential security breaches." The lab tech then asks, "Do I make myself clear?"

00 dispatch says, "Clear? Look. Guy wants a pizza. He calls up. Gets a pizza. Three minutes or less, or it's extra cheesefood for free. You can't lose. Right? So what? You want it under glass for this nobody guy? Get outa here. I got pizza going cold."

With nonscientific leniency, George Longley proceeds.

Alas, the pizza experiment will come to be known as The Great Pizza Experiment, as it changes LIFE for George Longley.

The experiment proves that pizza and a movie can cure mild dissinoma in the early, nonaggressive phase. George's first pizza arrives with the opening credits to a WarpFlix Movie, a sci-fi/porno thriller called *The Gynecologist of Lake Shore Drive.* George Longley attempts a double feature with the sequel, *The Vagina that Ate Chicago*. That seems odd, the title of the sequel foretelling the demise of the gynecologist in the first installment of the vaginal franchise. Did everybody else already know this? George can only speculate on his own naïveté. At any rate, data sets seem primed for gathering when anchoviekin smell wafts across olfactory receptors, as pepperoni and cheesy steam pour from the box. The scene would be promising if George Longley loved pizza, and a double dose of *Fatchuwant* hadn't numbed his chest. He paid the delivery person a hundred fifty dollars, hoping a forty-dollar tip was neither too little nor too much.

The delivery person smirked, "Nice hair, Georgie."

George Longley knows the dangers of cooled pizza; cheesefood congealing less than halfway down the esophagus can trigger pulmonary constriction in laboratory rats. But as *Fatchuwant* buzzes, the great lump shall emulsify. He surely hopes the far side of crisis will include regular breathing and normal viewing.

The “Georgie” moniker goes way back, begun by Warpanal reaching for levity. George doesn’t care. He laughs along with the delivery person and feels social, breaking through. The second movie opens on slo-mo zoom, close on macro bush whacking through the ancillary hair jungle, approaching the quicksand pit. George opens the box, hoping his chest will stay numb. He takes a bite. As the doughy ball and tepid goo mesh between molars, he senses adaptation and realignment. Hmm . . .

Meanwhile, in a dark stall of the dank employee bathroom at 00 Pizzeria Central, crosstown, a pizza delivery person writes on the wall: “Georgie eats it.”

Captive to his lot in LIFE, the delivery guy thinks he’s a cut above his socioeconomic niche; he’s a health nut after all, who would never compromise his sacred temple by eating an 00 pizza. Where do feelings of superiority get him? Grunting and groaning, an abject failure in the rudiments of sanctity, a person so tied up with self-esteem that he can’t relax, much less dilate and release. Stressed with survival in 00 and a low-totem job, he knows the load is in there and needs to eject, but so many sprouts and seeds have left him hanging high and dry. And there he sits, resenting a measly forty-dollar tip from a zillionaire. “Forty dollars,” he murmurs. “Like I got nothing better to do?” He draws a circle with a slash through *it* and inserts *00*, so the revised message reads: “Georgie eats ~~it~~ 00.”

The delivery guy is entitled to eleven 00 pizzas per week as part of the Dynamic Pay Package and thinks he might eat one or two now and then for economy and efficiency. Practicality rules, after all, and he won’t waste time or miss the freebie. In meaningful reflection, he writes a second message under the first: “00 eats it.” *What irony*, he thinks, in stacking messages to look like dialogue, like several persons sat here as part of the forum, and nobody knows it all came from the same person. Inspired, a third message is inscribed: “Eat me.” Trying a squeeze, he thinks the three-way exchange is enough.

“It’s like a story. Like real life,” he mumbles, and in a moment of growth, he gains passage. “Hard Luck.”

X

Where a Boy Can Grow Up to Be High Republican

Harry Wenk was born to spending power in 00. Bad kids from wealth were called spirited, not delinquent. Daddy and Mother Wenk smiled with benign superiority and sent Harry to military school. Out of sight was out of trouble.

The military school yearbook epitaph: "Give me a break." Other cadets followed Harry on weekend furlough, up and down boulevards seeking respect and from random females. Harry liked showing girls his pet hamster, Stanley. Stanley was not a hamster but his dingdong. Harry thought this wildly entertaining. His intro line: "Hey. Pssst. Come 'ere. I got somethin' I wanna show you."

The other cadets admired Harry and Stanley. Harry thought it natural and spun yarns of Stanley's quests. The cadets laughed and cheered. Harry basked, a self-made boy.

Daddy Wenk croaked long before retrieval or the splice, and a bequeathal of twelve million could get a kid started.

Leveraged spending brought warpage. Girlfriends and wives, mystery banks, whining contractors, bankruptcies and phantom loans established a pattern. Random groping, a chopper-gun hairdo and a game show completed the act to late middle age, when he needed more. His grown sons preferred gel over spray, leaving Harry no choice but to blame weak mothers.

The sons hunted with big guns, dressed like sahibs.

He called them spirited, a chip off the old block but not self-made, like him. They got warpage; Wenk spawn.

Harry Wenk's sons could shoot an elephant or leopard and get things hopping mad. Harry tried shooting small animals and liked the feel of it, squeezing off a little death. Rats and pigeons, rabbits and squirrels, the odd chipmunk or possum. He made up a little game and called it Disrespect? Taste this. Then he blew them away. Plastic lawn deer, raccoons or any twitch up a tree made him feel like Hard Luck casting thunderbolts, smashing silence on a moment of reckoning, *KABLOOEY!* It felt fair and balanced. Attitude and nature played out, with a tingling aftermath of fluttering bits.

It felt appropriate and, frankly, fun. He wanted coverage on his new power. Calling outragers as an east-coast promo man, he promoted the incredible Wenk, the father. He got nada but pressed on, borrowing and failing, gaming the system as it should be gamed, chasing tail in a LIFE of enviable affluence. It wasn't enough.

Finally, Harry Wenk sat under smallish urban critter heads for a warp profile: Wenk, playboy leverage artist. He could be global with one more connection in the borscht belt—not in the Catskill Jew resorts but in Moscow—and not in Idaho but in Russa. He said the little heads overhead were like NaySayers. "They die on cue. Perfect targets." Viewers thought him one more 00 nutter, hardly sensing a gifted antagonist would put them in the crosshairs.

He set out a salt lick, a barrage of name-calling, accusation and slur. He got coverage. "I love women like nobody ever loved women, if only they weren't so damned expensive! They're tremendous." The new wife emoted like a mannequin. He wore a blue suit with shoulder pads and stood straight.

What about the foibles and failures, playing his own promo man and the bankruptcies?

"I considered running. I could. I enjoy a flush and kill. I should run Republican. They'll believe anything. I'm self-made."

"Run for what? And why?"

"You're not being nice to me."

Just that quick, it was over. He seemed a nonstarter, until the double down a day later, when Harry Wenk said blood seeped from somewhere. "We don't know if blood was gushing there. We don't know about her blood-gushing thing."

What?

Harry Wenk got caught out, on camera, saying he liked to grab 'em by the pussy.

The many blinked, as Wenk wanked on, part of play, a grand script for leadership that could be. "Bomb the shit outa those guys!"

What guys?

The Book came next, as destiny came clear. At last, a Republican who made no mistakes. "I'm worth eleven billion dollars and will run a campaign, the likes of which . . ." Wenk got in with fewer votes. He went to romance and how he chose the new wife from a chorus line. "Her. I want her. Celebrities can do that."

What's that sound?

Business resounded. Products boomed. Steaks, tires, graduate degrees from Wheeler Dealer U. Wetback judges no problem.

What?

No. Not what but who, when and where. The High Republican had come to pass. *Nobody is more perfect than the Son of Hard Luck. So far.*

He soaked up praise: *Politics Today*, *Meet the Warp*, *Republican Forum*, *The Living Platform*, *FUX News* and *NEWSPLAT*. When lamestream media—*Meet the Press*, *Washington Week*, *Face the Nation*, *CNN* and *MSNBC*—failed to praise his policies, blind to his brilliance, he held The Book high. *Nobody loves The Book more than me!* He quoted Corinthians 2 and delivered *The Republican Prayer*.

Most Republicans had laughed at Harry P. Wenk as a quirk, a whiff, a spook, a nothing. What if he won? He wouldn't. They chuckled when he flung foul names like the Pudmizer Farms gorilla flung dukey. He lambasted disagreement and could take aim at . . . you!

With trouble raging across the land, the High One masterfully distracted with a name change. *We are the United Sectors of America. Executive Order rules. I win again, and so do you.* Outrage followed, even as the High Republican vowed to represent all Republicans all the time. He would fix what was wrong, find out what's going on and make things great again. The hotel nearby prospered. Elected officials who criticized were corrupt. Federal agencies dwindled, as he restored the dignity and purity recalled in a majority Caucasian nation. *We will fight to the end!*

Who in politics? Politicians? Doctors don't cause pain. Addiction. Scalpels and drugs! It happens. You can't win if. Risk. Break the eggs. Save the omelet. It's fantastic. Tremendous.

Outragers lurked, envious and hateful, like the toothy gal with the bee in her shorts.

Wenk smirked, unruffled. *Tell me, Erika . . .*

Back then, the many wondered, *Erika who?* Who would challenge the most formidable Republican on Earth?

Two-part question, Erika, yes or no, both parts. Were you ever had? How many drinks in? Do you still see him? Or her? Do you remember? His name? Where is she now? How many drinks since? Partners? May Hard Luck forgive.

Born again to Hard Luck, Harry Wenk, got the spin.

Swain got the knock, not the Pugnacious Prize. A billion searches in those days revealed Swain, Erika, frisky cub, Q.4 in no time, leveling to .3, settling to .25. As network correspondent, she pumped the jam to .28 and climbed to 4.2 with scoop and exposé over a few brief decades. She became Erika Swain, Warp News Anchor, rock solid at 1,256 and 1 on spin control.

News dogs called this Wenk Republican an uncanny politico who shot to kill, long range, out of range or up a tree, no problem. Harry Wenk shaped Republican imagery for a society craving justice and revenge, demanding a return to Elm Street.

Year One brought legislation to end tax on those investors who made the Republic great. THE LIFE could thrive without bureaucrats but not without investors. Warpanal bought in. Why not?

When Harry Wenk squints, pale sockets blend best with Man Tan. He blamed light bulbs for the orange tint. *Gimme a break!* Shifting bulk, lips aquiver, smoothing the coif without touching it, the High One is monumental. He confides: *We'll find out what's going on there. Won't that be fantastic?*

Would Hard Luck play Second Fiddle? *We'll see what happens.* Wenk has His ear and vice versa. Truth became indelible, as gangster tough compassion rose on an eerie smile.

Harry Wenk's face on a coin, profile right, shows grim resolve. Left showed the squirrelly drift every foldover comes to, so right seemed best. Harry Wenk on a coin will shore up the hohum for a hundred years. *It's the right thing to do. Why not? Money and love.*

Comfort, power, reverence. Who's laughing now? He laughs; one hundred percent of the many knows the High One will rule forever, if he wants to—until a blip in '84 puts stats in a spin.

He asserts: *Stats are cyclical.* THE LIFE *is ebb and flow. Not outrage. A blip. I give you HumanSport. My name is on those checks. I'm the only one.*

Great leaders through history had worries to ignore. Harry Wenk is a leader; the stat is 1. *I built the greatest economy in history. We have greatness like never before! Greater comfort lies ahead in* THE LIFE*, with happiness instead of the same old drudge.*

> Submitted on the floor of the Congress of the United Sectors, its protectorates and orburbs:
>
> We hereby resolve that the High Republican of the United Sectors of America shall be genetically spliced at his/her or whichever's discretion in twenty or fifty segments or combos thereof for immortality and greatness in the party and the republic.

A resounding NO-O-O! sends VU to pain threshold. Heads turn across the land. From out in the yard, down the alley and under the cardboard, a question resounds: "What the heck?" The bedrock bottom line is no, the immortality bill will not pass.

No-confidence shakes the pillars of Republicanism. Cracks open, debris falls. He asks. *After all I've done for them? Jenkins of Shoofly, Hotchkiss of Hogjowl, Mumford of Cornpone, Tarney of Red Dirt, Long of Louisiana, Rex of North Sluree, Phug and Graham in South Sluree know that disloyalty is a terrible thing. How do we play hardball uptown? They'll find out what bastards they fathered. They'll learn what assassinations they were in on and what country they were born in. They'll see where Hard Luckless treachery gets them. In the end.*

Warpanal frenzies on a Wenk defeat in Congress. Would a Hominy and Bubba Coalition deliver humiliation and mortality to the Republican of the ages? *Worse yet, holier-than-thou cornpone drivel oozing out the mouth holes of those molasses-drawling crackers practically makes their hats shrink. They sucked up to me in the early going. Asking for money and personal favors.*

Harry Wenk knows the game and hunkers down for the infight. He needs a populist frenzy, Memory Lane to penthouse condos. He needs rampant fear and Second Amendment emotion from loge boxes with catered lunch, to the riffraff with their soiled blankets and schnaps. He needs the home crowd standing firm, as OneEye snatches victory from the jaws of defeat. No more shout-down, name-calling conspiracy and so's your old man. This is a shoot-out.

Harry Wenk can grab a neck and hang on. Looking left and right, he's ready, whatever it takes. At the podium, he gives what for: *My fellow Republicans. I give you great works. You're welcome. Tremendous. We'll find out what's going on. More than meets the eye. I will continue as long as we both shall live or longer!* In pregnant pause, HR turns from OneEye to Congress.

OneEye blinks to point of view. *I see a city on a hill. Terrific. I run this outfit.*

HR polls by eye contact. Members twitch, smile and frown.

Erika Swain, *soto voce dramatae desperatae,* explains: "The High Republican knows they'll vote against him if he can't change three more. He's shooting fear bullets, flushing Republicans." Erika says a bloodletting could doom the one-party system. As if sensing her blasphemy, HR turns back to OneEye, hand to heart. *I pledge allegiance to the Republic, for which we stand. I will be blunt* (you has-been cunt) *on Earth as it is in heaven.*

"This High Republican will be around forever or as long as he wants, if he gets the votes. Or won't he? I'm Erika Swain. What's going on?" Erika holds a pregnant pause, as the High One steps down and strides out like a fearless man in a dark alley.

Three, two, one and cut to three shorts on *Avarax*: *Ask your doctor if Avarax is right for you. Dermatite*: C*inch neck wattles overnight with Dermatite. Rimsosoft*: *If other hemorrhoidal ointments let you down or keep you up.*

Back on the floor, it's a chat with Senator Brent Rex, Republican from North Sluree. "Aw, heck, he's upset. I think this'll blow over. I can't give the man immortality when folks in Sluree is keeling over so young and don't ask but one measly dam to shore up a muddy creek, more of a ditch, really, not doing nobody two bits o' good. All they get is veto, on account of this immortality issue. Well, Sir. I'm willing to look at a situation if you are."

Cut to Congresswoman Louise Long, Republican from Louisiana: "This ain't the time nor place to talk about Natasha, so I won't speculate. I darn sure won't discuss allegations of holoporn or gold digging. Don't forget: he chose her."

Back in the Oval Office, he who rules the world is sensitive as the next guy. Confiding with longtime warp confidant Slim Hackity of FUX, HR ventilates: *The nerve! A lifetime of incredible deals, and for what, a throwback to the old pork? It's a conspiracy. My face sits in pants pockets across the land. Someone is feeling for a chink in my armor, and I don't mean a little Chinese guy. That someone is Erika of the testicular fortitude. Something is going on. People are telling me. We'll find out. Bloody Erica and her haters. Terrible. Fooling around on Natasha? We still do it! All the time!*

Harry Wenk changes ties to show new confidence on camera. In the resolute chair, he explains: *Leather squeaks, pleading for mercy. I carry the weight well. This job is exercise, pumping my heart rate, running the S.o.L. gauntlet. Yes. Crazy. We'll win. We do.*

That didn't go well, and a tough season gets tougher when even FUX reports the Standard of Living (S.o.L.) index down. It feels like a low point, and the High Republican needs help. He mutters: *the S.o.L has declined for sixty years. Sixty-eight years, really. You want to nitpick? Who says yes when troublemakers ask if you have less than you did six years ago? Nobody. Why? Me! But instead of a cocktail formality, we got coup d'état. They need data to know how well off they are? Okay, here's data . . .*

He closes his eyes to better see. *The S.o.L. index won't change the vote. They vote as I say. As I say . . .*

Weighing options, he rises and wraps the executive person in a plush overcoat. He slouches from the Oval Office to the great corridor and down the sweeping staircase like what's his name, that dancer who didn't mind alleys or rain. *Yes, that's me!* At the front door, he commands: *Neutralize!* Across the lawn and out Manuel's gate, he murmurs, *Sneaky little Mexican thinks we don't know*. With a lip quiver to one and all, it's down the avenue to seek counsel from she who knows crisis.

With us or against us. I am the Republican. People out there want to kill. You and your family. That's why. To keep the war out there. It's terrible. Terrible!

Harry Wenk knew a woman, useful to a young man but left to poverty and weight gain. *Fat happens. Not my fault. Help a rising star. Look how great it turned out for the country. No time for footsies. We're winning the war on my watch. I'm good. Nice. She was nice to me.*

Striding the filth and degradation at street level, he thinks she'll ask for next month's rent. *Can do.* Or next month's immortality. *I love the little people. We'll see what happens. She can live forever for a month or two. We can work this out.*

He stops to savor, among the many at work and play. *What amazement, if they knew. I am among them.*

Hoodlums idle near the great statue of Himself, fiddling with spoons and rubber bands. Oldies nap at the base. *Foul Breath* jams the area with *Gong Yo Fonky Doodle.*

The High Republican in bemused disgust watches a geezer roast two rats on a stick. Stepping up, he says: *Without the FDA stamp, those rats are diseased. I'm in rats. Wenk Rats. Grade-A. Quality. Not from China. Not anymore.*

"What?" asks the geezer. "With the FDA stamp I can sleep better? So the Wenker makes seven bucks on a two-dollar rat."

Wenk Rats are best. Bigger and better taste. Much better.

The geezer looks up.

The High Republican freezes, as thousands turn to the familiar voice. Harry Wenk stands his ground, as he's pledged to do. But this is not airwaves. It's bricks 'n mortar, flesh 'n blood. The High hand rises to make it okay. He won't wave, less they misconstrue. The Big R doesn't stroll by every day, and maybe it's not him. But some wave back, and for a moment, it feels as it should. *These people trust me, love me, want me and need me forever.*

The crowd converges. The monkey wakes up. A finger pokes for holographic chicanery. A tugged sleeve and a knife seek a sample. Another finger spins hairs and musses the cotton candy.

The High Republican would remind these folk of his nuclear deterrent but breaks free instead, freeing the purple necktie and tossing it in the air. Eyes and hands follow it, as he ducks into his overcoat and out. He pulls up the beard, puts on shades and a hat and presto: Where'd he go? He was here, just here.

Into thin air is where the most powerful Republican on Earth can escape the monkey, who needs to feed on the only perfect Q.10 in history. What, he should stand by for a feeding?

In a few blocks, Harry Wenk can smell the underbelly. *Now this is Memory Lane.* Light dims in the cardboard abyss, festooned with rags, warp receptors and human detritus. *Yearning to be free, past shelf life. Hard Luck be with them.* Yet the Lane is mordantly appealing. *Call me sentimental. Children snug as bugs in their rugs, watching little radii. I did that for them. 25-inch minimum. Into the big tent. These people trust me, love me and need me forever.* He steps on a pile, and it shouts out. Up with insane grunting, the ogre grabs. *Hey! I'm the High Republican,* says Harry Wenk.

The ogre says, "Yish mmph ga dah . . ."

You should be euthanized. Harry Wenk pulls a card from his pocket. *Call my office.*

The ogre falls back into a heap.

Harry Wenk steps around, dropping the card where the ogre will surely find it.

Children stare, six or ten to the box. *Human* LIFE *is sacred, children. Save your money. Find out why. Don't spend it. Save it. Bless you. Bless the children. Save it.*

This is no time for campaigning. The Lane generates too much ammonia for a person from above. Harry Wenk feels faint. Covering his nose and stepping lively for three blocks, he comes to a gate. He knocks. Eyes peer through the gloom. He knocks again.

The whozerscope opens. On a gasp and a titter, tumblers roll.

He goes up and into a room that would fit in his closet. Two pews line either side with an aisle down the center. *This room will be dismantled and moved to the Smithsonian.* He regards the room where the face on a coin took solace, once upon a time.

Irene MacGonnorea was a dancer and a hooker with a good ear. *Make that a terrific ear. Fantastic. She heard everything and could chew gum at the same time.* Harry Wenk sensed value.

She told Stanley he looked like a honey badger in hamster clothing. Her little picker upper helped with esteem, as she garbled, "You must be Republican."

How did you know?

"Call it a hunch."

He winces anew as she opens the door, far older than her years. How did she get so fat? *I'm sorry*, he says.

"You're sorry? What can I do about that?"

I can get you a splice.

"Do I look like I need a few more years?"

A facelift? A nip and tuck? A what do you call it, where they, you know, cut out part of your . . . uh . . . thing . . .

"What do you want?"

I want your opinion.

"Okay. I don't watch. I got perspective. You don't come around. What's this, old home week?" Irene MacGonnorea waddles to her hot plate.

It's been a few years. I've done well. Tremendous. Maybe you heard. Something is building against me.

"They won't make you immortal. So what? If you can get me a splice, you can get one for yourself."

What good is life without power? How did you know? You don't watch.

"I got a pulse. Who doesn't know? The sky is gray. The sea is brown. It's daytime. What's to know?"

They're leaking quarterly stats. They want to do me in. Me! It's complicated, but . . .

"I believe it. Nothing is true, unless you say so."

They won't . . . You don't . . . I can't . . .

Her crooked smile finds a new wrinkle. "Speak up, Harry." She pours heated water into a cracked up and sips.

Grit with mothball aroma and saltine crumbs make ambient effluvia a thing to bear. *Why have I come to this hellhole?*

"Reprieve? You want a cup o' water?"

No.

"Don't tell me you came for . . . Stanley?"

No, please.

"You remember? The little picker upper?"

Yes. It was nice. But I . . .

"Save it, Harry. Here's what you do."

He leans in.

"I want to be an ambassador."

An ambassador? I could sprout cauliflower from my behind.

"Or live forever."

I can't.

"You can."

Where?

"I don't care. I want a condo big enough to turn around in with a staff and a . . . a chamber orchestra."

He laughs. *That's nice too, Irene. But ridiculous.*

"Your Secretary of Education can't read. Your EPA administrator is dirty. Your presence is ridiculous, here or anywhere. You come to an old whore when the chips are down. What's the risk on that? Harry. Are you blind to fallibility?"

I'm not blind. I know more about fallibility than anyone. Fallibility is my specialty. I point it out. Did you see the debates? I'm not blind. Or wrong. I'm not wrong. Look at me. I'm . . .

"You're going on the warp tonight, with a fire and the dog. Play the piano."

I can't play the piano. I don't have a dog. And not tonight.

"Harry. Poof. You'll play the piano. Don't show your hands. Play *My Old Kentucky Home*. Play *Waltz Me Around Again, Willie. Pumpkin Mush Your Head* for the kids. Get a dog. If not tonight, then tomorrow night. How can a yenta rule the world?"

I'll do better. I'll try to go on. Is that it?

"No. That's not it. You've been around too long. You can't fix this with one stroke. The fire and the dog are a good start. You need a theme. How about . . . Get America outdoors again."

America outdoors? All at the same time?

"Yeah. It's perfect. Why not?"

There's no room. We spend billions to keep them indoors. The whole shebang'll shut down.

"What do you care? Blame the NaySay! You want eternal power; don't be shy. Lead the many. Bang their head."

I do but . . . How do you know this?

"I don't watch. I get ideas. You need Jimmy Grimm up here Under One Roof this Sunday, dawn to dusk. Let 'em see you and Jimmy and the Hard Luck Guy getting it right. That'll help. One more promo can do it, if it's personal, on sporting victory. Not like throwing out the first ball. That's too tame. You need more dominance. More power. You need finality!"

A kill!

"Bingo. You're catching on. You want substance but casual, a natural outing for sport and history. Get it right, and you're in."

Harry Wenk wants to believe. Irene MacGonnorea's vestal viewpoint is pure as the driven snow. She's seen action on the front lines of two-dollar whoredom and remains politically untainted and alpha-free, a font of political know-how and clarity. She has not watched, does not watch, will not watch. She is preeminently qualified to counsel the Highest Republican in the world. He knows where she's headed.

Me? In Sector HS? He grins at the big picture and revels in the glory: *Two birds. One stone.* He chuckles, *Or three.*

Cogs mesh and spin to redline. Gears shift to overdrive, as she summarizes, "HumanSport is your baby, win or lose. I'd say it's an even bet. That McGunty buzzard got herself pumped full o' dead. Christ on a crutch, whatever happened to common sense?"

Yes, but . . . me? In there with . . . How can I . . . I'm not afraid of small game. I go in. I flush and kill. But Humansport? They have their own guns. That's armed combat. Like war! You know how I feel about that. I don't mean war. The war must go on. I mean . . . If I'm in it, who's gonna rule the world? I tell them what to do!

"Like you say, Harry, it's all attitude. If a million people get bagged in there, I'll still wait an hour to pay for groceries. Entitlement savings? For who? You go in looking fearless, OneEye over your shoulder. You bag a top Q. Boom. You're immortal."

Shoot a high Q? They'll hate me. They love the high Q-ed.

"They love the action. I didn't say it'd be easy. You want to rule the world forever. I want a maid. Same difference. You got to take some risk. You want to bring it home. Get shot at first, so it looks like self-defense. Take it in the shoulder, one of those hollow core jobs to put you in intensive care with a worried nation watching and praying. Self-defense on a justifiable homicide, critical condition and heroic recovery, OneEye stuck on you like a mama worried sick. You might die! Harry, wake up and smell the air freshener."

Irene reaches for a polypak of saltines warming on the hotplate. "Care for a cracker?" But he's lost in thought and painful visions of a shot in the shoulder. She crushes two saltines over her hot water. "Harry. How you ever got to be head hotdog is beyond me."

He scowls. *Nobody speaks to the High Republican that way. Nobody. Maybe Vlad, but he . . .*

"You won't get shot. They fit that in with synapse inserts or whatever they got now. Do I have to tell you that?"

He laughs short. *I knew that. Preceptor modulation. But how do you know, if you don't watch?*

She shrugs. "I used to work the alley. I saw. It won't be simple. You're gonna get a run from that bitch who won't shut up. That's where it's coming from. Mark my words, Harry. This isn't an opinion. You ain't the only Republican in town, you know."

Erika Swain. I knew that, too. I should eliminate her. But . . . How do I get her in there?

"You can't. She's too smart. You fried her giblets once already. You need the other one, the genius idiot."

George Longley?

"Yeah. Him."

You want me to kill George Longley in HumanSport? They love George Longley. I wish someone would kill him. But not me.

"Yeah, well. It's you, hotshot. He couldn't hit the side of a bus from inside. Besides, they only love him because he's crammed down their throats. Can't even guzzle a Pud without that creep watching. You kill him, what's gonna happen? They're gonna forget. That's what. They'll talk about the crazy scientist who tried to kill Harry Wenk. That'll fade. Hohum. Besides, it's time for a change, and you're the one to get changed, if you don't step up and dance. It's you or the egghead, Harry. You pull this off, nobody's gonna care about Erica Swain. You asked, I told. Do what you want. Now you got perspective."

But what if I . . . What if I get . . . in the line of fire?

"You die, dummy, just like most people, sooner or later. Difference is, you document your own retrieval before you head in. Do I have to spell out Full Republican Pardon for you?"

Harry Wenk tenses and relaxes all at once. *Yes! I knew that, too. I mean, I would have thought of it!*

"Like they say in the industry, no comment."

Four score and seven years ago, Irene MacGonnorea predicted the rise of a young Republican who made facts incidental to brimstone, who didn't drink or snort, except in private. And nobody cares about a little odd pussy, if it only takes a minute and feeds a hamster. He knew then as he knows now: *She's right.*

Standing into cobwebs, he drifts out. "Harry." He turns. "It's a hundred bucks. You got to admit, the talk is still tight."

I . . . never carry cash, but . . .

"Yeah, yeah, you'll send a man around. Boy. Republicans."

Yes. A man. Around. He drifts out. *Or a woman.*

"I want it warm!" She calls down the dark spiral. "And a driver! I want a cook! And a maid! To clean the litter box! For my cat! Two cats!" Descending like Moses from the mountaintop, Harry Wenk knows what to do. "And tarcaff! Would *you* like hot water every goddamn day of your LIFE?"

Out the black gate that slams into sameness with a million black gates, the most powerful Republican heads back on a surge of historical magnitude. It makes sense. Who is closer to perfect Q with residual resentment from the many? *George Longley is who. It's time for a change all right. Time to live Under One Roof with olden valyuz. Let's go outside.*

It's never enough. But why should it be?

Irene MacGonnorea poured the wisdom of survival into the most powerful Republican ear: Q fades. Q surges.

Okay, let's just see about that.

XI

With Utmost Humility

Sports & THE LIFE *Illustrated* still sells random event samplers of *The Greatest Debate that Never Was*. At eight easy payments of $39.95 plus S&H, it out-grosses everything but *How to Build a Cubeport*. It's not a fair match, given the gargantuan appeal of the how-to series. Beyond that, the Cubeport/Home-Compactor Combo represents unbeatable savings.

Governor Dick Upson, (R) Hardpan Sector, said, "Who cares? I don't care. Do you care?"

When Natasha painted those words on a jacket, suggesting that Dick Upson was a copycat.

Dick who?

But OneEye engorged on Dick Upson's every twitch, sigh and mumble; that's who. Then he had the testicles to challenge Harry Wenk in the primary.

Natasha wore the jacket again and said, "I wear jacket. So?"

The High One laughed and appointed Dick Upson to head a department, springing him from oblivia to Cabinet level, where he'd have billions to play with.

When national polling gave Upson a sixty-two percent approval rating, Harry Wenk fired him. *Dick Upson? He's terrible.* Nobody got sixty-two percent approval since the young NaySay President from Chowdersector, the one with charisma and sex drive.

The HR went down to Hardpan for some touch football and a picnic with—Hey, look; it's Dick Upson! He and the HR strolled in shirt sleeves for a photo op with winning smiles and Natasha, who kept her yap shut and wore spike heels and a dress that squeezed her mammary glands. She wobbled a bit but they didn't, not like real ta tas, but big counts most.

Harry Wenk proved that any Republican can have charisma, but only one can be High, and that would be Harry P. Wenk. Dick Upson's challenge was foolish and best forgotten. And that was that!

Governor Dick Upson threw in the towel and got to be Secretary of the Ulterior after all!

Thus quoth the conqueror: *See what happens, when power teams up with public service?* Harry Wenk ruled the world and would continue, which is better than three holes in the noggin hardly through a first term. With comparisons secure, talk of a hundred-year mandate became casual as a Memory Laner guzzling schnapps while peeing off a curb, which seems inappropriate but makes a playful post, in keeping with a sense of humor.

We'll see what happens, Harry Wenk thinks again after his recent defeat in Congress. *Adversity is the fuel of triumph.* The High One energizes White House staff, dredging old platitudes, hateful reference and reassurance on the sum of these parts for a victory that will never fade. *Never, ever, ever!*

When Mister Wenk first ran, he shared a family bio of vast fortunes dwindled to mere millions. He'd fought back, willful and intimidating. From humble parents and a humble home, the trumpets of destiny blared. Taiko drummers helped at the Republican National Convention, with balloons and greatness, rightness and hallowed-be-thy-Nameness of the next High Republican of this exceptional nation.

It seems like only yesterday. Next Sunday he'll recall humble origins again, to assure those unborn back then that humility still reigns. They'll thump and howl. They'll sway like wheat in a grow-house, ready for the reaper. *Harry Wenk wasn't born into incredible wealth. He chose two decent, Hard-Luck-fearing people of olden values, plain folk who bore a son in the image of Hard Luck. Mother spent time in Memory Lane. I'm not proud of that. Hard Luck shored up Wenk interests in the snazziest properties on Earth. You and I know what salt tastes like. I am Harry Wenk, your one and future High Republican of the United Sectors of America!*

Eternal High Republican? No. They love the stability thing but eternal might get them thinking. That can lead to resentment.

Harry Wenk buffs his speech and calls Jimmy Grimm. The road to power is a minefield of foolishness, and a kazoo seems safer than a piano without showing his hands. *I can speak through a kazoo, like a psychic medium, ordained by Hard Luck, Himself. We do not need a piano fraud investigation. They'd have a field day with that one. Besides, I'm terrific on kazoo.*

He orders a dog and a shampoo, rinse and tint for the dog and Natasha. The dog gets a flea treatment. Both wife and dog will emote by the fire. She'll pat his head. He'll lick her on the cheek where the salami got rubbed in. *The family is for values. We'll chat.*

He practices in the mirror: *The problem these days is living* THE LIFE. *We got more stuff on the warp than outdoors. That's good but confined. We're burdened. We suffer a national malaise.*

No. Scratch that. How about: We need to find our nature again, to fill our open spaces with people at play. As your High Republican, I support the Republic for which we stand, one nation,

Under One Roof. We'll take a long weekend, just me, Natasha and Woof, to an area so beautiful for spacious skies and amber waves of grain, for purple mountain majesties, above the fruited plain. And don't forget the sporting spirit. Your High Republican will score a sporting victory in that great old place called HumanSport.

Perfect! It ties everything together with seldom is heard a discouraging word. It'll play during Monday Night Slamball. Halftime! She wants ratings; I'll give her ratings. Ooh! How about a new initiative: a tax credit for children to take effect in the year of conception! Retroactive! That's money back on unborn children who are the future! The future! No, wait! A package deal, with felony banishment to a wasteland for any woman seeking abortion? Or burning a flag! No, best keep it simple.

Next thing you know, it's late, even for Harry Wenk, who sleeps and dreams. They went against him. It's bad. He'll get the lead back and stomp downfield on a warp chat to dumbfound the many. It'll shape up as a marathon Sunday with Jimmy Grimm *and* a national safari: big sky, big game, big money. A High Republican will gift-wrap the great outdoors and kill the rascal who pulled the rug on olden values. *He did a terrible thing. He's a techno-scourge, the Satan of Science, what's his name Longy, Lonly, whatever. Let the Swain bitch spin on that!*

Just so, it comes to pass: Harry Wenk's hearth crackles in subdivisions and condominia across the land. The wife and Woof sit on as overstuffed gurney, icons of obedience. He smiles. *My fellow Republicans. Let's spend some time together, just us. Me and you. I want to play some music. Music is a wonderful thing. My parents loved music. I love music. It's wonderful here and getting better every day. Natasha, say hello.*

"Hello."

Woof, boy, can you speak? Speak boy! Speak!

"Woof."

Isn't he something? I love dogs. We had many dogs when I was a boy in 00. It was New York then, over the rainbow. There's no place like home. And cats. I love cats. We had many cats when I was a boy in New York. Golden, olden times, with good, decent values. Not like now, people coming in here who don't deserve it. I want to go back. We're downtrending. It's a cycle, not my fault. A cycle. Remember when you were wrongly accused? Slandered? Demonized with vicious forespin when you tried to help? Cut me some slack. All right? Speaking of olden values and my boyhood home, I want to play my second favorite song, My Old Kentucky Home. What's my very favorite? Rock of Ages. You knew that. Ha! Okay. This one is for you decent folks in Hominy Sector.

So flows the oddly awkward yet endearing rendition of the classic plantation ballad, played on kazoo. Warpanal dissects body language, content, tone, tempo and rhythm, asking, "What? My Old Kentucky Home is his second favorite song?"

"Did he ask forgiveness?"

"He did, but without conceding guilt."

"Is this a second chorus coming on?"

"It is!"

"Surely, he won't do three!"

"It doesn't matter! Don't you see?"

What's to be seen, warpanalyzed, obsessed, refracted, reflected and gulped down in hopes of digestion, is that Kentucky was the only Hominy subsector to abstain in the recent defeat. The High Republican said he loves the kazoo. No substantive implications there, and after two more songs with no geographic reference, it's *Good night, all. Sweet Dreams. See you Sunday, you know where.*

Jimmy Grimm'll join me. You come too. Be there. You have your weekends, and don't forget Monday night for me and slamball with some hard outrage at half time. The HR dims to serenity glow, fade, hold and . . .

Cut to commercials, a subtly ominous detergent series with emphasis on cleaner cleans.

Sunday goes famously with a twelve-hour prayer session. Repose in stillness goes to freeze frame at six minutes. Stunt doubles come on, kneel and hold, so a High Republican and his righteous friend can break for a stretch. On a short nip, Jimmy Grimm praises Hard Luck for stunt doubles, allowing two old country boys to steal a moment for the good of the nation and the world.

The High Republican takes the bottle and raises it. *Reverend Jimmy, if I did imbibe, which I don't, I'd tip a snort right now. We're all stunt doubles, when you get down to it. The Republican Party can protect the values we hold dear, no matter who's at the helm. Preservation of wealth, living forever, maximum profit in global markets—that's what got us here. It doesn't matter who waves at them. I don't plan on getting shot, Jimmy, no way, José. If I did, Hard Luck forbid, that fool up front can wave at them every bit as well as this old fool.*

Reverend Jimmy Grimm takes the bottle back for another swig, "Mister Republican, I think we're gonna enjoy this."

The two great men of Church and State stroll back to the biggest stage in the world, where Reverend Jimmy rises to the pulpit, oozing warmth like a hot spud under butter. Honing to the heart of the situation, he decries olden valyuz gone away. "I beseech thee. Bring us back! Get off our duff and outside, where it all began! Olden valyuz can save us! Look at this! And listen to me! Forget electrons and protons. Frequencies. LIFE is fouled on particulate ionization. You hear? Let me show you something."

Reverend Grimm opens his lapwarp to the new King James version of George Longley's Random Event Sampler. "Look here what's fooling us." The inquisition is casual. "How about too much techno?" He shuffles icons and goes in. Thousands gaze at the Jumbotron, and in a blink, truth is upon them! "Let's sample a random fella, call him Bill Ding, and a woman Ruth. Let's add Bud and Sis, Spot and Puff. Let's tune in to warp programming electrospherically, say, all the time. That would be every waking hour of every single day. I'll punch in, oh, say, six months."

Like a maestro, Jimmy G gazes up as the giant screen defaults to ERROR CODE 666: *NO FUTURE. DARK AGES. NO FUTURE. DARK AGES. NO FUTURE.* A rumble resounds . . . Could it be direct communiqué from Hard Luck? Many forswear the presence among them! Jimmy murmurs, "Go to olden valyuz. Love your Republic now and forevermore. Aah . . . men."

Rumors riddle the airwaves. Did Jimmy Grimm sniff his index finger? Substantiation is nil. Beyond that, residual filth follows the ERROR CODE every time. The seven-second delay automatically snuffs subterfuge for eighty-two percent of the viewing audience. Yet careening off the electrosphere in shrill lament: "It's a guy in a fuckin' mouse suit!" With zero recog, the voice is quickly forgotten, a breeze, a starling, a lizard or something.

Beloved Reverend Jimmy raises his laptop high, like a tablet received on Mount Sinai. Slamming it to the lectern, he smashes snot outa the Luck-forsaken thing and brings the house down.

A single spin later, it's Monday night. Slamball! It begins well enough but hits rough terrain when the Reverend Grimm gets stuck in a crosstown jam and shows up for his surprise walk-on twelve minutes late! The HR is stretching his slamball rhapsody back to childhood in Sector 00, with the dogs, cats and toiling parents who remained unbitter in this great land of ours. Segueing to sport and THE LIFE, he urges the downtrodden to save their money. *Save it! Don't spend it!* And on to supporting our troops, who go where few persons would go for military pay. Pausing to ponder a brief vacay, he says, *A weekend will be perfect. Really perfect.*

Can that seed germinate? Like a tumbling tumbleweed, here comes Reverend Grimm, evangelically flushed, sputtering that word has come from Hard Luck. Grabbing the High One for balance, Jimmy blurts, "He wants for the Republican to be anointed by Congress: Sanctuarian." Reverend Grimm belches slightly through a holy moment. "Nobody knows like the Republican. Not. Even. Me."

Mixed agreement VUs make it good as done: Sanctuarian, the holy mantle. *They say you gotta be dead. We'll check our options.*

Warpanal buzzes over this apparent response to the Bubba/Cornpone offensive. All frequencies but *USS* speculate that Erika Swain will throw down. Is she up to something?

With nuance and timing that only the *USS* Anchorwoman can muster, she stays mum! Ready to strike, she's coiled and ready.

Bubba and Cornpone reps avow olden valyuz. Olden love echos across the land. Fundamentalist Republicans yank filters and receptors from their panels! A fogy from Muscogee achieves fleeting Q-in.4 with antique rabbit ears, dusting the contraption and telling OneEye that happiness comes in 2-D. "The day I need more'n Jimmy Grimm 'n H-1 is the day I hang it up."

How quickly a mood can change. Giddy with renewed hope Harry Wenk surges on a three-shot with Woof and the wife to cure what ails a nation. How well it plays!

Back on set, HR smiles and tells the Reverend Jimmy Grimm, *I owe you. I'm thinking some Second Amendment remedy to round things out. Snub nose .52 for fun, a .64 magnum for muscle, AK 91 for certitude. How 'bout a baker's dozen snipers from ATF to bring this one home. Misfits threaten National Security. They don't wanna bust their hump sixty hours a week and stay overdrawn, two months late and too tired for bumpity squish. They don't! I'll take that Longleg loser out!*

Reverend Jimmy sinks into a chair with a sigh, "Hallelujah!"

A problem remains: drawing out the Longleg loser. Harry Wenk banks on another walk down Memory Lane, this time in full disguise, quickly in, shushing shrill demands for servants and stuff, until Irene says, "How do you draw him out? You invite him! Hard Luck, Harry. I want a limo. I want call waiting . . ."

But the High Republican is back down and out and up to the pinnacle in a blink, inviting George to a hunting weekend, just them two. *Forget Woof and the wife. Nobody wants the soft stuff.*

"I don't hunt," George Longley says. "More to the point, chromosomatic aberration in humans compelled to kill other species to extinction may be . . ."

"Yes, well, I think . . ."

My staff will interface with your staff. See you, George.

The High Republican dissolves.

Hm. The line went dead. It could be a bad connection, but not with synaptic-bridge backup? Harry Wenk must have one or two, if he has the backup and delay with the secondary delayed backup. Wouldn't he, after all?

XII

Pizza Karma

Meanwhile, back at HumanSport, business holds steady.

Shy of booming, the place meets projections, once Echelon analysts factor trepidation relative to violence and death. A many so long out of the hunt is bound to shy on first blush. Initial price resistance kicks in, compounded by the unLucky Wanda Ann situation. At least Wanda Ann is grist for progress: many Republicans sigh wistfully, "Wanda Ann would want it this way." The sentiment rings true. Nobody doubts Wanda but the fringe—bums, misfits and NaySayers. Her legacy will preempt her tragic demise. Wanda's taxi torso exhibit draws record crowds to Pudland.

Bunghauser Deuche submits a request to HumanSport Admin for taxidermy right of first refusal on high Qs. The prospect boosts quarterly projections and consoles sportspersons willing to stick it out there, from the relatively known on up.

With growing entertainment value, acceptance gradients also curve upward. Naysayers can't drown out consensus. The HR summary: *You have crime. Terror. Mass murder. Mayhem. Famine. Pandemic. Drought and dysentery. Much negativity from lying, crooked people. Low energy scum. Bad hombres. What can you do? Give in? No. You shoot that sonofabitch!*

Sonny Wayne Wyoming sits by, ready to douse the sonsabitches, they try to get funny. His new position brings THE LIFE. With material gain comes insight to Hard Luck and the hohum at operational levels. He learns that a Hard-Luck-fearing man knows humility, that faking it is a place to start, that he has something to lose. The job—the position—gains meaning.

The RV Graveyard becomes a dynamic exercise in recycling. Ultimate sportspersons can bivouac in the dead RVs at no extra charge, except for the ultimate price on bad judgment. Judgment comes to Sonny Wayne as well. He'd imagined rocking on the porch, taking potshots at strays and stragglers, but that fantasy withered in the light of consequence half a dozen firefights in.

He winged a couple of wannabes early on. One stayed in but got bagged the same day. Realizing his error, he pledged on local Warpanal that he would hold fire, even if a grazing shot looked like fun. He advised: "You cain't come in here loaded up for killing and go shufflin' up to a RV for a little nappy poo. You fittin' a stay one dern minute, you best be fittin' a give, lest ye shall receive. Heck, you gonna receive no matter what. Second feller I winged headed home. I'm issuin' that one a free pass, thirty-two hunnerd *plus* expenses, to make amends. Why would Sonny Wayne do that? Good for the Republic. At's why."

Sonny Wayne bagged another the second week, not really looking for a kill but testing his Featherlight Trigger. Sure enough, he wished he hadn't done that, too. At least it was an oldie nobody missed, and he wouldn't make a claim. Pinkos cleared the debris with nobody the wiser.

Rocking in the floodlit haze, he reflects on personal growth and Lucky stars and talks personal into his handhold diary. "Who'd a guessed it'd get s'good? No need to fuck it all up now." He senses movement yonder, maybe a lizard, but you don't grow up on a wasteland without steel-trap lizard recog. He murmurs to the handhold, "Besides, ain't no lizards without some Japs close by, and especially ain't no hundred-eighty-pound lizards." Sonny Wayne raises and snugs. There again! It's a nose pick or head scratch one. Easing whatever the fuck smack dab 'twixt a crosshairs, he exhales easy as a daybreak turd on prune popovers, and . . . BLAM!

Whelp, groan, stagger, flop and out, next stop eternity. "That'll teach 'em. Bastards think they can come in here at night and just lollygag around Wyoming HQ. Well, they cain't . . .

"It goes to show, you cain't decide on nothing. You play it as it comes. Still and all, ain't nothing like banging it right on the money. Bingo! Lights out. I have to admit, it's fun. And there's one less careless sonofabitch a Republic has to pay for."

Sonny Wayne ponders follow-up coverage on this one, "like it coulda been inappropriate or some shit, which it weren't, on account of stalking in the bushes at night. But them follow-up fuckers can show up *any* time and make a mess o' things."

A hunter wants to see if his kill was big and dangerous. Sonny Wayne's wounded quarry squirms from the bush, moaning for somebody to finish her. Sonny Wayne won't do it; next thing you know, every dang staggerpuss'll crawl into porch range begging. "No. She'll die just fine all by her lonesome. Oh, I'd like to have some fun with them there in the flood lights. That whimpering sounds like my cousin Burt, crying like a girl over a damn broke bone or something. Old Burt. That's funny. But this don't seem good neither. Seems like the Hard Luck feller might get right pissed off. Folks work and save for a weekend to turn THE LIFE around; it ain't right, gettin' bagged by the ticket taker and then gettin' left to squirm on top o' that. After all, she is human." Hearing her whine a bit longer, he finishes her and goes in to bed with an end note on the way. "Ain't no end to mercy, once THE LIFE turns around for you."

A pinko detail heads in at first light. Shoot. Some old deluded grandma or librarian out for a fling, chamber still full but for three shots, likely potshots, she shows no dirt nor blood but her own. Probably saved up. Might have been happy to fire off a box of shells and go home, maybe bag a sloppy Joe or a couple decrepits on the way. Sonny Wayne winces, resolving to stay out the fucking way from here on. Game warden can't be bagging game. He laughs but thinks he'll laugh alone, word gets out. Hell, he didn't mean no harm and learned his lesson. He might potshot but only to show HS is for keeps. Anybody gets winged ought to be grateful.

With Q and cash flow, Sonny Wayne settles into the sporting LIFE. Follow-up is sparse, local color crews now and then. They're a pain in the ass, but it's good to hear admiration and envy. Folks passing through the turnstile ask, "You get to do this for a living?"

"Just another shiftless day in a wasteland," Sonny Wayne says. They laugh. He laughs. As he plans his first splice, he gets wind of the bigwigs coming in. It seems, as they say, appropriate. He would have spit off the porch a time ago. Not now. He sends pinkos to clear foul kills ahead of schedule. Bigwigs won't want to see a bunch of last week's stiffs and dried splat. Attention to detail and attitude are part and parcel to Q and money. Sonny Wayne has tasted THE LIFE and likes it. No reason to mess this one up. The place looks good, a snag here or there, some fool stuck up a tree or hung on a ledge, "but you cain't tell a stiff from deadwood once they dry out, without gettin' close up to see the teeth and eyeholes." Hell, that's color and flavor. Another year, the place'll look real as Disneyland, and *THE LIFE with Sonny Wayne* will be ready to go.

Sonny Wayne takes a rest on a dusty afternoon. Action lulls. Unwritten truce settles on the sector like any campground, when folks hang it up for a quiet time. Some set booby traps. All keep a wary eye; like the man says, "Defend yourself at all times."

He goes in for some alpha on his new warp, only a seventy-incher, but hell, goes good with a Warp-Feed Banquet, ready in two seconds or double your money back. Contributions the autobiopic are nonstop. "The new banquet is amazing, leaving the apple-flavor sauce cold, if you outline the sauce pocket with your thumbnail. It's a miracle, cold sauce next to lizard 'n peas and real-style mashed potatoes 'n gravy hotter 'n fresh-fucked sheep dribble. Talk about miracles: three bucks for lizard chunks 'n peas? Good lizard, too. On the skinny side, but hell, a man can hunt lizard for days and not do as well. Leave it to the Japs, selling us back what used to slither on the porch, come up with a meal outa what white folks used to gag on, keep the tails for theirself. Hell. Still, it's hard to beat." Letting the handhold down gently, he thinks a man can see the dang LIFE is more than middling good.

But on the first fork poke, electrons preempt Lazy Susan . . . what the hell . . . Hardly a grab yonder after two years of nothing, Darla Jo says she's coming home loaded for bear. "You know what that means, Sonny? It's a saying, like when you want to kill a bear and you're ready, a round in the chamber and that other part all loaded up. I mean like when they had bears. See you. Don't get excited, Sonny. I got a boyfriend."

Sonny Wayne plays it again. Two years, and she went and filled out behind his back. "Why, that little . . . Ain't it just like her to hold out on her old man when she'd have so much more to give. It didn't hurt her none and helped me out." She looks more woman now than she did at home. Why would she head home when she swore it'd be springtime in Hell before she laid eyes on these rocks again? Is she coming for Q and cash? Darla Jo got so ornery, you'd think she never had a decent home to grow up in or the love Sonny Wayne could show a daughter.

Darla Jo Bojoli got excited as any teen over rock star Qs, till she felt old. Girlfriends bit the dust, ran the foreplay circuit and got married, cashing in on the Republican rebate for first marriage and a ten percent splice credit for each new baby. Darla Jo said no. Why should she hunker down with a lug just because he felt her up and pressed his groin on her? Even if he wasn't jumpy as a vibratwand, she wanted more and aimed to get it. A girl couldn't just pick up and leave an RV graveyard, even if her daddy helped, which he didn't. He was about rich as a flagpole and just as single-minded.

Darla Jo got to Sector Western Heritage the hard way, walking, bumming rides at the recharger, fending off gropers. One offered money. Darla Jo said okay, if he'd up the ante. He didn't. He moped. Sorry sumbitch. If he only knew what he missed.

Getting out in Sector Western Heritage, she could feel the wilderness spirit in subdivisions like Cowboy Hills and Double Buckaroo Ranch Estates and Lone Cactus Ranch Estates and Buckboard Hills and Chuckwagon Ranches and Steerhaven Dream Castles and Sodbuster Ridge and Darla Jo's favorite, Little Dogie Manufactured Homes. Darla Jo loves little dogies. She tingled at the Western Heritage River pump. She'd seen rivers on the warp and knew she could work it as a raft guide. One day she'd float downstream to where a thing or two might finally happen. She plunked down her paltry few bucks on a single for a week, unpacked her washrag, wiped herself off, hiked on down to the river and applied for the job. She lied on her résumé, but any nimrod knows a résumé is to show improv skills. She got on and got the hang of it, losing a few overboard, but the tourists mess up no matter what.

Ten months working the river was enough. Western Heritage is good for saving money. Shopping malls are bigger in WH but pricey. It was work and sleep for Darla Jo, with some alpha when she wasn't fagged out from smiling all day, talking about the guy catching the fish on the second bend, fielding questions about fish, who could live on their own without being fed and how many there used to be and how people caught them. She wanted to make a sign: *I don't know!* Or, *Who cares about a fish?* Sometimes she said there were twenty-four hundred fish. The tourists went slack-jawed, *Twenty-four hundred!* Sometimes she said there were about a million fish. Nobody believed it. Mostly she said it was one fish, and he gave three wishes if you let him go, and all these people caught him and wished for stuff, and that's how we got Western Heritage. The folks liked that one, not that they believed it, but it was a good story with a nice ending, like Disneyland, and the gift shop sold the daylights out of the little plastic fish like the one the guy on the second bend caught. Darla Jo got a raise and praise on her attitude.

She dreamed of drifting on down but caught a ride. The rafts were on guide cables, and the Western Heritage River ends four miles down in a settling pond for pumping back up. Ten months times thirty days times four trips daily times twelve fish questions dimmed her lights but not her drive. She headed out with enough for two weeks in the city—*the* city, 00—three weeks on a pinch.

She didn't love the city and sure as heck wouldn't stay for long. She came for cash and Q. Ten months and twelve million tourists asking about gills, scales and slime can numb a girl's wits. Maybe that's good; the city is so hurried to catch up with itself; a little numbness helps to dull the grit. Everything before yesterday has no meaning in the city. Yet everything onward seems hinged on what came down. You can't break in, but you can fade fast. The writing on the wall says, *You're nobody.* Cash and Q? Well, it has to happen to somebody.

Meanwhile, the breeze is dirty and stinky.

Faces sag and look down. Nobody says hey.

Look out.

Keep moving.

Hey!

Darla Jo isn't your normal gamma normal. *Keep moving*, she tells herself. Don't stop, don't pause, don't think. Just move, stay alert, and when the big O sticks its head out for a millisecond, grab it by the throat, stand on it and make it say, "Yes, Darla Jo."

She gets a job. Some would call it a great job. A week in, she's breaking even on a room, something to eat and carte blanche privileges in an 00 bathroom; sinks, running water and sit-downs with locking doors. She sings, "If I can make it here, I can make it anywhere . . ."

She hasn't made it yet but took a giant leap, getting on with 00 Pizzeria—*00, to Taste the Sector without the Hazards.*

That notion might be a stretch on the Pigflavor & Cheesefood Supreme. Now there's two pounds o' glop you wouldn't wanna step in. It's a toxic spill to stop your heart, but 00ers order up and gobble down. In all fairness, they couldn't very well get unhungry if they didn't eat pizza. Darla Jo doesn't care what they eat, but talk about hazard; delivery persons get two bucks an hour and tips. Tips run eighteen percent on average. You get hung in traffic, lost, chased or late, it isn't steaming or the grease and cheesefood congealed; you eat the load. Oh, sure, you can resteam on arrival, *if* you shell out the twelve hundred clams for the portasteamer. Who'd work this taco stand if she had twelve hundred clams to spare?

A good day has time for thirty-five deliveries plus the twenty bucks on the shift. She can load three pizzas for a circle loop and pencil in two bucks, plus twenty to thirty on tips and maybe pull a few traffic aces and make the first stop three minutes out front. She's busting her chops with the scuz and cheese glop dripping on her shirt and pants. She got those secondhand anyway, but grease stains are embarrassing, till she realizes she fits right in. Everyone wants to break out. She's getting it, sure enough, and *BLAMMO!*

A jerk scans her up and down through the whozerscope and zeroes in you-know-where. The seedy voice asks, "Are you hot?"

She says yeah, steaming, guaranteed.

The voice says, "Prove it."

She knows it's a loser, a perv looking for you-know-what or a freebie pizza, but she cracks the box anyway, and steam doesn't matter when the perv says, "Too cold. I don't want it."

She says okay, look, half price. It's not cold but will be in a minute or two, not to mention the load in the cube. Sometimes she just walks away, cuts her losses and goes.

But sometimes she eats it herself. It's in her shift quota, but sometimes she was so hungry, she already ate one, and this would make two, but she sure as hell won't give it to the perv, so she stands there eating it and lets him watch. Chewing with her mouth open and grease running down her neck, she moans, lets the perv get himself going, and she splits, hurrying to save the load and praying to Hard Luck for no pervs or gropes on the next stop, or at least grant them the cash to pay for the pizza with a regular tip, pulleeze.

She risks life and limb on forced aces back to 00 HQ just to offload. Nobody holds a gutful o' double 0s more than an hour, two at the max. If she's down forty-six bucks on her first run, she sure as heck won't pop three bucks more on a public sit-down.

It happens like that to Darla Jo Bojoli not two months in, farther from first tingles than a wasteland from 00. But tingles come in mystical ways. On a thick, gray day in 00, a girl's spirit bogs down. Losing more time on a major offload, she can only hope for clean and easy and a few decent deliveries around the corner.

Aching in her heart and gut to hold the load, Darla Jo races back to home base, double parks and trots down the alley to the 00 sit-down, ignoring sniggers in the delivery hole. Those pervs snigger at anybody racing down the alley. Barely beating the clock with hardly time to drop her drawers, much less paper the seat, Darla Jo cuts loose halfway down on a double pepperoni and anchoviekin paste, shooting the gap like a qualifier in the stretch at Indy Sector, neck-and-neck in a photo finish.

Breathing deep on pizza whiff, she feels relieved and not too soiled. But the other alien inside her, the Pigflavor & Cheesefood Supreme, creeps inexorably homeward like a naughty child dawdling in the mud, squishing, gurgling and threatening mischief.

She has no choice but to wait it out; neither time nor tide can stop a Pigflavor & Cheesefood Supreme. She wonders: *Why me, where now and what for?* Darla Jo Bojoli is tough, but a girl far from home sees omens stacking up. Doubt darkens the little sit-down; this isn't working out. Squeezing to make this a rush order, she grasps at happy thoughts. Closing her eyes, lolling her head, breathing deep, she opens, glances to the right and reads: *Georgie eats ~~it~~ 00.* That's a good one. Rebellious sentiment helps in hard times. She feels better, seeing stuff on the wall about a rich Republican who has it made. People share a special feeling on the

00 byways. The many murmurs in a little wall talk. Wall talk lets her know she's not alone in the world.

Someone slashed *it* and wrote in *00*. She likes that, imagining the phantom profile of George Longley engorging a Jumbo Oink with Burger Bits. George Longley eating 00 pizza? Doubtful! Maybe Georgie is a closet perv who likes to scan through his whozerscope. She laughs. That feels good. Things start to move. Someone wrote a third message: *00 eats it.* That's good too. Under that, someone wrote: *Eat me.* Darla Jo hasn't eaten anyone, not really, not anyone who was anyone, but she thinks she might, if the price is right, because it can't be worse than a fatlink or the 00 sit-down waiting on the Cannonball Express.

She nearly ate Rolly Raymer. He sorely wanted her to and was about the best ever at eating her. But when a girl has her mind set on leaving, it doesn't seem right to be eating her first boy. Letting a boy eat her was one thing, but eating a boy would be like going steady, or should be. He had a Great Mesa Salami for a joystick anyway, so it couldn't have worked out all that well, even if she wanted it to, but a girl wonders.

Should she have stayed in Wyoming? She could be taking it easy, no worries, eating Rolly and getting used to it, but no. She had to go. Boy oh boy . . .

And there it is, chugging round the bend, one Mongo Jumbo XXL Pigflavor & Cheesefood Supreme hardly a half-hour from one end t'other, no place left to go but back out on the road. She knew there'd be days like this, but knowing doesn't change the day. Tears form. Maybe a good cry is best, so for better or worse, a girl lets it all hang out and sobs like a baby. Yet the tears become prisms that refract in a fuzzy gleam, and Darla Jo sees the tiny head peek out. Call it running for cover in a downpour; at least it's something to run for. With sudden insight on coincidence, she says, "Huh." Never a lollygagger, she cleans herself, washes up and strolls across the alley to Dispatch.

Dispatch is a spitball perv. He leers, "Why aren't you on?"

"Because I'm off," she lies.

Like jumbo olives sliding down the cheesefood, his eyes slide down. "Why don't you wear something slinky? Show off your chest. Outline your vulva. Make more tips that way."

Darla Jo's smile slags like hot mozzarella. "I'm saving up for some slinky wear."

The perv warms like a man given the go-ahead. "You don't have to wait to make more money," he says.

"I want more. I want to learn to make money like you."

"That could take a while."

"I'm not going anywhere. I learn fast." His lips curl to reveal sausage and pepperoni bits riding high on the gum line. Maybe they can drop this charade and get down to progress. He can show her the ropes while she gets comfortable with the you-know-what. A girl makes more with the right connections. Everyone knows it.

But he turns quickly to three calls at once for Gargantua Extremis with extra cheesefood, all half pepperonis but each with a different second half. The rinds and crunchy wet things are on hand, but some nervy bastard wants round-Os, and once you open a five-gallon bucket of round-Os, you move 'em out or go to SPECIAL. Then the board lights up. It's like that in the pizza game. Twenty minutes of nothing, and they gang up boom, boom, boom. Three, twelve, twenty-nine pizzas online in less than a minute with the rush order charge on every one.

A girl from the wasteland goes tingly in connective mist again. Telephone turmoil and people shouting for pizzas right now is a big distraction for Dispatch, a now or never minute, make it or break it for the whole damn shift, a demonstration of worth, which will be the same bunch o' nothing in ten minutes as it was ten minutes ago. But the noise covers her slide sideways and around the console to the back-up file. The opening stays open with thirty-six delivery persons to cover calls pouring in.

Darla Jo breathes deep. She punches in *Georgie* . . . No. *George Long . . . ly*. No. *George Longley*. An address and phone number pop up in brilliant simplicity, green on green. Feeling like Darlarella, Darla Jo sees her invitation to the ball.

Slipping out, she hikes back to her room and counts her stash. A few hundred can't bankroll a future but might capitalize a magic bean for a beanstalk to heaven. She's seen enough movies to know when it's time to go for broke, hang it out there, roll the bones and pray for snake eyes. Washrag fresh, she dabs some blush and eyeliner and sets out to execute. Left, right, left, don't look back, zippity do da, wonderful day, la de da de da . . .

She ignores the questions buzzing like flies. *What in the . . . Who in the . . . Do you think you can . . .* Banished from the sacred temple between her ears, these pesky distractions dissolve in thin air. Stubborn niggles fade in her wake, testament to the will of women. She left her delivery cube double-parked with about half a zillion dollars worth of hot glop stiffening in back. So what? Is a girl supposed to put her LIFE on hold so three dozen pervs can scorch their tongues on time? Maybe it's time for a change.

1: *Attitude is all we have.* She reads it from a billboard, dead ahead, right on time. Like a part of 00 at last, another a cog in the great wheel, she fits in, blending with the flow, one more of the many having a nice chat with herself, hurrying to catch a dream around the corner. She must have allure, so many men want to grope. But what chance can she stand with Georgie? He can have any woman in the world. Well, she's not any woman, and the world can fool you. She squeezes the paper with the magic address in her pocket like a voucher for anything a girl could ever want, splices and tiled sit-downs, shopping and real food for starters. Darla Jo Bojoli understands: immortality is only as good as the cash to back it up, and George Q. Longley has more cash than he could ever spend alone.

XIII

Oh, Little Darla, I Love You So—Oh, Oh, Oh

Did you ever see a Mrs. Longley? No, you never did. You never saw Mr. Longley for that matter, not live on the warp anyway. If there were a Mrs., you'd know about it. She'd be in the fashion blurbs and Q-ups. She'd be regular on *Q's Who* and *Q Review*, *The Few with Q*, *Half a Q*, *Luncheon with Q*, *Q This Week* and the rest. She'd have worthy opinion coming and going, if she existed, which she doesn't. You never heard of her or anything she said or did, because she isn't, and nobody ever said boo, till a spunky gal from a wasteland had a sit-down vision one gloomy day at 00 Pizzeria.

Maybe she's shy.

Leanne is the Longley daughter and anything but shy. She must have a mother somewhere, unless she was adopted, but why would a guy with the best chromosomes in the world want to adopt? Why wouldn't he slip the goods to any old flawless woman he wants? Why wouldn't he keep a harem of women with perfect chests and not a hair out of place and the humma hummaroma oozing from every nook and cranny?

Hey, maybe the sky oughta be plaid. Darla Jo can't count herself out on long odds or oughta be. Averages might rule, but few situations come out average, and in this stratohaze, a merest margin can make the diff between pizza delivery and high mucky-muck for LIFE. She can scrimp and save or put her money on a number and give chance a chance. She loses? So what; today won't change from yesterday or tomorrow or a few weeks ago, which was nowhere.

What if the Mrs. is around? A man still needs a girlfriend, doesn't he? Not that a girl wants to play second fiddle to an old frump, but practicality is a thing. No doubt about it, even if the gut-bomb jitters still play havoc on her rosy-red composure and give her a dose of the sweats to make her foundation clot. She has no choice but to roll with it. Or wait for another shot. And wait.

It was twenty bucks on a wash off that went to two hundred with the shampoo and remake, clean underwear and a dress to show off her chest on a delivery that might count for more than chump change on a maybe tip. She didn't want to spend it and thought she could get by without it but went ahead on the whole hose over. "I come this far." A girl feels confident. She has allure and fresh scent to back it up.

"Oh, this'll get him," the saleswoman said, like it was written all over Darla Jo that she planned to make a play for the face in the Pudmizer can. A lift, a spread, a tuck, a tweeze, a squeeze and there. Darla Jo chortles, thinking what fun she could have with a low-rent perv in a whozerscope. She laughs short; that may be where she's headed, except for the rent, which has to be sky-high. It has to be.

She wonders how old George Longley is. He's been around forever. She doesn't care. But if she had her druthers, she'druther he comes in under a hundred, or at least under a hundred twenty. Do guys that old still like to you-know-what? She doesn't care about that either. Just deliver the pizza. The little dogies of destiny'll deliver the rest. If he has any potential left for you-know-what, Darla Jo is the gal to bring him out.

What if it was only a spitball doodling on the wall, waiting to squeeze off, and she's chasing dreams? Many concerns of the reality/fantasy interface swirl in confusing eddies. What if George Longley is a lie, a ruse, a logo, another empty icon in this crazy freaking 00-ed world of ours? Doubts buzz like flies on a pile of fresh negativity. Yet she strides north, perseverant as a great explorer of the past, onward to the top of 00, to the source of Maximillion Boulevard: #1. It's real. His name came up in green. But what if he doesn't live on this street, or in this city or sector?

He does. If he doesn't, no big deal, she can cruise and smell good and knock on the door anyway. Someone has to live at #1 Maximillion Boulevard, someone rich and maybe not too old, maybe a specific male who'll appreciate a spirited specific female who can swing t'other way if someone wants to. Or maybe a girl can just cruise and meet someone. Or something.

Anything.

Please . . .

All the houses on Maximillion Boulevard are bigger than a girl from the wasteland ever imagined. Peeking through iron bars and spreading shrubs, she beholds domiciles at once terrible and fantastic. Festooned and gargoyled, each parapet is lined with a flashing eye all its own. Some have security gates with electron control, voice or thumbprint. A sign says, "Be." But she knows she isn't meant to be, not really, not here.

At #1, she finds a modest if tremendous security gazebo with a single, outdated OneEye that blinks on her arrival and asks who she is and what she wants. "00 Pizza," she says, knowing her plan is silly and weak—and over. What will she do tomorrow with her cash gone and no job? Heck, what'll she do in five minutes, when she gets chased off by the butler or wife or anybody who says scat?

Tiny tumblers whir. Old hinges groan, and the iron gate creaks open, as if humans passing through are few and far between.

"What a beautiful evening," she mumbles. At twilight, a genius scientist will be done in the lab, unless he works late. Later might be better. Late night better still. But then she might wake him or interrupt a movie. Maybe tomorrow morning . . .

Thoughts plummet like lint in her wake, left, right, left. Stepping softly, her long legs feel like pendulums, and time has come tonight. What if he's not home? What if he has a date? What if he's, like, in there with the High Republican or somebody? The long walkway canopy arches with perfect renditions of pink and white flowers, silk leaves and chintz petals. The flowers hang over silk shrubs around the wishing pond, scummed over but lovely with small rodents suddenly still on her arrival. Or would that be the intrusion of a . . . A what? A spitfire slut from nowhere looking for a freebie feedbag, come to roll snake eyes on the biggest stakes in the history of the world?

No, arriving now is a girl from Wyoming with generosity in her heart, a girl who might struggle with attitude but knows that steel doors sixteen feet high with a whozerscope to match and a monkey-paw knocker must open to receive a pizza. Lifting the giant paw, she wonders what she'll say. The paw falls with reverberant doom into abysmal emptiness on the other side. She breaks a sweat, squirming like a tongue-tied interloper. She must speak surely, but what to say? Tugging her cleavage for a better view of her innocence, she wipes perspiration from in between with the hem of her dress and hopes nobody sees. She looks down her dress to see what George Longley will see: snow white and flawless with a modest heave and succulent shape. She reaches in and feels herself to sample what George Longley will feel, if he—no, and besides: stop. They look bigger and feel bigger, and that's the idea, but the wires are a stiff price to pay. Never mind, the payoff can be stiffer still.

She waits and waits. She needs an adjustment but knows she doesn't have time but what the heck; sliding her dress down, she reaches back, unhooks the push-em-up sling and takes the darn thing off, suddenly sensing the whozer sensing her. Spinning to one side, she shimmies back into the dress. Twenty bucks for the sling; who cares? Flinging it to the bushes, she breathes easier, wishing for a mirror to double check her innocence. Is it back in place? What'll she do if her presentation draws no response.

"Yes."

"Oh Oh."

"Oh oh?"

"Pizza. 00."

"Oh."

She waits, realizing that a man as great as George Longley wouldn't answer his own door. She wishes she brought a box; the place has so many whozers and little eyes. Any fool can see she doesn't have a pizza.

"I didn't order a pizza."

It's him! Or an underling—just her Luck.

"It's a freebie. On account of . . . um . . . a special for people who order three in the same month." Sliding gently into whozer view she hears a moan, not a perv moan but a moan of calculation, of thinking out loud. She loses a tiny sigh of her own, nearly a whimper. He knows. How can he not know? He's the smartest guy in the world, and she's nothing but a . . . a . . .

"How did you know what flavor to bring?"

"The computer knows." That's it. No more. Down and out in 00 is better than jail. She steps sideways, turns back down the walkway.

Ten paces out, the tall door groans. She stops near the rodents, who watch curiously. She turns back to a stoop-shouldered man in his second prime and a ratty flannel shirt, gray eyes bigger than a rodent's but just as round. Tattered khakis and a pre-Reagan pompadour that's hedge-rowed across the top seem experimental, just as the man seems chronically inconclusive, circumspect, undefined. Yet with certain vibrations of power and intimidation, his rock-wall countenance fractures the stillness.

"Do you have a pizza?"

"No."

"What do you want?"

Well, she can't very well say she wants it all and will do anything, enn-nee-thing, for a chance at a LIFE of leisure with no work, endless shopping, alpha soak, opinion rendering, Q-Ups, *Who's Q,* the works.

Tongue-tied, she can't say anything.

Dumbed down and choked up, virtually gazing upon the face of Hard Luck, she feels her brain tell her feet to end the agony and right, left, right back to where she belongs. Yet the inner woman who lives apart from rational fear advises her to let it happen. Shut up. The many see no diff between Georgie and Hard Luck. Her feet feel as one with the pavement. The woman within gooses her.

The man in the door observes her empirically.

She looks for perv potential in his gaze but sees none. Only emotionless objectivity shines from George Longley's eyes, which is good and then again bad. Stepping to within a foot of the face in the bottoms-up of the few Pudmizers she's drained in her tender LIFE, she gazes at the strange hair. She wonders why, when everyone has great hair. Why thick glasses, when nobody wears glasses anymore, much less thick ones? Why such pale, fair skin?

And why lips so plump and red, quivering on the verge of speech? She smiles sweetly, as a fairy godmother from deep within mellifluously says, “I lost my sling.” She stoops to reach it just so, and her dress cleaves on her perfect pink bosom.

From the far side of the precipitous threshold comes the second whimper in an 00 minute, this one his.

Bingo. Home free.

“How did you lose it here?” asks the smartest man in the world, his voice breaking.

Darla Jo eases into a different posture. “I . . .” She looks down, then up. She blushes. “I took it off.”

“Why did you take it off?”

“It was too tight.”

“Why did you have it on?”

“Because . . . Because . . .” Rationale fails her, leaves her out on a limb, on the edge of the cliff, high and dry all at once and out on the tidal flats with the flood coming on. Or does it? Does not the strength of simple folk derive from instinct, which is the simplest truth? “Because I’m poor and from the wasteland but work at 00 where I read on the wall that you ate it and you’re richer than anybody and I came here for a chance at . . . you know, everything. You could give me a chance, but I don’t mean give, like for nothing. I mean, not nasty, but I mean, I’m young and smart, not as smart as you, but I’m pretty, and I have a good figure, and it’s real, and I don’t need a sling, and I’m honest and loyal, and I can be your friend, and we can, you know, just . . . have fun. Get to know each other. I’m Darla Jo, I mean, if you’re . . . free. I don’t mean right now, but maybe sometime, if you . . . want to.”

“Come in.” He turns and leads the way.

She follows down a hallway to a great room, through it and others to a labyrinth of halls and bathrooms with sit-downs, running water and showers, all of it sitting empty! *Slow down*, she thinks; *don't offer too much at once. He'll think you do that with everyone and might be a whore, and nobody wants to get tight with a whore and spend time and effort where a few bucks would do the trick.*

"I'm watching a movie."

She nods.

"A love story."

She nods.

"Do you like love stories?"

"I . . . Sometimes I do. If they're good."

"This one is slow. I might not get it. Do you care to watch?"

"Yes. I do."

They repose at opposite ends of the gurney for a movie called *Grounded Feet, Orbital Hearts.* Neither he nor she move a muscle for an hour, till he asks, "Do you want a pizza?"

"Oh, no. No, thank you. I mean, unless you do."

He smiles and turns back to Lazy Susan for another hour.

Darla Jo's eyes get so heavy, her brain so tired from a day beyond belief. She woke up in a scuzbox hole in the wall in the depths of 00 with nothing to bank on but faith in Hard Luck that she might average out. Fat chance, it seemed, beginning with a perv loss, bagging the job—she must be fired by now—coming up with a crazy scheme, blowing her dough and walking sixteen miles north, across parts of 00 that make HS look EZ. And into a casual evening, watching a love movie with *George Longley!*

She nods out but shakes it off with the fortitude of a player keen on a win. "I'm awfully tired. Do you mind if I lay down?" He stares, his fixed half smile not so different from the flinty version common to the wasteland. "I mean lie down," she says, smiling back, laying her head gently on his thigh, as if they were already friends. She senses several thousand volts coursing from his toes to his head and hopes she's done the right thing but suspects she hasn't but knows she has to give it at least a few minutes or look like a boob.

George Longley's hand slides off the graback and out to thin air. It levitates like a whirly cube looking to land but not knowing where. He dreads ambivalence. He's seen movies where the hero touches the love interest, uncertain on receptivity. He cannot tolerate hostility. He's seen movies where the hero is too timid for contact arousal, and the love interest falls for the hero's old-fashioned shyness, a refreshing change of pace, going from brazen sexual advance to gallantry in this brass-testicles world of ours. George Longley can only hover, fearing faulty data; what if the moviemakers are wrong?

Oh, it can happen.

He waits for his hand to make up its own mind, which it does; tensor muscles weaken and the hand descends.

Darla Jo can tell: he's a very strange man. She doesn't mind. Everyone is strange in their way, but she dearly hopes he isn't a perv, because she can learn to love anyone who isn't a perv, and if he's a perv, well, she'll give it her best, but she hopes he isn't. His fingertips touch down on her waist gently as a lunar module, and his palm settles on the lunar landscape just below the pelvic horizon, from which the moon's curvature can be felt.

She knows she's dreaming; it's so natural, like she's having a date with George Longley. In a few minutes, she is dreaming.

George Longley as well experiences ethereal modification in an unearthly effervescence, fingertips to aortic region to his own pelvic interlude, all beyond rational behavioral response.

Darla Jo snoozes.

George Longley observes.

She awakens when he squeezes her hip. "I don't know," he says. "It seems remote."

Does he mean the warp control, that the voice activator is unresponsive? He's dropped an octave on account of a surface grope, which seems appropriate, since she still has her pants on, and he is George Longley. But maybe not. "What seems remote?"

"Romance."

She sits up to rub the creases from her face. "It's not. Not when you really find it. Not when you really know."

"Have you ever?"

No girl could hope for a better approach to this, the springboard of romance. "No."

He stares briefly into her eyes, up at her hair and down at her ruffled dress, then away. She thinks it likely that he, too, has never found love. Or he's as good at a mutual grope proposal as he is at saving the world through science. Many questions rush forward. She picks the first one that seems propitious. "Are you sleepy?"

"Yes."

"Shall I stay?"

The fixed smile twitches in frenetic ecstasy and fear. The great one is clearly a perv, but then perversion seems, perhaps, only a potential, not yet proven. A girl can clearly see he's no spitball. Are you kidding? With that kind of money? He moves his lips to say yes, but no sound emerges.

Darla Jo plays him easy, as she once imagined the man on the second bend should have played the fish, if he wasn't a machine, and the fish was real. Where a woman of gamma-normal instincts would peel her dress, pull down his trousers and straddle the wild rooster, Darla Jo Bojoli seeks a different pace for a different need. She touches his face. "George. Do you mind if I call you George?"

He shakes his head.

"What time do you get up in the morning?"

"Four," he squeaks.

"Four?" She whispers. "What's the rush?"

He rolls his shoulders, sort of, in a noncommittal shrug.

"Do you have breakfast then?"

"No." He concentrates, as he must have done when first conjuring his Theory of Relative Absolutes. "I breakfast at nine."

"Nine is a good time for breakfast," she says, like he's a child who needs approval. "A good time to breakfast. Would you mind if I . . ." She hesitates. ". . . if I make breakfast for you?"

"I wouldn't mind."

"Would you mind if I . . ."

"No."

"You mean you don't want me to . . ."

"No. I don't mean no; I don't want you to. I mean no, I wouldn't mind. I mean I do want you to."

She hasn't said what she has in mind, and he wouldn't mind, indicating approval of whatever. Something is going on that seems as unlikely as an easy win on astronomical odds. The guy is a perv but not a normal perv. Who cares if he wants tickle hairs and Dream Whip? It's time to go ahead and get it on, before things change quicker than a kick in the head, like Mrs. George showing up at sunrise, even though she doesn't exist, or the jealous girlfriends start streaming in at four fifteen. In rare synchronicity of pizza delivery, loneliness, lovability, need and chemistry, opportunity swells to proper size and sways like a top-heavy drunk. A girl will grasp it by the throat for submission, given the chance, or not.

George Longley, himself, reduced to quivering perv pudding, knows chemistry like nobody's business but is stumped on this mixture. Wobbling like a plastic pooch in a rear window, he'll nod on anything, including what he's not yet imagined and she has, all of it relatively absolute and within the margin of error.

Darla Jo shares his willingness on whatever comes to pass. A girl isn't a whore for knowing what to do. Two people on the verge must start somewhere, and a woman will get no closer to doing the Hard Luck Guy, Himself. She stands to brush the rumples off her dress. She turns and takes his hand to lead him off the gurney to a huge door, until she giggles, "George. I don't know where to go."

"Where should we go?"

Son of Hard Luck on a crutch. "We need a bed."

He nods, recognizing familiar steps in the human mating procedure, sensing as well that his preceptors are dazed in preemptive override from penile perambulators.

Down the long corridor, arm in arm like royalty to a coronation, they stride. The bedroom is big enough for one-on-one. He says, "On, please." Lights beam from every angle.

"Not so bright," she says. They dim. "Romance," she says. They flicker faintly as moonglow.

He waits.

She steps near, wondering if he wants her to drop his pants and get down to what every perv wants. A girl walks a high wire on stakes like this, when the stuff has to go where it counts. She's seen enough warp trials to know that.

He waits. Opportunity stands clear of its burrow.

The play is hers to make. Giddy with a power few women have ever known, she teases perfection. "You . . . You don't do this, I mean, usually?"

"No. I don't."

"Not with women or men?"

"No. I don't."

"Why not?"

"I don't know."

"But you . . . you have a daughter."

"Clinical extraction."

Perfection eases nearer.

In the end, it's no tickle hairs or Dream Whip, no sweet gums or floggers and no eating, except for a brief demonstration to give the poor guy the feel of the thing for once in his strange and powerful LIFE.

Not bad, she thinks, with opportunity on her tonsils. *My first real blow job, and it's George Longley!* "You want to try it?"

"I . . . I don't think I can reach it."

"No, no. Not on yourself."

"But you don't . . ."

"George. Don't think. Just take a deep breath and put your face right here, no, no, up a little bit. Okay, open your eyes. Now do whatever comes natural."

He looks up in disbelief.

"You don't have to do anything, George. But if you want to try it, you put your tongue out and move it around." He sniffs, processes, sniffs again and tastes it like a cat on iffy cream. She thanks the Hard Luck Guy for the presence of mind to spend twenty bucks on a shower. Can you imagine, George Longley gnawing on a smelly bone? George commits, driving with fervor to the end zone of love. "George." She pulls back. "We can do more of this later."

"All right." He waits.

She would say, "Come and get it, buckaroo." Or, "First time's the best time." Or, "Dive in, swamp thang." Or something playful like that, but the atmosphere is not playful. It's clinical, merciful and more or less. A man so isolated he's never done the you-know-what quivers beside her, awaiting guidance. "Love me, George."

"You mean, make love to you?"

"Yes."

"All right." George Longley has the instinct, and he's seen it in a book or a movie. Up and in, he's gone like Old Faithful in two blinks. He breathes short, "It's supposed to last longer. Isn't it?"

"It will. It will." She pushes him off.

"Now we sleep?"

"If you want to."

He says nothing.

"George?"

"Yes."

"That was your first time?"

"Yes."

"It was my first time, too."

"You're supposed to say that. Aren't you?"

"But it was. I let boys feel me before. But that's all."

"How did you know about the tongue part?"

"I let a boy do that. But I never ate anybody. Nobody but you."

"What happens if you . . . If you . . ."

"If you what?"

"What happens if you keep going?"

"You mean the mouth part?"

"Yes."

"I'm not sure. We can experiment."

George Longley shivers; here is a woman willing to approach love with scientific method.

"We'll find out. It gets better as you go. I mean, I think."

"Do you . . . Could we . . ."

"What?"

"Could we try it again?"

"Already?"

"I think so. Yes. If you can . . . I mean, you know, the mouth part, and don't stop."

Oh, brother.

XIV

Fun and Games

George Longley is a man of few words, speechless at the romantic summit. He can't sleep for need, please, once more. Through the night comes want and give, getting his fill, lolling over words and deeds.

A woman can only assume satisfaction. She knows by sunrise she could have saved twenty bucks but regrets not one nickel.

Breakfast is late. Who cares, waking to dreams fulfilled? Soft sheets, a fresh if gamy scent and a glow just yonder, where the sit-down awaits her tush. And a shower for free. She smiles in a second waking that does not, cannot, will not default to stink and grit and the jar under the bed.

Large, soft hands knead like kitten paws. She rolls over to George Longley easing into the driver's seat with his signature moan to begin a lovely new day. "Good morning." Does he remember her name? "Darla Jo. What's your last name?"

"You're quite a man," she says.

"In what respect?"

"You just keep going."

"Is this abnormal?"

"It'll be fine. I think we'll adjust."

"I would like that."

"George?"

"Yes."

"Why haven't you done this before?"

"It never . . . I don't . . ." He looks away.

"It's okay, you know."

"I've done it now. I'm doing it now."

"Yes, you are."

He grips for traction. Songbirds sing the refrain.

Darla Jo can't help breaking a Cardinal Rule of Clean Living, that showers shall be under one minute. This is George Longley's shower for Luck's sake, the man who gave so much, and she gave some back. She's earned the steaming cascade. Will friendship materialize? Maybe, if things stay light and cozy. She insists on preparing breakfast and wants the kitchen staff relieved. Maybe they never saw a woman in the morning, and Darla Jo buck neckid under George's shirt would be too much. Best ease the outrage gently.

George nods, and the kitchen is vacated till further notice.

The kitchen is bigger than an 00 Pizzeria. She fixes wasteland French toast, though she's never had eggs; they're so creepy, with the slime and yellow stuff, but hey, if that's how rich people live, then cock a doodle do.

They eat on the terrace, serenely. He stares.

"George. Never a hooker? They got some you'd never know were hookers. How could you go through life being so famous and never have a woman come on to you?"

He thinks. He looks off. He says, "I don't . . . It doesn't . . ."

"I'm curious is all. You're good at it."

"I think you're good at it, too. And you said you never . . ."

"I haven't. But a girl can tell. I mean I've, you know, fooled around. Have you ever fooled around?"

"No."

"Fooling around is fun."

"Fun?"

"Yeah. I think you haven't had much fun."

"Mm." George Longley considers fun as a concept.

"I love fun. I haven't had much either. We can have fun. Together. You know?"

"How?"

"It's easy. You don't worry. You go shopping and eat good things and go places and have fun."

"This is fun. Isn't it?"

She touches his hand. "This is fun. I love this."

He stares at her. "Do you love me?"

"I think I could. We only just met."

"But we made love."

"That's a figure of speech, because people don't like to say you-know-what when they talk about themselves."

He ponders. "I'm very busy."

"I know. You're the most important man in the world."

He grins. "No, I'm not."

"Who is then?"

"The High Republican. Sports heroes. Many people."

"But you . . ."

"Tell me who you are. Why did you come here?"

"Just a crazy thing to do. I had no idea."

"You had an idea. Human behavior derives from rational thought—or irrational, if psychosis factors in the neural matrix. If you had no idea, you're a perfectly random being. No such human exists, ergo, you had an idea."

"I'm a wasteland girl looking for a LIFE. I started at the top."

"I'm a scientist looking for a LIFE. I'll start with a wasteland girl." They eat, aglow. "What is appropriate frequency for sexual relations?"

"My mama left when I was a little girl because my daddy wouldn't leave her alone. He always said she was no good for staying and not much better for leaving. He's mean like that. He said it's not like a bar of soap—you can't wear it out. Mama told him to get himself some soap, and when he ran out, he could get some more. He bothered me for a long time, but I never counted it. Anyway, I think we shouldn't worry about it."

George Longley ponders soap and bother. He wants to know more. "How long should we wait?"

"Maybe this afternoon. I'm sore. Aren't you?"

"No."

"Well. Let's think about this afternoon. Okay?"

He nods. A knock announces an incoming holovisit. "Excuse me." George speaks in the mellifluous tone of an important person. He takes the visit inside, in the bedroom.

She woofs her French toast, famished from the exercise and emotion on so little to eat. Hurrying, in case he comes back and she needs to be dainty again, she peeks through the glass. George Longley sits on the bed talking casually with the High Republican.

She's famished but can't eat. Will ultimate reality dull her hunger till she fades away? She slips in to watch like a fly on the wall; French toast seems mundane with history in the making—

A busy schedule is no excuse. Your country needs you, George. Natasha and Woof agree. Get out and breathe some wasteland air.

"This would be . . ."

A holiday. You've earned it. Think of the many, knowing you're out there enjoying one of our great new parks.

"I don't hunt. More to the point, chromosomatic aberration in humans compelled to kill other species to extinction may be . . ."

Perfect! It's a date!

"Yes, well, I think . . ."

My staff will interface with your staff. See you, George.

The High Republican dissolves.

George looks up. "He wants me at HumanSport. I can't."

"Oh, George! That would be fun!"

"People kill each other there."

"George. My daddy is the game warden at HS."

"So what?"

"He'd just die if I brought you home."

"I might die if I go."

"We don't have to go *in*."

"I'd have to go in. He ducked the question. It's plain to see. A big fat Q like me? Not go in?"

"Nobody will hurt you, George, as long as I'm around."

He stares from the edge of the bed, wondering why this archangel has descended to Maximillion Boulevard? "I . . ."

"George." She steps in to shimmy free of the baggy shirt. "Let's not wait till this afternoon." Presenting a new outlook on LIFE at eye level to the most important man in the world, she brings him home from outer space, down through the stratohaze to terra firma.

He takes it in like he's never seen it before.

She recalls the guy catching the fish on the Western Heritage River and imagines tour boats passing, enjoying the show. She waves, like the guy on the bend. Tourists are downing Puds and seeing George at the bottom, and so does she. She hears stupid questions about fish, but a wasteland girl will spew answers no more. To think, she could have been right here all along, caressing the most important head in the world in its search love.

XV

A Day in THE LIFE of a Family with Destiny

Peony Lu beseeches Hard Luck: Just say it ain't so. Tell me Billy Moline did not stray to the arms of another. She harkens, but it's only the lump beside her, snoring like a bellows. A woman ignoring tangible evidence is only fooling herself. The prosecution builds its case, as the defendant saws logs.

The test will be simple: a man awakened to a luscious buffet will respond or not. Indifference to the hottest cream puff in the subdivision will prove infidelity. In darkness, she rises to shuck her jammies for a negligee from the glory days—from her first season on the pro tour. Even in low light the mirror heralds loud and clear: Baby, you still got it! Yet she simmers alone, molten magma on the flow, as the village below sleeps. She writhes, pumping the dingdong Richter to seven point eight—make that nine point ten. At least that's how it would peg, if she was appreciated instead of coming up nada with the bum in bed. By the wee hours she sees how a woman's best years are easily wasted on fools like Billy M and what's his name, the first one. She could be prosperous and thin, lying beside a man of substance with a LIFE of mobility and immortality. She could be a woman with needs met and resources all her own. She'll soon prove her case beyond doubt.

Up again in the dark, to enhance the flimsy crepe number for optimal magic, Peony Lu waxes and Satin Sheens the pitcher's mound. She trims the infield, rats and teases the batter's box, and, just for fun, slides her tongue over first and third, arches her back on the squeeze play and slides into home. *Ooh*, she murmurs, mouthing a silent, "You're out!" Let him get out of this one. She crawls back in, a bit relieved but fidgeting again at four. That has-been bum spent it elsewhere. She knows it. Look at him.

She drifts. She'll get by on her own. The girls are young enough to find splice money down the line. But a modern woman needs more than getting by. She needs to run a proper home for her children and guarantee them a LIFE better than hers with a future they deserve. She doesn't feel vindictive, but if this deadbeat cockhound can't cut the mustard by sunrise, he'll pay. Oh, boy, through the nose, he'll pay.

Old Sol rises in the haze.

Old Billy snoozes deep.

Peony Lu flips on the warp, and a new day begins.

Leanne Longley is George's daughter and Head Specialist at the Rosenfeld Clinic.

Peony Lu laughs scornfully. Just look at that hussy with her degrees, telling OneEye how things ought to be. Hardly daylight, and Leanne Longley is mouthing off on sterilization required for any splice and a bunch more sterilizations too. Leanne is plain unRepublican. Warpanal calls her the polar bear; big, toothy and cold. Everyone knows she got mixed in a test tube, or maybe a tumbler, on the rocks. George Longley won't share Leanne's radix ovulatum, but conjecture runs from Memory Lane to Allana Titana, former point guard for the Nutcrackers Northcentral. Leanne was cloned the year Nc^2 lost the championship to the Village

Lezbohemians, denying Allana a posh retirement on astronomical wealth. Yet she lives way beyond the means of a runner-up. How does that work? Most people think Allana is Leanne's test tube mama on account of Leanne's length, girth and skin tone, and that's how Allana got rich. Who cares? Leanne is George Longley's sole heir, of worthy opinion from the first WAH! She would stop gene splicing to ease the human overload. Does it matter who her test tube mama was?

Sterilization brokers support the idea. Duh. They want the splice contract to stipulate that the party of the first part will bequeath assets only to a party of the second part if the second part agrees to sterilization as well. Warpanal speculates on a second-part class action, requiring first parts to take the hit after a hundred years or at age two hundred, whichever comes first, because it's not fair, waiting for money and stuff in vain.

In re: *Brown vs. the Board of Propagation*, the Court of Supreme Opinion ruled that sterilization undermines the Miracle. The unborn many shall not subrogate Constitutional rights to a diabolical scheme.

In a formal statement, Leanne Longley calls the Supreme Judge a fecal-brain motherhumper. Held in contempt, fined two billion dollars and six months in the slammer, Leanne will not cower but sasses OneEye and the judge in what could be her swan song. She'll be caged tomorrow! Not really. Leanne will do no time. Are you kidding? Georgie's daughter? Daddy'll pay the measly two bil, and a few people will pay a few other people, till the situation hums on down. Leanne will be confined to quarters: bedroom, lab, kitchen.

"Oh, tough LIFE," Peony Lu grumbles.

Billy wakes. "Huh?"

Peony Lu grumbles again, "You don't cut back overnight like that without a reason."

"What?"

"You're seeing another woman."

"No." Peony Lu dangles a darn-near-perfect breast—after all these years—in his face, but the lug only yawns, "I'm not."

"I don't believe it," Leanne Longley says.

Peony Lu stops to listen, as Leanne goes in for the kill:

"Whacking off ought to be illegal without a temperature-controlled test tube to save it and flash-freeze capacity to keep it. We lose ninety percent of living sperm in every shot. Those little swimmers are alive! They have feelings and a conscience. They're trying their darnedest! They have rights under the Constitution! Guaranteed! Splooge is sacred. And the twinkle in your eye! Don't lose it. You're committing murder! Undelivered man snot and unborn twinkles deserve funerals! If you're a nutter!"

"Off her rocker," Peony Lu says, coming back on a seductive profile, calling back to Leanne. "You're the nut!"

Also coming around, as cued, Billy rolls her way to lap her up like a frisky pup. *Sunrise Today* breaks for a few important messages, and just that quick, Peony Lu is appeased. Well, a girl loves the attention. That's all. She also loves the thirty-second spot for Full Cram Truck Cubes. Her fave is the hunky guy who says, "Cram tough! When *you* need to cram it in!" Where is he already? Then again, who cares? Billy's on it! The hunk gets to his punch line, but it's too little, too late. He can't dink like Billy M. Or cram!

The new spot on Hot 'n Cold Warp Dinners, brought to you by Pillsdown Laboratories, is okay. But the best one is the two cartoon stiffs plugging into the hot socket at Emeretrieve Systems Ltd., Subdivision Retrieval Specialists. Showing the process much faster than it happens in real LIFE, the stiffs go smooth from crinkly. They turn pink from gray and finally sit up.

Hot Shot the Wonderdog lopes up with a ball and says, "Woof!"

The elderly woman stiff throws the ball as the other stiff, an elderly man, sits up to ask for a dance. They waltz.

Hot Shot retrieves the ball. "Woof! Woof, woof!"

Peony Lu loves it when Hot Shot smiles at his two people, alive again, but she misses it because Billy M is on a romp. The prosecution rests, figuratively speaking, when Peony Lu cries, "Yes! Yes! Yes!"

Billy watches sideways for Hot Shot or someone to say that Emeretrieve is open Sundays. Why spend money on a warp spot and 00 ad execs for two stiffs and Hot Shot and play it on a Sunday and not stay open Sunday?

"Yes! Oh, yes!"

Billy goes full court, like three points down, two point six remaining. Closing moments stretch, but what the heck. A good night's sleep is a new lease on LIFE, and he's an athlete, after all.

Peony Lu gasps at last, "Nice save."

Save what? Women are complex. Billy won't question oblique comments. Besides, he's already working on a vital equipment list for the family outing only three days away. Three days. He hopes Hector won't be groggy after two days of dead. Well, maybe a day and a half if he gets down to Emeretrieve right after brunch.

Peony Lu says there ought to be a limit to Leanne Longley getting so much attention from OneEye. As Leanne calls for sanity in human reproduction, Peony Lu turns to the man she loves. "Oh, Billy. Do you love me? Do you?"

"Yes, I do." He pecks her forehead and rolls out for a rinse. "Come on, Peony Lu, we got a big day ahead of us."

"I'm coming," she says, drifting to sleep.

Sleep can be good for a slump. He watches out the window as Danny shoots a few and practices his reverse dribble. Billy waves, but Danny is all focus; you have to hand it to that guy, still buffing the rudiments. Billy wants a big breakfast, with the Moline family gathered to join the nation in table talk on HumanSport. Gosh darn though, the Moline table will be different with the Big BM heading in to crunch time. He feels Mo alongside on his way to pancakes, scrambled eggfood and baco.

Rozomon snores on her cot in the hall.

Marya sits in her alcove under a naked bulb facing her antique computer, a picture of literary color. She grimaces at Billy, "That was disgusting."

Billy nods. "It always seems that way afterwards. Then you want to go again. If you do it regular, you don't get disgusted at the end, not like I got disgusted if we lost, I mean, not if we got beat because they were better, but like with carelessness, like when . . ."

"Go make breakfast."

Billy smiles; Marya breaks quicker than three on one. That's why she's a good writer. He hasn't read her story yet, but she must be good; she's so smart. He and Mo break for the kitchen.

Little Alysyn says she was up for *Sunrise Warp with the Hard Luck Guy* and saw the whole service before switching to *Binky for Kids*. "Honest, I prayed! I swear it!"

Billy mutters, "These kids. Who do they think they're fooling?"

"Okay! It's Binky! Pay attention! You're waiting on a light! Six lanes to the right, six lanes to the left, a few lanes on the cross planes. Everybody waiting. You wanna pick your nose 'cause you got a decent snag on a fat woolly in there itching for a pluck. You wanna flick it out the window. You'll never see these people again. Whaddayagonna do?"

Alysyn squeals, "Pick it!"

Billy loads the perfecooker with pancakes and eggfood.

Rozomon's snoring sets up a rumble, like she ate all the baco. Sure enough: it's gone.

Never mind; Billy fills in with piglike links.

Between the rumble in the hall and the nitwit in the kitchen, the literary voice in the wilderness sits in her chair, stifled in domestic pollution. Can't these people see? The question buzzes like a power pylon, exuding electromagnetic toxin that melts creativity and mutates thoughts till she could scream. Marya wants to be a writer, they say. What is she in the meantime? Is she not writing now? Is the present tense preempted by petty subdivision ideas of what a writer is supposed to be? Must a real writer get calls from 00 and Hollywood? Must a real writer have a warp agent and a gifted director? Does this hillbilly burb ever get literary? Have they read her story? Do they care? The buzz thickens, stuck again with her nemesis, her block. Gripping her table, her knucks go white, eyes shut. She holds her breath until exhaling, exasperated.

Marya wants her pages turning with thump and gore and real love to hold a reader's interest. She thinks she can. She may be a natural. She may be destined for importance. If she doesn't feel her greatness, who will? She feels it. Greatness surges in the throes of divorce, with introspection and the meaning of love in 00. How can she go wrong on a winning combo? She loves the soft men and bitter women who populate these byways. She's resilient, a modern woman who can take a punch and keep on coming. Her men aren't simpleminded like Billy. They're sensitive and romantic.

But enough of Billy M, a no-count, has-been rimballer in denial. Billy can't even get on as a sportscaster, and they got some nitwits calling those shots. At least he's a standout in the dunce column, foursquare stoopider than most when it comes to LIFE in the city.

Speaking of which, she needs to be in 00 for a week or a month or six to get up next to the literary action, with the lunches, cocktails, workshops and personal contact a great book needs. She could find a champion to help build a platform of greatness. With a solid platform, her story won't even need reading! But that takes money, and primetime seems better spent on craft. But in Foxwoodburrough Hills Estates? The vicious circle goes nowhere fast. Fastly? Quickly? Yes: going nowhere quickly.

She's up to 00 standards and feels free at last with a stack o' genius under her arm but still bound by no money for a room or lunch or cocktails. And no platform. And no greatness or importance. She'd shuffle along in the stoop-shouldered crowd, one more gob hole looking for a stuffer and a lie-down, not to mention a sit-down and a place to rinse her washrag.

She labored a year on her story and another on the rewrite. One more year passed on refinement to perfect flourish. It's right, or will be after a bit more tuning. It's old style but perfect for a warp special or serialization in *Vanity Flair* or *Real Women Today* or *Cosmo*. The turn of phrase, majestic ellipsis, acerbic yet inoffensive inference, flamboyant omission and wickedly twisted syntax make it a delicious read, a riveting tell, a smash hit, a blockbuster, a laugh and a cry. Why the heck not?

Marya's story follows a little man who wants to be the Universal Wrestling Federation World Champion. Nobody pays attention. He's a little guy. She can change him to a woman, if a woman editor thinks that would be more passionate. His name is

Larry but could be Lorraine. Call her Bronco or Rozomon; it doesn't matter. He's *The Monk*, drawing on secret powers of meditation in the wasteland, far from subdivisions and convenience to church, schools and shopping.

She fondles Bobb Fjord's latest masterpiece about a used-cube salesperson on the Jersey shore. Fjord is important for sharing the sensitivities of a modern nonspecific in a used-cube context, a salesperson who opens his soul to the needs of others. Marya saw Bobb Fjord at the FHB Mall. Easily compensating size with importance, Bobb Fjord opened his soul to inspire Marya and *The Monk*. The magic lingers. She might change the title from *The Monk* for more emotion. She ponders *The Monk! The Monk! The Monk!*

That notion brings and eerie chill. Goose bumps rise like omens of painful sensitivity and importance. When Marya reads her story at the mall, she'll praise Bobb Fjord's importance and inspiration. Guzzling her triple tall tarcaff, she feels the magic. She imagines a child of the future in a distant subdivision, a child who will become a young woman with her own story of greatness, who will one day read at the mall, where she'll praise Marya Blanda.

Maybe Marya should go to 00 and enroll in a Bobb Fjord literary workshop, except that it runs five grand. Sure, you get a money-back guarantee on lunch connections, but you still have to spring for lunch, and what can you do, after laying out five Gs? Go for sandwiches? More dough for a lie-down and pleasantries could run seven in a wink. What price fame? Seven grand and change is a steal, *if* you got it.

Bobb Fjord's second installment of the sensitivity trilogy got a whole page of praise! As if that wasn't enough, at the bottom it said: "Turn the page for still more extraordinary acclaim!"

Heck, some ordinary acclaim would fit Marya's schedule. Setting her triple-tall tarcaff aside, she dives back in, on her way to power and flow, except that so much tweaking makes it read like a mantra. Words lose delineation; wor dslos ed elinea tion. Worse yet, she hardly gets them into place when adversity stacks up. What writer could transcend this soulless place, its constraint, the snoring and piglike stink smothering her thoughts? Best hang up the creative side for now and work the mines, sending out more solicitations on *The Monk! The Monk! The Monk!* Hey, the mines, mindless, mine own flesh and blood . . . Hmm . . . She feels that her ideas will tap the mother lode of discovery, celebrity, wealth and acclaim, somehow. She sees her thoughts as spermatozoa; one will break free to pierce the golden egg. She knows it can happen.

Becoming that little seed, racing through the protoplasmic gloom, she drafts her personal greeting. The *Wannabe an Author Guide* advises a curtsy and a blink. That's not Marya. She'll plop onto their desks in 5:1 aspect ratio, lean on a lamppost and say, "Hey." She keeps it brief on intro fluff and slices right into the prime fillet. Each electrogram includes a riveting sample and bio to titillate an 00 frontline perceptionist. She'll wrap it up with a refusal to fail: "Please confirm receipt of this electrogram instead of ignoring me, you sanctimonious, self-important piglike link!"

Well, she'd best revise that little chestnut, but she'd surely like those 00ers to know how she feels! At least thinking it over gives her a chortle, and a chortle amidst travail can uplift a struggling authoress. She feels like a lottery ticket gizmo punching numbers. Each electrogram is another eight-dollar ticket on the literary lottery. Never mind that she does the muse's work for nothing! The next ticket might come up in clover. She works to fever pitch.

Finishing her daily quota of submissions, she tiptoes up the hall for a money number to transmit. She'll pay it back someday. The electros are free, but the scavengers in 00 charge a buck and a half each to receive and another six-fifty to read. As if . . .

With twenty new electrograms on their way, she hits the gurney for a short soak, because ideas jolt from the hologrid any time, and a writer needs to soak warpage just as literary fabric needs thread. Hey, that's pretty good. She makes a mental note to write it down when she gets up anyway for a Coke or a pee, or a *Pepsi.* And maybe a pizza if breakfast isn't ready. But maybe not.

"Flick it out the window!" Alysyn squeals.

Rozomon snores.

Marya shakes her head; her sisters know nothing.

Peony Lu drifts into the kitchen, a breast flopped out of her bathrobe. Worse yet, verging on bilious, she presses up to Billy, who deals plates, forks, ketchup and syrupy stuff.

"Hey, hey, hey," he says, like he can't be bothered after he got her all goofy in the first place.

Danny picks up steam outside, taunting imaginary opponents. "Come on, big man. Big man. Let's see whatcha got. Come on."

Boy. These people.

Rozomon grunts, "How's anyone supposed to sleep around here? Cheeze whiz." The eldest daughter struggles up with gooey eyes and drool jaw. Snorting, hocking into a swallow, she grabs the remote and holds it beyond Alysyn's reach. "I gotta pee like a hydrant. Binky stinks. She's a stag dyke with an ass fetish. What sexist bunk. *Binky for Kids* is dumber than dog yak."

Alysyn squeals, "Nooo!"

Marya sneers, "What a bully."

Rozomon snorts, drops the remote and shuffles to the kitchen to watch Billy spread prune jam on toast, as Peony Lu rubs his belly from behind. Rozomon makes puking sounds, snags a piglike from the perfecooker and eats it quick; it's so hot. And off she waddles. "I got a load queued up oughta make the highlight reels."

Billy reminds her it won't mean squat without weigh-ins before and after, and a quickshot wouldn't hurt. "Please, 2D only and hold the scent-around."

Danny smiles in the door, rimball orbiting his body front to back, hand to hand. "Looks like a training camp feast."

Billy nods. "We have outrage."

"Looks like you two had a heckuva workout."

Peony Lu says, "Mmm," laying her face on Billy's back.

Billy turns quick for a tongue thrust to her ear like the anteater reaming termites in the old nature warps. He playfully whispers for all to hear, "He remembers Sunday morning, doesn't he?"

Peony Lu backs off. "Why do you bring that up?"

Billy shrugs. "Just playing around. It's only Danny."

Danny plays along, "Sundays were tough without you to make breakfast."

"Here I am, and here it is." He calls over Peony Lu's shoulder, "Come and get it!"

Rozomon shuffles back on a weary note. "Not even close. You feel the pressure, but it's just flaaatulence." Plucking another piglike, she juggles it sprightly, pops it into the hopper and breathes like a dragon. "You know, gas ought to count for something, when you think about it."

"Rozomon. Please."

"Not bad, Billy boy. You're gonna make some lucky little lady a fine husband."

"He already has," says Peony Lu.

"Must you?" Marya whines, shuffling to her seat.

"Attitude, Marya," Billy admonishes. "You want to be a writer someday; you need attitude today."

"Attitude shmatitude," Marya says. "What I need is a change. I think the hohum stifles my flow."

"Boy," Billy shakes his head. "How can anyone be stifled with so much food on the table?"

"Yeah, right," Rozomon says. "Four hundred sitcoms. Four hundred special reports. Four hundred made-for-warp movies every week based on hohum situations and adventures, but it's not good enough for Ms. Tight-panties-wants-to-be-a-writer."

"I am a writer."

"Yeah, and if I strap on my leathers, I'll be a bathing beauty."

"Alysyn!"

"I can't!"

"Alysyn!"

"Go ahead. I'll be there in a minute."

"Young lady!" growls Peony Lu. "Get in here this minute or no primetime Sunday!"

"Oooh!" whines Alysyn, not liking this one bit.

Just so, with denial, assertion, complaint and affection, a family convenes for a Sunday feed.

"Let us give thanks to Hard Luck for this, thy bounty," Billy says in his sincere, grave voice.

"Do you think it's enough?" Marya asks.

"I darn near emptied the freezedrier," Billy says. "Unless you want reptile dinner with hashgreens."

"No, I mean enough thanks for this, thy bounty. Do you think Hard Luck wouldn't like the Billy M clan and Danny if you didn't mumble for this bounty?"

Danny Blanda stares at the syrupy stuff oozing over his plate.

Peony Lu sighs with Rozomon and Alysyn.

Billy M, in no mood to tease Hard Luck, shrugs, "No. I think Hard Luck likes us. I'll do the honors on account of I'm the center on this play."

All bow their heads, except Marya. "Relax, Billy. I got this one. You be the center. I'll be the pom-pom girl. Okay, you don't need to bow your heads. This isn't a request; it's a connection. Close your eyes or let them droop. We beseech the magic holding us together." Squinting, she leads the meditative repose.

Peony Lu sighs.

Alysyn kicks the table.

Marya shushes.

Rozomon belches.

Alysyn giggles.

Billy peeks.

Peony Lu frowns and fidgets.

Danny fingers the syrupy stuff to stop it dripping over the edge.

Peony Lu says, "That's enough."

"It's not," says Marya.

"It's getting cold," says Peony Lu.

"It got hot in a minute. We have all the time in the world."

"We know what you're driving at," says Peony Lu.

"What, Mother? What am I driving at?"

Rozomon lunges across the table but changes pace halfway to drop on the piglikes and pluck three, skillful as a buzzard at the dump. One slides down her eat hole as she juggles the other two.

"Trah'n uh kee uh fuh eah! Dah wha!" Dousing the fire with red drink, she huffs and puffs and gobs the other two.

Billy waits.

Marya glares.

Peony Lu ignores her difficult middle child and gives a direct order: "Now eat!"

Billy pours syrupy stuff that runs into his eggfood like Danny's. "Darn. I hate that." He laughs, all in good fun.

Rozomon says, "Eat, yourself."

Alysyn giggles, "She said eat yourself."

Peony Lu says, "Shut up and eat," and eats, herself.

Danny eats quietly, humble as an extended guest.

Alysyn pokes around.

Rozomon gains momentum, two-handed.

Marya eats and observes.

Billy eats, itching to break the news.

Alysyn drowns her pancakes in syrupy stuff then whines that it ruined her eggfood. She needs a new dish and can't hold any more piglikes, so take them away.

Peony Lu insists that syrupy stuff enhances the flavor of anything, if a girl has attitude, and on that note Billy opens up.

"Anyone care for an outing? Say . . . Slonerosis?"

Everyone perks, even Alysyn. She's seen warp promos for Slonerosis.

Peony Lu grins for what's coming.

"Yay!" says Alysyn.

"Yes. Yay," says Billy. "We're going there. You too, Danny, if you want to. We're going there on my way to HumanSport."

Marya blurts, "What?"

"Oh, Hard Luck," says Rozomon.

"Watch your mouth, young lady," says Peony Lu.

"Don't call me that," says Rozomon.

"I wanna go I wanna go I wanna *go!*" cries Alysyn.

Billy breaks into scheduling, assignments and equipment.

Slonerosis was a Recharge, Food & Lodging exit, last chance before crossing a wasteland, till HumanSport pumped a pulse for a hundred-mile radius. Now a boomburg with terrific convenience on a diversified economic base and low to average unemployment, Slonerosis is poised for prosperity. The Slonerosis Ultimate Sport Center is the location, location, location of investment speculation. The Echelon praised the SUSC for peripheral niche fulfillment, turning a grease spot on the road to a low-risk amusement destination for Mom, Dad 'n the kids.

Slonerosis has games and rides with great odds and fabulous thrills like *You Make the Rules, Win or Die, Terrifying and Satisfying, The Itch You Can't Scratch at Home, Wipe the Bastards Out, Get Even* and *Get Even with Blood!* Slonerosis took off like nobody's business, drawing the curious, the timid and the many not quite up to Ultimate Sport, who still want some action, lights and whistles. A family of five can get up next to the fun till exhaustion or midnight for one easy payment of six ninety-nine ninety-nine. The fee includes parking, hookup and waste disposal hardly a ten-minute walk from full sit-down comfort and a snack bar. Another ninety-nine ninety-nine gets the same hungry five a spot at the feed rail for burgers, fries, colas, hotdogs, sausages, cheesefood snacks and much, much more. All you can eat means Round O's, Fatty Doodles and Sweet-o-Reenos too!

The place is Everykid's dream, with paved hiking trails and a bear monster just out from the camping area. The kids whistle and sing and shake giant jingle bells to keep from startling the bear monster, but he lunges across the path, growling every time, eyes lit up and nose holes smoking. Then he slides back into his bush. It's more fun than any subdivision or condo.

Eight bills busts Billy's budget, but what the heck. He can stash the family at Slonerosis mere minutes from HS. They'll love it, and he'll feel better knowing they're nearby. Eight hundred bones'll be chicken scratch after a decent day on the range. Shoot, eight hundred? He'll make twice that on a postal worker in second prime! Shoot, he'll have money for a matinee in Romance Gardens, Peony Lu's real wish. They slow dance at Romance, all the parents proving that Slonerosis isn't just for kids. No way.

He smiles. "Things are gonna change around here. Slonerosis is just the beginning. I'll be hunting a couple of days with friends, then I'll catch up with you."

Marya says, "You're going in?"

Billy grins, practically proud.

"I'm going too," she says with admirable resolution.

"No," says Peony Lu.

"I want to watch. What's the harm?"

"No. It's no place for a little girl."

"I am not a little girl. I'm developing a career, in case you haven't noticed."

"No. You can come along to Slonerosis or stay home. You're not going to HS."

"I'll stay home," says Marya, sliding out for a mope.

Easing onto the gurney, she sees the break a young woman needs, first-hand exposure to some wasteland nitty gritty. For once, Billy M, stuffed-animal athlete and live-in pogo stick, makes himself useful, and dumb old stupid old horny old, wrinkled, flabby, saggy-tit Peony Lu bitchface wants her to miss the action. Hard

Luck, this is HS! Or it should be HS, not BS. This is dimensional, possibly passionate and definitely important. The place is political, controversial and bloody. A decent writer can wax carnality in every scene with the original perspective of a subdivision woman on a critical look at sport in America. The muse is singing! This is it!

Time and circumstance call for action, covert no problem.

Marya rises and drifts back to the feed.

Billy reviews canteens, backpacks, towels, pillows, blankets, flashlights, bug spray, mess kits, toilet paper and on and on.

With a pleasant smile, Marya sits, takes a piglike and dips it in the goo. "You're right," she says. "You can eat this glop on anything, if you lather up an attitude."

Peony Lu doesn't like to be mocked and can do very well without her daughter sucking on a piglike to make a point. Peony Lu knows the teen-year frustrations. She already had study dates, laundry dates, library dates, movie dates, discussion dates, Coke or *Pepsi* dates, cruise dates, game dates and heavy dates at Marya's age. It didn't hurt anybody. It relaxed her. Everyone called her abnormal, too, as if a fine firm figure was for one thing but not another. "Wait till you're a mother," she says.

"Not to change the subject," Billy says. "Hector's in the garage."

"In the garage?"

"Yeah. He's dead. He needs a retrieval, and it's Sunday."

"He's old," Alysyn says. "Fatty Rozomon ate all the hash, and now Hector won't get any."

"I did not," says Rozomon. "Besides. Dead men eat no hash."

"Yes, they do," says Alysyn. "Or they starve to death."

"Dummy. He's already dead."

"Yeah, but he'll wake up hungry, and it'll be your fault."

"Girls," says Peony Lu.

"I asked you not to call me that. How would you like it if I called you Ms. Horny Butt?"

Billy laughs.

Danny covers his mouth.

Peony Lu is not amused. Rozomon isn't too old for a spanking, but she is too big. Peony Lu glares at her eldest daughter, wondering if some pencil-neck power forward who could slam-dunk and keep his mouth shut caused this unlikely spawn. How long does the motherhood contract run, and when can she get back to free agency? She loves her children, but a woman misses the thrill of victory.

Rozomon redirects. "You do not eat when you're dead."

"Do too."

"Yeah? How's a dead guy supposed to eat, Stupido?"

Alysyn cries that she is not stupid.

Marya says it takes one to know one.

Alysyn cries that she is not, not, not!

Billy scoops the last of the hash and heads out to the garage. He draws it into a still-functional transfuser and shoots it into Hector's thigh, smoothing lumps as best as he can. "There. No complaints. Hash is better than nothing."

Hector can't complain that his neck is stiff as polybrick, and jamming your ancestor into a pizza oven is plain dumb. Dead men stay mum, but who wants a fifty-two-million-dollar score rounding the rim and falling out, sore and hungry. Well, a few tubes of Flaccigel ought to soften things up.

Billy comes in low on a murmur, "I'm sorry." He pulls the body out, drapes the bag over the load, lashes it on back and arcs capacitors to lickety split, a man fast-tracking to destiny. Next stop: Emeretrieve Systems, open Sunday, he hopes.

"Okay. They're open," Billy tells the family on his nasalink. "Drive-thru only and backed up around the corner on lattés. Everyone's amping for the Sunday lineup."

"Smoke 'em, Billy!" Alysyn yells. "Money in the bank!"

Billy hears a slap and Peony Lu yelling, "Young lady, I will not have that kind of talk in this house! Do you hear?"

Poor little Alysyn screams wah, wah, wah, running away.

"She makes me so mad," Peony Lu says.

"Hey, she's a kid. You shouldn't hit her."

"Hey, yourself. She's my kid, and I don't want her making jokes about killing people. Okay? You think that's funny?"

"No. But she didn't . . ."

"Let it rest, Billy. It's been a long day."

"It has? I thought you . . ."

"Some of us didn't get much sleep last night, and we had a strange man at the table again this morning. My kids need low voltage therapy, and you're out on a half-cube with a stiff in tow."

"He's not in tow. I laid him over the back seat."

"Sometimes you don't . . . You don't . . ."

"Hey, the line is moving. Hey, they got a warp monitor here, and . . . Hard Luck! Peony Lu! It's the playoffs! I forgot!"

"Billy! You're not . . ."

But the call is over. Billy pulls out of line. Later will be better anyway, when he won't have to fight the Under One Roof traffic or wait for a latté line. Round One of the playoffs will be in the record books in a few hours. Squeezing thrusters, he shoots lightning on a sixty-degree lift.

What a nut, those waiting in line agree.

Billy can't hear, gaining stratohaze for the three-mile hop. *Getting older, Billy boy. Two space outs in a row, first the replay, now the playoffs. What'll it be tomorrow? The rudiments?*

How could a man anticipate a thing for weeks, discuss it, bet on it, dream about it and forget it? How often will the Vengeful Warriors, Western Division Champs, look to fourpeat against BloodSuck, Scourge of the East with the highest field percentage in eight years? This game has more amperage, live birth and promo than Woodstock IV. It's a rampage going in. It's Hannibal over the Alps, Attila at the gate and Robertson casting the NaySay to Hell. It's the dirtiest, nastiest, most unconscionable gang of rimballers ever. The Vengeful Warriors come onto the court in formal attire—with war paint. They shake hands with the refs, the other team, scorekeeper, timekeeper, fans and outragers, asking, "How do you do?" Then they crush their hapless adversaries. They finished the regular season at ninety-six and two, suffering two losses when Discus Harrow got suspended on a second-degree murder wrap that *anyone* could see was self-defense. Besides that, the suspension coulda waited for off-season. Well, it coulda.

BloodSuck wear big teeth and bite their opponents in the fray, claiming innocence—the rim did it, or the goal post is sharp—to the dismay and frequent rebellion of opposing fans. Billy retrofires in compensation, clipping the neighbor's hedge and thwacking a guardrail. "Get the freak out of my way!" he yells. Billy M is a Warrior man, do or die, searing in for the playoffs, opening round!

Back inside with a major shush, ignoring Peony Lu's major mood, he goes airborne with a "Clear out!"

Rozomon rolls in time. She knows this other guy, Sunday Billy.

He surfs to Vic Vinninny's closing comment, "It isn't right."

Peony Lu slams a few doors.

Vic says, "But you have to hand it to the Suck, pumping season tickets to twenty-nine thousand nine hundred ninety-nine clams and charging extra for the playoffs! Come on; you can buy what, six, eight 1 Moons for that. You'd be facing LIFE without rimball, and you really gotta ask yourself: Is that the THE LIFE? Man, oh, man, we got a doozie here tonight! We'll be right back after these important messages. Stay tuned and find out what you think."

Billy wedges in for rimball, the playoffs, the Cokes or *Pepsi*s, the Puds, the chips and dips and waaay too much pizza! Yeah! Woohoo! Who needed piglikes and eggfood with a playoff coming on? Well, he forgot. Never mind, a couple *Swill B Gone*s with *D-Greezit III* and a Postgame Suppositron will flush him quick as flash floods in a wasteland. He works over a couple pizzas but holds off on a third on account of some temporary unpleasantness. That's okay; he needs to eat prudently now anyway.

The Warriors take it walking away. He knew they would, but what a fray, with the fangs and blood and biting. It's anybody's guess who'll win tomorrow, with so much blood lost. That's how the Suck comes back. It doesn't get much better, not since about ten years ago, when the East Northeast Inbred Gothics went in drag. The ENI Goths doubled ticket sales and warpage and doubled again when the Nonspecific Coalition for Equality in Sport came out to cheer them on. The ENI Goths got trounced by the Central Midwest Rotarians but proved once again the power of show biz in sport.

Billy feels good about the game and his team's prospects. He shuffles to the kitchen for a Coke but on second thought grabs a *Pepsi*. The taste that comes alive brings him back to his senses, so he tallies needs, like flowers to swing a major mood. Maybe he'll take her out for burgers or fishy sticks and fries. This is hardly the time, with the budget squeaky tight. But he can't handle a mood now. He heads back out to the alley where his half-cube leans with Hector's body bag on back.

Timing looks better on this approach to Emeretrieve. No line at the drive-thru and receiving chute open looks like easy in and out, till a guy pulls up right before Billy with a Big Tow full of stiffs.

Billy groans, "Aw, gee . . ."

The guy says go ahead, you first; you only got one. A good sort, the guy says his brother-in-law's RV is old, with wheels and overstuffed furniture, strictly surface, no lift, no matter the octane.

"No lift? Octane? They still make those?"

"He's a vintage RV nut. Look where it got him? Over a shoulder and down a ravine is where."

"Jeez. Are you sure?"

"Yeah. That was three weeks ago so this could take some time. They didn't get bleach-misted, and the little ones on the bottom might need extra juice on the revigger and more time in trim 'n clean. I'm Deke. Deke Gerring."

"Billy. Billy Moline. Thanks, Deke." Billy goes ahead in front, unlashing the bag and pulling Hector halfway out when the window nurse says, "We'll take care of that. Drop it on the chute and go around to the cashier." Billy nods and heads around.

Deke Gerring says he has to get his retrievals done today, because he's headed up to HumanSport in three days.

Billy double takes on this first real opponent in ages. Not a bad guy, but none of them ever were. Hey, it's a game for Luck's sake. He wonders what Deke Gerring might be worth on entitlement tally.

Deke looks worried, like Billy might be nonspecifically motivated.

"Me, too." Billy says.

"Yeah? Whatcha carryin' in?"

Billy shrugs. “Not much. I’ll hang back. Pea shooter is all.”

“Hang back, heck. I’m takin’ me a peashooter, a triple ought *and* a long gun with a forty-six clip.”

“You ought to clean up on that arsenal,” Billy says, practically feeling the hundred, hundred fifty grand or whatever Deke will pay out. Triple ought? What a hick. Billy M will take him at two hundred yards; guy won’t see who got him. “Good luck.”

“Same to you, stranger.”

That’s odd, the guy calling him stranger like in the old movies. Maybe he’s getting pumped—pumped for a loss. Billy pulls around, but the cashier can’t total charges till Hector takes the jumpstart for a time-remaining readout on the trickle fibrillator, only another minute or two. Then comes the same old same old: you want the Chemtone Detox for your loved one? Or the Ajax Plaque Inhibitors? Deluxe Trim ’n Clean? Dukey ream and dermal steam? Minicure, maxicure, manicure, pedicure, lasercure? The real kicker is dental.

“No better time than dead,” says the cashier. “No pain, no drugs, no soft touch. In and out. Dental special this week at four ninety-nine ninety-five per quadrant with unlimited drilling plus surcharges for prosthesis or gum disease. Does it have its own teeth?”

“Just the basics, please,” Billy says. “He’ll bathe at home.”

“We’d like to tell you about some other great programs at Emeretrieve. Three things last forever, and one is Aural Sheen. On special this week only . . .”

“Just the basics. Please.”

“Would you take a brief survey on . . .”

“Please.”

The cashier smirks; some people. “That’ll be twelve hundred sixty-two dollars.”

"Twelve sixty-two? Holy . . . What's the sixty-two for?"

"You want him Flaccigelled, don't you?"

"Nah. He'll loosen up at home."

Shaking her head, the cashier rings twelve hundred even.

Billy thumbs the screen and says, "Unixpress," hoping it'll fly. He glances up to see Deke Gerring, watching, scouting, putting Billy M in his crosshairs.

The waiting lounge has a warp, but two hours can crimp an attitude. What-ifs can get to Mo. HS will solve Billy's problems, one way or another. The bigger problem is now. Hector hates retrieval, always asking what's wrong with dead. What if he stays dead? Hector's money could start a—wait a minute! That's it! Be Not Proud Termination Services. Dead in thirty minutes or double your money back AND a free kill next time for you or your loved one. No, wait, not a free kill. Something softer, like sleepy time forever, on the house or something. Why not? You can't know if you don't stick it out there. With hardly time to jot a few notes, the swinging doors bang open so the old man with the crooked neck can stagger through to the waiting room. "Mm . . . Mghh . . ." Head bent and a grayer shade of pale, he cuts loose where he left off: "Blow the . . . bastard away . . . is what."

Billy doubts Hector can ride bitch on a half-cube, but what can they do? "Come on, Hector. You must be hungry."

Hector grumbles, "Hung . . . Hungr . . . Aww . . . Billy." He feels his jaw. "You didn't . . . dental. Did you?"

"No, Hector. I didn't let them do anything."

"Mm . . . Good boy. Let's get . . . get outa . . . Go."

"Hector, I have to get some flowers."

"Mm. I'm not dead anymore."

"Not for you. For Peony Lu."

"The cheerleader?"

"Yeah."

"Mm." Hector rubs his bruised thigh. "I might puke, Billy. I think they shot me up with piglikes."

"I think they used hash. We'll go for burgers later."

"Burgers? You eat that stuff?"

"The kids like it."

"Kids? Take me home. Eat what you want. What day is it?"

"Sunday."

"Three days, Billy. Don't blow this one."

"Yes, sir."

XVI

A Weekend of Sport for the Many from All Walks of THE LIFE

Nobody on Earth, not in the subdivisions and condominia up top or the cozy labyrinth underneath or the orburbs overhead, nobody doubts my commitment to HumanSport. I build things. We build together. Tremendous.

The High Republican reminds the many of who, what, when and where, for which they must be grateful. Strolling boldly in pink across the DMZ, he stops at the biggest, most comfortable RV ever seen. *This is the great outdoors, roughing it like Zachary Taylor and Teddy Roosevelt and me. Good to be back.*

Hot off the production line, *RV 1* glistens in orange blush with pink piping. The Spread Eagle spans its flanks, symbol of a world starving for democracy and corporate management. Harry Wenk turns to OneEye in pregnant pause, unzips his pinks and steps free. *Hard Luck, I love ultimate sport! Hard Luck!*

Clatters in the distance include hatches closing, a can tumbling, bolts sliding, hammers locking. The High Republican ducks, dodges and bangs his head on a backdoor shingle, too low, with an old banner tacked on for inspiration: Mission Completed. A bump on the HR noggin is terrible, but oversights happen, and the shingle can come down after the show. The hair is not mussed, but somebody's gonna get fired. Carry on.

Any political event with Eye-op would begin with stats on growth, low unemployment and job creation, vital components of the Standard of Living index. But the S.o.L will have to wait. Every whacko ever fantasizing early retirement and posh conditions is out there, firing at whatever moves or doesn't move. *Realpolitik* calls it joy in sport and in faith. Hard Luck will pick the winningest winners and trounce the losers. Winning sportspersons are requested to bow their heads in prayer or genuflect or point a finger Luckward. No surveys on your HS experience will be taken for now.

Who will Hard Luck favor? All take cover and wait for the richest game in the world to begin on this day of days.

RV 1, emblem of a free and dominant society, has anything an exceptional family could want for camping in the great outdoors. The Republican imagines a warp series, *Travels with the High Republican*, or *Road Republican*, or *Hitting the Long, Lonely Highway with the Most Powerful Republican on Earth*, or *I'll Take the High Road.* It will capture the spirits of freedom, wanderlust and power. *They'll never get this thing off the ground. Who cares? Dudley can wave out the window as well as I can. Let him soak up the bumps and miles—and bullets. He can sleep on that Luck-forsaken lump they call a mattress.*

Dudley Lipshitz of the Republican Guard is a stunt double to the High Republican: same plump movement, delusional posture, citrus pallor, horizontal pompadour and Macy's Parade bloat in perfect replica of Himself. Just like the High One, Dudley smirks if he's in the mood or scowls if he isn't.

Like now, he isn't. Praise Hard Luck, Dudley sits square in a few dozen crosshairs, framed in the big bay window like any old day in the wilderness. Billions watch his complacence. Who can deny immortality to a High Republican at the wheel, ignoring death, slurping tarcaff and gnawing braised ground sparrow, casual as you please? Hard Luck, you can't beat the great outdoors for drama. If Dudley gets nailed, he'll get a round of Hail to the stunt-Chief for protecting the leader of the free many.

The Park is full but can always hold a few more. Ultimate sport has self-adjusting density control. How crowded can it get? Who'll mind? Who'll complain first? When a hole in your head is somebody's jackpot, you shut your yap on cramped conditions. You hear grousing at HumanSport about as often as sportspersons through the ages have complained about too many critters to kill.

Warpan punditry seeks perspective and calls it a strange and beautiful thing that we have yet to comprehend.

A personal problem remained for the High Republican right up to the last minute, when the inspired solution came to the genius Republican. Would the Republic be best served by bivouacking Georgie boy in a separate, stupendous RV with no stunt double and a stray sniper to cure things quick? Or should Georgie camp here in *RV 1*, where Dudley or one of the Joint Chiefs or stewardesses or, what the heck, the High One, Himself, could ease on up and pop goes the weasel? *Hey, you mess around with guns, there's gonna be some misfires. Somebody's gonna get whacked! Capiche? Guns don't kill people. Sportspersons do. Accidents happen, even at this level. After all, we're only mortal. Darn. Too bad we don't have old Vice High Chump Chinnley in here. He'd pepper Georgie with birdshot and call it home, home on the range. Old Chump might need a retrieval or two after, but we could set that up.*

The High Republican reflects.

Not too far away in a newly burgeoning theme park and a rented RV, a family approaches a scenic overlook near Slonerosis. Along for the ride: their former father and the great-great-great-great-grandfather of their stepfather. The panoramic vista of HumanSport is a marvel to behold. They agree: it really is something. It just goes to show what attitude and leadership can accomplish.

Billy sums it up: “It was nothing but a wasteland last month. Add a little organization and elbow grease, and it shapes up with rollicking good fun for the whole family!” His effusion hides the flutter in his gut, but that’s how it was and is, pregame. It feels biliously good! More importantly, Billy M is home, center court, on the comeback fantasy of many years. He’s in it and on it, scanning ridges and scrub lines, boulders and stumps. He counts dead RVs and notes the decrepitude of each, assessing each for bivouac or cover in a firefight. He feels good, really good, on his game and eager to get in there.

Alysyn chatters over rides, the nature trail and the bear monster.

Rozomon hopes they have decent burgers.

Danny agrees, “It sure is.”

Peony Lu makes the best of it. She and Danny Blanda are not on a camping date with the kids. But what if they see anyone they know? What is she supposed to do if Danny gets hormonal? Nah, not after such stamina and consistency at Billy’s end of the court. Gosh darn him; that Billy is tough to stay angry at.

Marya points. “Look. RV 1. The High Republican. Erika says Georgie’s here, too. Erika says it’s a last ditch between the big guy and political slaughter. She says it’ll show what kind of . . .”

“Shut up,” Hector interrupts. “Get out.”

"Not here," Billy says. "I'll head on down to the campground and hook up to the sewage treatment lines and get some power and water. Then it's you and me, Hector. They got a shuttle."

Alysyn begins, "I want! . . ."

She shuts up too when Hector's red eyes bore in.

Retrieval hangover is worse than the day after the Unibowl. This one is the worst yet, with maladjusted children in his face and nagging doubts that his chosen heir can protect the estate from these gamma normals and their needs. The ride downhill to Slonerosis is silent to the entry gate, where the ticket scanner says, "Nine hundred eighty-six dollars, please."

"No, no," Billy says. "We want the special. Hector and I aren't staying. We're going to HS. I want to hook up to sewage and . . ."

"Nine hundred eighty-six dollars, please. Pay now, please. Pay now, please. You're blocking traffic, please. Pay now, please. Pull out of line, please. Now, please."

"But we're . . ."

"Nine hundred eighty-six dollars, please. Pull out of line, please." Through amplification louder than Billy has heard since Woodstock IV, the scanner booms. "Security! Security! Security!"

"You . . . fucking piece o' . . ." Hector struggles forward.

Peony Lu gasps at the language.

"Gi . . . gimme."

Billy pulls the thumb printer in through the window.

Hector spits on it and presses. "Kiss my ass, please."

"Hector, Let's get out here and catch the shuttle."

"Thank you, please. Move in, please."

"Move it, Billy. I don't need their noise or yours. I want a big bang, over and out. Any dough goes down the rat hole on the way; that's your loss. You want to cry, cry quiet. Now step on it."

Billy bites the bullet for big cash, moolah of magnitude.

Hector gets still to improve his odds on two more days without dying again.

The rest ride silent. Soon they can rant and rave all they want without Jerko and Prune Face breathing down their necks.

Meanwhile, up the road and over the line—the fine, thin line between an amusement park with family values and the great HumanSport experiment—real LIFE or death await. Nature plays out in exceptional ways for exceptional people of an exceptional nation. It's a nation surging with freedom, which isn't free and doesn't run like some colors do. Take a man nestled under a thin layer of cold, muddy scuz. Not a bad guy and not big or brawny or rich, he's suburban, average in every way but exceptional for living in the home of the brave. He sprung five days ago for a Big Tow full of in-law retrievals. He's that kind of guy. He brings decency to ultimate sport. Deke Gerring doesn't want tons of money to live like a high mucky muck, and he doesn't want to live forever, not yet. He only wants a new warp, a new gurney, some mid-level appliances and food on the table. He wants a nest egg, so he can rest assured that his children and all the generations will be grateful and may hang a portrait of Old Deke over the heater.

Deke Gerring covers his face with detritus and digs into the waste of the wasteland. He assumes the position briefly before bursting through ground cover to spin and fire on a field rat at thirty yards. BLAM! Free-range burger meat, coming right up! Oh, Mama. Deke has the crosshairs gene, and how! You think thirty yards is too close? BLAM! BLAM! BLAM! Two crows in flight and a starling at sixty yards, how do you do, plummet to Earth, D.O.A.

But wait. There! Deke hits the drift.

Just yonder a man and a woman stroll carelessly this way, guns lolling in the crooks of their arms, reviewing strategy. He says, "No. The old ones are better. You need more of them, but—"

BLAM!

The man falls. The woman freezes before lunging for cover. Too late. A moment of doubt is like dribbling before shooting. Believe it quick and shoot quicker or BLAM! Deke Gerring, up from the scuz, strolls over to check his kill, his piece of the rock, a two-bagger. He hears a rustle and believes it, zigzagging, rolling to the dirt for a belly crawl—ground sparrow. That's okay. Only those with unflinching attitude will walk out of this weekend. Back at the kill, he finds their licenses. Let's see. He's fifty-four. She's 26. Hm. Old wicket dipping some young wax, but . . . wait! Can it be? The dog tags show an 00 address that looks pretty dang exclusive. Who lives on Maxy . . . Maximillion Boulevard but the richy richos? Luck. These two might be Q-ed!

Deke Gerring feels pretty darn good with expenses covered not two hours in. But here's the iffy part. Any sport calls for pushing the rules now and then. Two easy marks with a good address, possible Q and entitlements ought to pay out better than bureaucrats. They are absolutely positively not foul kills, but if he doesn't foul-kill tag, he's hauling a load as the action warms up. How fair is that?

It's not, unless you make an exception and fire a couple foul kill tags in their necks. "What'n hell you want me to do? They's high mucky mucks that never worked and won't but cover my costs!" Deke Gerring explains to an imaginary jury of hardworking, Luck-fearing Republicans who can't help but understand. With Mo on his side, Deke tags and drags the corpses to a nearby ravine and rolls them over. She snags a scraggly stump in an armpit on the way down and hangs there. He snags nothing and falls two hundred feet.

Dang! The pinkos ought to find him, but dang! That whole pinko process'll take another three weeks. Or months. Deke doesn't like to disparage but can't help mumbling, "Dang bureaucrats. Wish they was in here."

Aw, heck, he's done about as good as a fellow can do, chalking up a double and 00ers at that. Deke Gerring snorts up some raw victory and heads back east on his belly with a winning spirit in his heart and the taste of dirt and money in his mouth.

Hardly an hour from the park but worlds away from its anxiety, George Q. Longley and companion cruise westward on their first outing, their fourth day as an item, their hundred and fifth hour in reach of each other. If somebody would step up and tell George that his neighbors got bagged and foul-tagged, he'd show no emotion. He never met the Bluesteins. It's that kind of neighborhood. He sighs at Darla Jo. So much behind them; so much ahead.

She smiles serenely at the great thinker. Boy oh boy, she concurs, a homecoming queen never rode a float like this one.

Down at the hub of the action, Sonny Wayne Wyoming feels a new LIFE surge on perspective and values. In the money is a fur piece from broke, and here comes a hoi polloi weekend, with the cubecaids and steady stream of female women with their clipboards and high heels swooping in like pigeons homing to roost. He laughs at not too long ago, when Sonny W. Wyoming pooh-poohed relaxation programming and all that calmness crapola. The condo crowd and their chronic stress relief. Look who's tuning in for harmony now. In, in, in to the tippy top of his crown of consciousness and hold, hold, hold . . . Then gently release, out, out, out . . . Visualization can help a thing come to pass. Trouble is, them high heels and tight skirts, clingy blouses and lip-gloss turn the harmony thing to a containment issue in his dungarees. Next thing you know, he's gonna havta . . .

But KABLAMMO! BLAM! BLAM! BLAMMO!

Hey! That was you-know-where!

Warden Wyoming is out like a shot with his Hilite oculators—Hilite: for smart-zoom oculation to bring every rat hair and gnat's ass into focus. They're so durn pricey, most wardens can only drool. Zooming to *RV 1*, he scans for clues on what the fuck just went down. Gunfire blazes. Polychip debris flies. In the smoky havoc, Sonny thinks it's a Secret Service cannonade. Why would the HR go offensive now, from his hub? Who they takin' out?

On a gasp, the scene comes clear. Blown to smithereens, the bay window frames the gore. OneEye zooms in for the feed:

The High Republican of the United Sectors of America slumps over his breakfast of tarcaff and tiny hindquarters. Pooled in red sauce, his head cleaved like a melon, steam wafting from breakfast and split skull, he has no more to say.

Guns blare, OneEye strains, sniffs, scans and moves in, wending fearlessly to engorgement on carnage galore.

Sonny Wayne prays for *somebody*, for Luck's sake, to jump aboard and steer the beast to somewhere else, some other who, what, when, where. And why? But the many has a right to know.

Inside *RV 1*, Harry Wenk cowers, hardly smug as Huck Finn at his own funeral, looking more like the young Wenker on an early deal, down by eleven million on a triple net ground lease with nowhere to go but deeper in the hole. *Victory is ours. Never fear. I pardon people and expect the same. We will make this work. I never said I wasn't perfect. We move on. Into the future. I am The One. This is terrible but can be wonderful.*

BLAM! BLAM! BLAMMO!

Hard Luck, hear me now!

In abeyance to the greatest power on Earth, violence stops. In stunning aftermath, OneEye trills his many-tongued message like happy hour at Babel and proceeds. Warpanal will digest, assess, regurge and conclude, reassess and reconclude so fast, the many will merely blink between realities. OneEye sniffs the hot, bloody trail of urgent news. Sharpshooters won't cough up a syllable. He peeks under the table, behind the gurney. In sidebar color, he murmurs, "Plush enough to die for!"

Drifting down the hall to the executive sit-down, he peeks in at the High Republican peeking out: *Never fear. Never. Never.*

Across the warp, sporting and political endeavor merge, abuzz and swarming. OneEye goes to pores and wrinkles on the High Republican and hold . . .

Warpanal won't cut to personal and parental bios or the whole memory panoply from teachers and childhood friends—the standard transition on a fat Q. This is different—close, so close. What to do? How to play it? Hmm . . . Opting for time to figure, Warpanal goes for S.W. Wyoming's 2¢ for immediacy, depth and color—easy on the reds. With a background scramble B-roll to synch commercials in the off markets, the Wyoming clip forms up and soon fades to new truth affecting LIFE as we know it . . .

THIS JUST IN!

"How was Deke Gerring to know what *RV 1* stands for?" Mrs. Gerring asks, subtitled below her sputtering spew. Behind her, poor Deke is leaking worse than last year's cider sieve, bound, gagged and hoisted by the hind legs for weigh-in and Eye-op. The G-man beside him shrugs, calling it procedure, for the perp's own good. Foregone among top-level analysis analysts: executive dispensation on retrieval, so any and all conspiracy potential can be pursued and fleshed out.

Heather Heatherington, not a big woman, is known for penetration. Standing on Deke's far side, she confides, "Trouble is, they want to make this man an example. Skin him like a springbuck. This is patriotic country, Erika. Reaction runs deep. Folks here want Deke Gerring stretched and tanned for Pudland. Comments from some zero point zeros might help form up what's happening here. Sir! Excuse me. I'm Heather Heatherington with *USS News*. What happened? What should happen now?"

The passing man sees Heather and OneEye. "Guy . . . got shot, I guess. I don't know."

Deke Gerring looks drained to irretrievable.

Jade Boren, on an improv podium nearby, prattles on with the obvious, the first assassination attempt in an ultimate sport park. "Sporting ritual. What does it mean?" Profile left in pregnant pause, staring at Deke, she turns slowly right to *RV 1*. Eye to Eye she seeks poignancy but seems oblique and more obscure than random samples who don't know. Jade Boren loses two points fast in her most dramatic chance since grad school.

The ratings winner on the Deke Gerring story is clearly Mooja Slovac. Known as Alpha Bitch or the Queen of This Just In, nobody denies her hard nose for outrage. The Deke Gerring fiasco is the story of the century. Deke preempts Wanda Ann as the turning point, the identifiable, isolatable, most profilable point between then and now, not to mention what might be. Mooja knows how, stretching OneEye, greasing a VU and stroking the melodrama to a head of steam. Short of breath, hair mussed, soot streaked on her brow and beautifully down one cheek, she gets close to Mrs.

Gerring. "Look what they did to your husband. Was he part of a conspiracy? What do you feel right now?"

Fresh angle, nice twist, history in the making.

Mrs. Deke can't speak for sorrow flooding her banks.

Mooja lets her gush.

OneEye eases in to microscrute the essence of utter agony, so the many can join this intimate wallow of emotion. Resting a hand on Mrs. Deke's shoulder, Mooja urges calmness and sharing. "Come on now, Mrs. Deke Gerring. Let us in. Share your pain. We're here for you. Speak for Deke. Speak."

"No!" Mrs. Deke cries. "He was . . . He was . . ." She's done.

Mooja steps aside, effusing pity, asking, "What can you do with a nutty woman who can't talk because her husband tried to off the High Republican?"

Warpanal This Week will call Mooja's coverage bold and daring, "the result of a career dedicated to elucidation, uplift and insight in ten seconds or less." WTW will profile Mooja from youth to now, bagging a record share for non-primetime on a hard news bulletin. WTW will call Mooja a shoo-in for the Pugnacious Prize.

Mooja stoops for a OneEye 2-shot with poignancy *and* immediacy. WTW will size up the move as "all the difference in the world." Mooja Slovac and Deke Gerring pose for posterity at ground level, count one, two, three and: "They're rushing us from the sidelines now. There's talk, Erika, of giving the late Deke Gerring a taxi fit for an assassin. Innocent? Or not innocent? Sport or politic? You tell me, Mooja Slovac. Press B1 on your receptor panels and emote now. A vote for innocence will be charged one dollar per emotion. Guilt is fifty cents. Erika, this man, Deke Gerring, opened fire on the High Republican and will live forever in infamy, which is not the immortality these folks want. Poor Mrs. Gerring. You know she was quite calm before the truth sank in. She called her husband hardworking and Hard-Luck-fearing. I'm afraid that sentiment is lost on the wind here, Erika. Deke Gerring got blown away like chaff in a storm. On a group squeeze, he's part of history. The tally is in, Erika: Fourteen percent innocent, eighty-one percent guilty, five percent undecided. Deke Gerring will have a hard time beating those numbers. I'm Mooja Slovac. Back to you, Erika."

Erika Swain rarely takes it back on a pregnant pause but does now, wagging her head more somberly than anyone can remember. "We'll be right back after these important messages."

Across the plateau, Game Warden Wyoming blasts an emergency ceasefire. "I mean now, and I mean you, and I mean every square dang inch o' this place." The big squawkers bellow.

Strolling casually as one more Friday in the park, Uncle Hector Moline and his despondent heir-apparent take in the scene as they cross the front lines.

"What a break," Billy says. "We can see their defense. We can tell what they're gonna do if we try what we're gonna do. I mean, with an offense that hasn't been . . ."

"Shut up," Hector says. "That idiot took out the stunt double. Numero Uno's got a bench of doubles. He's worried. Put his best one in the window. He's got more. Not so good. A pimple here. Skin cancer there. We'll see it. He's worried. He knows we're out here. We're a moral threat. Republicans feel it. Ha!"

Billy thinks the old man's common sense got left on the retrieval table. Billy *is* a Republican, not a threat. He wanted a weekend of ultimate sport, and here he is, harnessed in ultimate drudgery. It's okay. For fifty-two mil, he'd do floors. But how much longer can a charade play at this level of extreme hazard?

"Talk about breaks," Hector says. "I think the Lucky Guy up there might like me. Look: the High Republican. George Longley. All these outragers and Warpanal. Billy, we can't miss. We . . . Let's stop right here and pump 'em full o' lead. Are you game?"

"It's a cease-fire, Hector!"

"Fuckinay, fool! Cease-fire my ass!"

"They'll see me. What good is your money then?"

Hector mumbles that fifty-two mil can buy a defense team to get you off anything, with enough left over for a 50 and a couple three 20s and maybe a few shorts.

Billy mumbles but won't argue.

At least the weather holds, gray and hazy with nominal inversion and no thunderheads inside the ridges. What a day, the High Republican walking around a big as LIFE, close enough to yell at, standing in the open and shaking hands with the many, including armed sportspersons, everyone calling it glorious, especially with George Longley showing up.

Billy wants to go shake hands with the High Republican, but Hector's in a mood.

Hector stops fifty yards from *RV 1* to listen and watch the High One greet George Longley with the gladdest hand in politics.

It was nothing. We anticipate. This is sport, after all. Look at you, George. Are you experimenting with women these days? HR turns fatuously to OneEye. *Can you come up with some improvements? Maybe a low maintenance model? Ha, ha. Is this your prototype? I'm glad to see it.*

George Longley contemplates nothingness relative to *it was nothing*. He considers nothingness on a parallel plane running tandem with chaos, i.e., on similar non-trajectory, random formulation effectively yielding a state of nonbeing, albeit our very special order residing therein. Mass coverage seems similar. Violence blends with cordiality in diametric opposition to magnetic attraction of opposites approaching critical mass, begging tough questions sooner or later. Who could be attracted to violent death? The question bores down on a tougher question oppressing an exceptional nation since the Republican Mandate emerged: Who would vote against his own best interest?

George Longley factors risk and exhilaration, the heroics intrinsic to sport. The many *is* watching. Many watching enhances sexual attraction in the watched. But something itches. Oh, yes, the money. "What am I doing here?"

Darla Jo pipes up. "Having fun, silly."

George contemplates antecedents of *we* in *we anticipate*, bringing another instinct to play. Sensing false data, unlogic, non-parallels tracking for manipulation, he blushes. Like a cephalopod in love, he doesn't know what to say.

Darla Jo Bojoli senses discomfort. In a OneEyeful she tells the most powerful Republican on earth, "I'm no prototype, Sir." She plucks ultimate greatness casually as many women might tweeze an eyebrow. "I'm Darla Jo Bojoli. Born here in Wyoming before my father was Sonny Wayne Wyoming, when he was only Sonny Wayne Bojoli. He's game warden here, kind of a wasteland version of you, but I won't be helping him out anymore."

In situation-control, the High Republican says, *Well, well, well,* peeved at this pedestrian hamming an Eye-op that neither money nor power could buy, not cheaply at any rate. This no count hick is bombing a High-One-Georgie two-shot at the matrix of sport in America? *Gimme a break!*

Darla Jo shows obsequious affection.

George grins, continuing the series of historic firsts. Gazing with empirical fondness upon this wise young woman who found him by chance, George Longley is revealed for OneEye and the many. His abiding faith in random events paid off, it seems. It's not the same as faith in Hard Luck, fulfilled, but it's not exactly not, with staggering odds abounding.

"George and I are an item," croons Darla Jo, as if soaring to Q.7 for a female person in public display of affection *with Georgie* needs a narrative! Blasting through to Q.9, she bats lashes to 9.5!

Shake the earth. OneEye chokes! Pandemonium erupts! OneEye rolls back, as news dogs yap on which bone to chase, the one in tow or the one reflected in the water below. They want both bones now! Deke Gerring tried to off the High One *and* Georgie got laid! LIFE in the pursuit of outrage can be unfair, and every news dog knows there can be only one story of the century at a time.

Deke Gerring hardly stands a chance. Bloodless and pale with that chalky mask that usually gets the gore rating, he is a mere mortal who took an unLucky shot. He pales further on each and every blush pulsating between George and Darla. Here is the gristle a news dog can chew. Here is outrage in the making of outrage in the making; here is the story of the century:

High Republican SHOT DEAD!

—Almost

Yet the story of the century is quickly preempted by the story of the century:

GEORGIE AND DARLA JO TO WED!

No hype, this is for real, a moment of ultimate outrage.

"Come on," Hector mumbles, shuffling past a OneEye engorged to full bloat. With Billy in tow, he ambles to the far end of the dead RVs to claim a bivouac for impending action. A prime hunting blind should be easy to find in a ceasefire. A knock on a door ought to do it. "Hello? Anybody in there?"

The action will resume soon. This is HumanSport. What can they do? Call it off for a weekend romance? Hector doesn't think so and double times his shuffle to easy cover.

Billy lags, humping all the modern weaponry one caddie can carry, bemoaning the no-cart rule but maintaining attitude. He'd be a sitting duck in a cart, relaxing for a few minutes down the fairway and getting pumped full o' dead. How convenient is that? Reality is a Supralight 909 small bore automatic with telefinder, laser marker and a can't-miss accelerator that gets darn weighty in no time, especially bundled with a couple AK 91s and extra clips for fire power to spray a grandstand. Heavy son-of-a-guns, but jeez, the final bracket of the ultimate playoff will demand some spray fire. Sadly, poundage increases with distance. A single-action, local-infection mortar is twelve pounds that'll bend your knees between parking and digging in—and can make the winning difference. You can't hit the jackpot without heavy hardware. The old man was buying. What could Billy say? I think that's enough? Let's squelch on firepower and ammo? He could have had Hector buy one of those sport utility cubes with refractoshields, so expensive the Pentagon bought some! Then they could have scooped some gold. But no civilian vehicles in HS. Still, it's fun to think about.

They slog past a Live 5 Warp Weather woman from Southeasternorange County on a sidebar interview with a sportsperson from Southern Cosmic. Billy feels a tingle. He can outrun, outjump and outshoot this LaLa joker in any given quarter.

The Southern Cosmic sportsperson bagged a geriatric four-pack to cover costs early, then got a young urban professional couple in brand-new weather suits with telemetry helmets, night 'n radar goggles, flotation boots, polysteel long johns with flak skivvies—the works. "Had themselves trussed up till they couldn't get out of their own way. It's the honest to Luck truth: I did them a favor. Who wants to live like that? They went over the edge. Had to foul-kill tag 'em," claims the SEO County guy.

Billy M reads the lie; the guy is sleazy, with his condescending happiness, pierced ears, crystal amulet and B.O, hiding unsportspersonlike conduct in bliss, common to Cosmic Sector. What a creep, pumping himself up after stalking Deke Gerring all morning, too scared to stand and fire. Then he over-tagged Deke's foul kill that should accrue to the widow and children. Boy, Southern Cosmics and their cheeselike subterfuge. The over-tagging penalty is an hour in yellow out front, and this guy talks like a hero.

"Nobody wants to fire effective weapons on humans," he says like a colonel, "but when you train and plan and get ready, it's a thrill and a privilege and an honor to participate in an activity like this one." He over-tagged. Billy knows it on game-day instinct.

Billy offs some scorn in passing. "I'd like to see your spinals in yellow out front for an hour."

The Southern Cosmic guy and the Live 5 Weather woman turn to Billy, as the Cosmic guy asks, "What's the matter with him?"

Billy movies out, up to present tense and ditching at last the burden of former potential greatness.

Holing up with Hector in a dead RV isn't so bad. Hector gets close to croaking every few hours, but spirits stay high. Whiskey revives him. Billy gets into camo-fatigues and helps Hector change. The uniform works its magic. Billy smears their faces with olive drab greasepaint. It's bonding time for a benefactor resigned to mortality and an heir to carry the legacy. Camaraderie warms the air. Billy wishes he was around back when sportspersons could camo up and hit the bush, and some big old four-legger worth killing would come along casual as you please.

Hector says he's hungry and has to pee.

It comes down to good times and laughter, eating beans right out of the can, expelling gas out loud and trading jokes. Billy shares his old, secret love for Peony Lu, back in the days of potential glory.

Hector tries to remember youthful love. "Hey, Billy. When does a cheerleader only have seven fingers?"

"I don't know, Hector. When does she?"

They share man-bonding smut unfit for polite society, the grit that brings men and nature together with some decent whiskey, death on the doorstep and living fully in the moment. They pee in cans and set them down the hall. Billy says he'd give anything for a Coke right now, or a *Pepsi*.

Hector lobs a clod and knocks a can over and says a place like this ought to smell like piss.

Billy thinks it over. Night falls.

Through the haze, Sonny Wayne Wyoming announces ten minutes till the ceasefire ceases. Five minutes, one minute, ten seconds and three, two, one: "It's back on, campers. Defend yourself at all times."

Wasteland mosquito swarms hum with the outrage corps, as the many feels the eerie wonder, hazard and potential of ultimate sport through the night. Outragers agree, "This is THE LIFE and death."

"You can feel it in the air."

"THE LIFE."

Nobody builds a fire but some start glow heaters. Billy read the pros and cons of glow heaters in HS. The con is disclosure, but every dead RV is occupied, and everyone knows it, so what's the diff? Half froze in the dark might be a purist's paradise but won't fool anybody. Warm, limber hands are quicker. Anyone approaches; you blast some manners their way and pick up a few bucks.

Out in the scrub, a young woman nurtures an ideal of sacrifice for art. Shivering between a rock and a tree, she estimates barely punting distance to the last RV on Bivouac Ridge. Hardly a cozy campground, glow heaters give it a neighborly feel, even as front-line hunters go tooth and nail for more of THE LIFE. She writes it down: tooth and nail for more of THE LIFE . . .

Marya's approach may be naïve, but she's halfway there. She needs in for warmth. If she makes the door, her own kith and kin could blow her away. If she calls out, she'll draw fire. She jots another note: it's amazing, what a woman can suddenly know. She's seen warp coverage on those who come early to HS to claim a dead RV; scrimpers and scratchers, coupon clippers looking for cheap cover. Paying the thirty-two hundred entry fee makes them feel proprietary or left them too broke for camping gear. Not proprietary. Scratch that. How about privileged? Yes. Nice.

The Park is the future; it will shine or stop. Let the chips fall. Thirty-two hundred smackeroos weigh on a thousand brains. Many eyes fix crosshairs on payouts—or is that a tumbling tumbleweed?

Marya senses a red dot on her forehead and shudders. She's no Hindu, and a nose wipe can trigger eternity. It drips. Mosquitoes land on her face. Like an ice sculpture in slow melt, she knows the move is hers. She wants to shout out the madness of cold-weather mosquitos, but survival requires stillness. The beautiful irony and impossible paradoxes demand notation, but stillness rules.

She must reach Billy and the old man. How?

A dead RV nearby has an awning over an elderly couple and a few second primers, likely cousins. In the center, a portawarp on a portaSue warms the night with applause and laughter. It's another

Special Presentation with Binky Stardust paying tribute to select Hollywood stars for their incredible talent and opinions.

A cousin brays, "Haw! Haw!" Taunting return fire, he dares long-range laser cannon and capacitating oscillation lock that can take out a frog fart at five hundred yards. They're out there.

Marya waits for the grunt cousin to draw fire, twitching now and then. If she had a laser cannon, she'd take out a few jerks. Some people need it, so obnoxious. On the bright side, when return fire breaks open, she can zigzag through the confusion. Another delicious moment of anguish and mosquitoes sucking blood makes her brain swirl, like thoughts in a blender—no, like . . . like stuff in a blender. No, uh, fruit! Like fruit in a blender, yes. That's what blenders do. Fruit in a cake?

She can't move but won't forget the blender idea. Another idea needs no mental note, already indelible on the quilt of her wildest dreams—no, the drawing board. No. On the, uh . . . the canvas! Yes, like a painting, a swirly one where everybody flies around. Her only approach is a belly crawl to Billy and Hector's door, where she'll bray her own Haw! Haw! Other sportspersons will think it's the grunt cousin and open fire. She'll call, "Billy. Open up. It's me." Inside, with no mosquitos, she'll gather her wits, buff her notes and interview Billy and Hector at the ultimate scene for feel and flavor.

She drifts briefly to the future, not the material future these so-called sportspersons want, with appliances and immortality, but a future in 00, of great works, insight and importance. Her towering achievement will be crowned with humility, in deference to Bobb Fjord, a most important writer.

Even a place like HumanSport has room for perspective.

XVII

HumanSport Sunday Wrap-Up

They laughed at the guy in pregame trance who looked more like a zombie than a dinker legend. Some players hold hands and pray. A few look up and point up. One or two take a moment in private entreaty with Hard Luck. Back in the day, Billy M went still as a freeze-dried lizard, clearing, so victory, the reality, could pump his thought vesicles to second nature. Snake-eyed, transmuting all, the winning view was the only view.

Decades later, Billy pregames again. Bagging an easy stray in the night has no more consequence than hitting five-pointers in warm-up. It bodes well and puts him back in the game.

The HS Weekend Report normally takes an average viewer share. This Weekend preempts all programming, including Under One Roof with Jimmy Grimm. Billions watch. The overview overlooks an ex-R-baller of former five-point glory. The anti-sport wing of the NaySay gags on the Weekly Bag Dump—it includes a young woman of the subdivisions with no equipment or weapons, ventilated. Their noise is predictable; they gag on anything. Who watches Warp 86 anyway?

Saturday morning in HumanSport pegs global viewer ratings again. Billy feels it, trancing like never before. His weapon rests in reach. His mentor sips whiskey. Outside lay the corpse of the gamma normal who couldn't enjoy a night of semi-truce but had to try an easy score on a sneak attack, approaching on a Haw! Haw!

Who did she think she was fooling? Billy can't feel good about bagging a teenager, especially with the iffy payout. She looks healthy enough to accrue the few thou it would have cost to get her a job. But savings get amortized, he'll see what? Ten, twelve bucks a month? Forget it. She's best off where she is, in a heap. Darn teenagers; they shouldn't be here, not when you shell out hard-earned money to bag someone loaded with entitlements. Best to pass on the young ones. Trouble is, she helped her inbred cousins next door fix their audio markers. Some families have no scruples, using their young as decoys. Nothing for it but slamorama.

She's out there, maybe thinking differently now about sneaking up on Billy M, who blasted enough firepower for three clans of bumpkins. He had no choice. Now they got his number—number dead serious. Factor that in your sporting averages.

Hector grouses. "I told you not to kill anyone. You think I'm puh . . . pussy . . . pussyfooting around?"

Billy says self-defense is a kill-or-be-killed situation.

Hector fears Billy's Voodoo beliefs in Mo and weaponry. As a bona fide sportnut, Billy could blow the whole show.

After tarcaff, they head out, low and slow on their bellies. Unwritten is the rule of odds enhancement. Capacitating oscillation detectors shut down at sunrise. Otherwise, the game gets stuck inside, where nobody scores with nothing to shoot at. Seasoned sportspersons set up false oscillator rhythms before heading out. It's a ruse. Everybody knows it and does it anyway.

Clearing Bivouac Ridge takes two hours. The work is grueling, belly crawling with an ancient uncle in tow, one who gets heavier on every groveling inch and won't shut up. Hector wants to walk. At this rate, somebody else might smoke the big target.

Billy has half a mind to let him get up and walk. "Yeah, yeah, yeah," he says, painfully aware of the compromise a sportsperson makes for money. He turns to say that stealth will be key to success at this point . . .

But he goes mum. Hardly a three-iron to the east in glistening dew sits *RV 1*, still as a stump in a wasteland. OneEye is still. With no action for minutes, Billy realizes it's a commercial break, so sponsors can catch up after so much breaking news. The outrage ticker strip at the bottom of the Jumbotron assures that any action will preempt these important messages.

Billy signals to Hector: time for a break. The old man deflates and breathes. Billy watches and waits, waits and watches.

Meanwhile, it's nice to hear about the taste that comes alive, the all-new cubes for '85, rich, roasted flavor, whites to be proud of, rectal, dental, vaginal, penile, mental and skeletal comforts now available with all new ingredients doctors recommend. "Coming up: Does it matter how much you sleep? Or when? We have highlights of an amazing rescue. Meet a man who loves hangnails. Tragedy strikes in Hurricane Sector. The five-day outlook is gray and hazy. Details up next. Stay tuned and find out what to think."

Inside *RV 1*, the High Republican shouts *NO!* The curtain will not rise on Don Dietz, stunt double for emergency only. *When I find out who put this fellow on the stunt-double team, they'll wish they never heard of GS II.*

Don Dietz hangs his cow-licked, mole-flecked head over a cup of tarcaff in HR essential slump.

The crew shares a chuckle.

The High One does not laugh. He paces. Billions are watching, as they should. The most powerful Republican on Earth utters not one syllable. What could he say that wouldn't tip his hand? No. It's time for sportspersons to lock and load, including Himself in camo-fatigues with a pink-fob reminder that THIS is a casual stroll. Nobody would potshot the HR on a neighborly visit!

Check that. He'll run, roll and swerve—no, no, casual strolling is best. He'll knock on the door. When he hears it opening, he'll pretend to scratch his head and accidentally blow away George Longley. No. An accident will undermine heroism. He'll turn to OneEye, disavow techno and *then* blow George away. No, an accident may be best.

All is still next-door, except for undulating quilts. Free of sunrise contemplation, George Longley and Darla Jo Bojoli wallow in LIFE. Pleasantly dazed, George contemplates the scene outside and suggests a day of RV repose, them and catered brunch. Either a love saga plays on, or they shoot to kill. Tough choice. Duh.

Darla Jo murmurs, secretly fomenting a sweet payout just yonder, over the line. She won't break the law but can lure a wasteland varmint into no-man's land. Up for a quick pee, she tapes her panties to the back window.

Just yonder, eye-rolling like a hungry lizard, Sonny Wayne Wyoming watches the rig with the big, bold emblem in green on yellow: RV 1a! *It's a tough bone to chew on. Left him in the clutch is what she did. Counted on her. It wasn't all that often. Gave her a roof and all. Comes home like Mrs. High Mucky-Muck, like we should be proud of George Longley stirrin' the puddin' instead of an old fogey, except that it ain't Sonny Jo Bojoli no more. It's Sonny Wayne Wyoming, by Luck! Boy, she makes me mad. Hey. What's that? There in the window. Why, it's . . .*

Farther yonder, a family reunites. They had imagined fun at Slonerosis but had no idea . . . All you can eat burgers, fries, cola, hotdogs, sausage, cheesefood snacks, Round O's, Fatty Doodles and Sweet-o-reenos make a day dreamlike. The feed rail loaders don't even care if folks fill polybags to chow down elsewhere in the park! The kids shut up, stupefied. Marya is lost, as usual, likely run off to mope and write things down. She'll turn up.

It sure wasn't Danny Blanda's idea to share a room with Peony Lu, but five won't fit in a single, so it had to be. Nor did Peony Lu think seduction, breaking out the old chintz. Billy never noticed that chintz, but it cast a spell on a few top draft picks, back in the day. It was hardly premeditated, even with the short hairs still waxed. But a woman likes an ex to see she still has it. Call it one of those nights of happy fatigue. Add fresh colas, the negligee, old Danny looking sheepish, and let's face it: Peony Lu has it. They both wanted to use it, only for a few minutes. What could they do? Deny nature? She finally said, "Come 'ere, you big lug." Team spirit and attitude don't fade away. She shrugged. "We did it about fifty thousand times. What difference can one more make?" Her eyes threatened death if he told anyone. Danny's no talker, and they both felt bad about doing it behind Billy's back; he's such a great guy.

Getting down to it, there wasn't much difference between fifty thousand one and fifty thousand six, except that a night of rigorous understanding makes for a morning of concern. What if? How do they tell him? Can they still live together as an extenuated family? Worries slide to the back burner at sunrise, as front and center comes to a boil: fifty thousand seven.

Back in RV 1a!, window panties get spread, so a perv with Hilite oculators can see the lace and dainty crotch skids from yesterday. Bait never looked so good.

Sonny Wayne rises to it. She's inviting him over or making fun. Either way, it's time. Donning his pink vest, he heads over and around to the back door, Sonny Wayne's homecoming of choice.

Reading him like a book, she turns the page on his approach.

Billy and Hector pause at the canyon rim where Wanda Ann took it in the kneecaps. Billy calls time out in a game of utter magnitude. The place tingles, but even on a belly crawl, a sportsperson won't hang here long. They inch along.

Starlings take flight.

A murmur ripples the wasteland.

The High Republican steps from *RV 1* in camo-fatigues with a pink fob and a sidearm. He strolls over to RV 1a!

OneEye zooms.

For better or worse, Darla Jo wants to bag her father and call it fair game, after all. She packs a lady derringer, large bore, perfect for a perv come calling. Out back seems appropriate, but a wasteland lass soon has to choose between opening the front door on the Big R or the back door on sweet revenge. She senses opportunity out front and lowlife in back. She figures Sonny Wayne will be around as long as fungus grows in dark, wet places.

George Longley hears a knock and perks up. Look what the last knock got him. George is a fool in love, so he answers the back door with an AK 91 in hand—a perfect replica in a squirt version. The squirt gun is a joke, because a man so long without love was without humor, too, and that's all changed.

Things change to something else when he finds himself dead center on a zero percent margin of error. Crosshaired on a single datum that marks him dead, he breathes deep, staring down the black hole of eternity, as presented by his father-in-law.

As if by Hard Lucky convergence to that same instant, Darla Jo opens the front door in her bathrobe. "Hello, Harry."

All's fair in love and Sector HS, but with All Hell about to break loose, OneEye swoops close to Georgie's gun. It's dripping! The AK 91 is a squirt gun! Georgie is defenseless! It's got to be misfit saboteurs! And a High Republican impersonator in pink is carrying a magnum hand cannon at the front door, not dripping! Pinkos have no guns! It looks like misfits want to kill Georgie!

The sidearm at the front door rises.

The guy at the back door hefts his bazooka a tad higher.

Billy knows what twenty-nine hundredths on the clock feels like, but this is no time for nostalgia—no time for anything but a heartbeat. He needs a long dink and another!

Casting caution and himself to the wind, he leaps for glory in a fallaway skyhook, arching to full altitude on a midair half gainer and uncanny levitation. At the apex, he squeezes ever-so-gently with the accuracy of a lifetime on the buzzer sounding and the only trajectory in the whole wide world to keep things spinning.

OneEye blinks. HindEye opens for split-screen coverage of *ℛ𝒱 1 and* 1a! From the edge of the historical cliff, Billy is up and stays up! Beyond the edge, over the ravine, he's in range!

Worldwide warp whispers, "Story of the Century!" BREAKING NEWS is the unreal hangtime for a long-baller past potential. Billy M in midair makes global impact, squeezing five at the peak, and it's . . . *double swish!*

Greatness will be his epitaph. Two shots wing Georgie, shoulder and calf, downing him for his own good.

Shot three gives Sonny Wayne Wyoming a new viewpoint, a dot on his brow in Punjabi red, as his spiritual aura begins and his era ends at Sector HS.

Spiraling through a flip, Billy's fourth and fifth shots relieve Harry Wenk of ambition and need, self-loathing and anxiety, removing him to where all the king's horses and all the king's men can't retrieve the High Republican.

Nobody should shoot a woman in a bathrobe first thing in the morning. Billy knows this and hopes that other sportspersons in camo-fatigues can learn it. One last shot goes skyward in sheer, poetic joy of an ultimate long dinker, at the summit at last. Billy M kisses the rim and falls to his death as beautifully as he rose in THE LIFE, potential finally achieved.

Bouncing off the canyon wall, he bangs the bottom, a crumpled mulch of bones, blood and dirt, mixed with tears of sadness and joy.

XVIII

Peony Lu Moline of Foxwoodburrough Hills Estates in the Great Sector of SuburboLIFE, Becomes Keynote Speaker at the Republican National Convention, as Happily Ever After Retrieves Underground

But first: farewell and *das vedanya* from Natasha:

"I first lady. I want for you call me first woman. America! Now I give great pleasure introduce from you . . ."

Opening acts are warm-ups, also-rans, wannabes. The donor class will not arrive until minutes prior to the ultimate name formally placed in nomination. Still, up-and-comers clamor for a prelim spot. Who cares if 48 percent of the seats are empty and 92 percent of the home viewing audience is on refresh? It's still a zillion eyeballs on hand, and competition for time up front is fierce, like the nomination itself used to be.

Openers in '84 include Jorge Sontos, whose grandfather developed the outrageous home audio system. His other grandfather was president of Brazil. His father won the Notable Prize in literature the same year Jorge played goalie for Brazil in the World Cup, sacrificing both kneecaps, winning the championship, blocking every kick. New kneecaps allowed mobility to serve as Prime Minister of England and undergo transgender procedures to prove a point: that a global leader and rock-solid athlete can win a Ms. America Pageant, and she did. Switching back to manhood, he went on to win a world title at a hundred forty-four pounds in MMA octagon fighting, no holds barred. He also won the Notable Prize in economics and medicine. He owes a few bucks and gained a few pounds. So what?

A few Republicans trickle out for a breather. Next:

More relevant to the moment is Adgery Marlow Cream, pistol packin' mama from Boll Weevil Precinct, Bubba Sector. Nay Sayers say she used to be a guy. Again, so what? In her first campaign, she sang a ballad. *Lookin' for a home. Lookin' for a home. Ohohohoh oh. Lookin' for a home.*

It didn't work. Her new message worked: "I will fuck you up!"

Not so long ago, Warpanal asked the HR if Adgery Marlow Cream's profanity was appropriate.

Profanity? You want profanity? Listen to the Nay Say. Smell 'um. I wish she'd fuck 'um up. I wish somebody'd fuck 'um up. Fuck that sonofabitch up! Punch 'um in the nose! Fuck 'um up!

That was then. Representative Cream waves to the mingling crowd. A few wave back. She waves the other arm and whispers, "I will fuck you up." She gets a better response and leans into the microphone to boom, "I will fuck you up!"

Six fans whoop. A few more bang seats. One howls.

She waves with both hands and says, "Peony Lu?" Response ticks up a notch as Adgery Marlow Cream descends and a fan fave slowly rises. Isolated howls and cheers grow to a unified chorus.

Peony Lu Moline never sought greatness. It is thrust upon her. With ebullient cheer, she waves both hands, flashes Vs for Victory, throws kisses and embraces the space before her.

When the crowd calms, she speaks sweetly. "THE LIFE is a bittersweet mix of the bitter and the sweet." She shares personal tragedy poignantly for OneEye and the Republican base. Moving to meaning in LIFE, she says, "A woman's greatest sex appeal is in middle age, when heft and creases suggest experience and know-how."

Danny gives two thumbs up from the wings, as the Republican Convention goes gaga for a woman of heroic tragedy. Nobody sees her sniff her index finger, because she doesn't, not really. Nobody asks, *Who cut the whiffy?* Whiffies occur, and asking who is gross and childish. She calls for quiet.

"If you were hungry in the last six years, I say down with hunger! If you were raped in the last six years, I say down with rape! If you got raped and preggers, I say Hard Luck bless the silver lining. If you were cold or got beat up or really wanted something but no matter how hard you worked, you couldn't get it, I say down with cold and beat up and not getting what you want!" Thusly beams the Queen of Pixies at 26 times the size of LIFE on the MegaJumbotron. Peony Lu pauses like a pro. The many amp to maximum surge, proving her a natural-born cheerleader for all seasons, an up-and-comer—a Republican to keep an eye on.

"To everything bad, I say enough! To everything sad, I say enough! To the teensiest tiniest stuff that gets you so mad every day, I say enough!"

Warpanal agrees: they could drop the balloons now and give Peony Lu the Republican Party mandate. None could foresee her stellar rise to Q. Nobody predicted this formerly obscure housewife as the perfect woman to nominate the name in the heart and mind of a grateful many: Erika Strong Swain.

Like a glowing comet, Peony Lu sears the seams of speculation. Will she be Vice-High on a Swain ticket pledged to Olden Values? Peony Lu has credentials on OV with experience in the field. She's a woman among women who made the semi-ultimate sacrifice, giving her daughter for sport and art in America.

Erika Swain, Republican candidate for Highness, calms the crowd. Her expression, designed for Campaign '84, transcends conviction to rock solid faith in growth, olden values, an impenetrable hohum, more and better stuff and much, much more. She does not sniff her index finger or cut whiffies in series, including black bean, spirulina and piglike whiffies. She does not feel herself up or blow raspberries. No, she cocks her jaw at eighteen point eight degrees and veers slightly right to beam for OneEye, teeth clenched in grim resolve. She bellows, "Sacrificing a daughter!"

They cheer.

"Giving up your own flesh and blood!"

They roar.

"Meeting ultimate with ultimate!"

They stomp and howl.

"That might sound trivial to some of you."

They vehemently deny triviality.

"But it's pretty darn wonderful! Right! Here! At the Republican! National! Convention!"

They frenzy. They bring the house down. Some will later attest to OneEye fogging up.

"Make no mistake! Marya Moline is the—"

"Blanda! It's Marya Blanda. There was another guy!"

"Marya Blanda is the most important writer in America!"

They romp and ballyhoo. From under the din, Erika Swain presents the Republican Award for Merit in Literary Success to the Marya Blanda Memorial Foundation, with a grant from the National Endowment for the Warp. "These funds will open a writing workshop seminar in Sector 00, where aspiring writers can work and think at the hub of literature." Erika laughs heartily and looks unstoppable. "Believe me, ha, ha, ha. I've been!"

Tumult transcends. Republicans rejoice, hailing a new era of leadership and growth. Balloons fall through a blizzard of confetti. Delegates pump signs for OneEye, and the big squawkers blare *Happy Days are Here Again*, which is pretty darn obvious. Taxicube drivers outside can feel the rumble, and so it goes, hither and yon, from the highest high rise to Memory Lane.

Many miles away, in a hunting preserve much quieter since the recent commotion, business is back to normal. On a stable daily regimen, sportspersons come and go, sitting up or lying down. Nobody misses Game Warden Sonny Wayne Wyoming, who did too much but didn't do enough. Chester Coyote is the new warden, and things seem settled. Folks do their best for the Republic and leave, as heroes or stiffs or both. Many make self-warpo segments before crossing the DMZ, to confide on why they might fail. Viewers at home enjoy insights with winning sportspersons on the Sunday wrap-up and share doubts and fears with the losers too.

A nagging question lingers.

For practical reasons, not all stiffs are recovered in Sector HS. Non-recoverable corpses are visible and blend in, once withered, except for the stiff formerly known as Billy M. When the pinkos got to the bottom, Billy M was Q.6.2 and rising. His following does not take his absence lightly, but the pinkos searched high and low. No stiff, no foul-kill tag.

Mike Dunce, Vice-High under Harry Wenk, took the oath a month out before the election. What could he do? Build a campaign and run against Erika?

At least he qualified Billy M for retrieval. The legendary long dinker did not get smoked but went over the edge. That doesn't count. Dunce ruled that a five-point shot on a flip and half gainer was trickier than dinner with a woman, not the wife. What about Billy M? Can a hero take out an HR? Analysis analysts chew this gristle through a few cycles to arrive at last at HS, HR's problem child, and what a red, white and heck of a blue way to go. The High One tried to take out Darla Jo, and if that doesn't spell all's fair, then HS might as well be a bridge tournament.

The uproar fades to hohum soon enough. Far from HS, non-sporting persons deep in a cave chuckle over the mystery of Billy M.

Billy is also amused but can't laugh: too sore. He's not alone; two companions hung in at crunch time: potential and Mo.

Billy M, shortest odds on the long dink ever, is retrieved to bond with his patron. No hangover compares to this. The room spins with Berber carpet, fluorescent lights, shabby furniture, bag wine and strange tones. Stimuli tumble like flotsam in a kaleidoscope.

Hector sits in a lawn chair.

The misfit commando leader is Leanne Longley.

Billy thinks she's nuts, prattling updates on a better tomorrow. "Your wife is fucking her old husband. They think you're dead. We got the girl. Hector wants her in."

"Hi, Billy," calls Marya from a bleak alcove, perfect for organizing notes, getting it right for art and history.

"Marya . . ."

"Isn't this neat? You didn't mean to kill me. I'm better now."

"Aw, gee," Billy moans.

Colonel Longley assures: "Listen, soldier. Catching on takes time. Meanwhile, we can use a maniac like you." She grasps his chin. "I need a man. You might be it. This is the future. We make the world a better place. Hector carried the baton on warpwarp interceptors, filter worms and foul cadencers. He's tired. You'll do. It's a future we have to win. We want what is rightfully ours."

"What's that?" Billy asks.

Leanne curls a lip over excellent incisors that sparkle with revolutionary zeal. "Stuff," she says. "New stuff for the meek to inherit. Get it?" She steps back. "You saved my father. I'll reward you later. Hector? Final comments?"

Uncle Hector slumps over a Gopherbroke tallboy—Gopherbroke, the homebrew from underground. Tossing the empty with a feeble nod, he says, "The end."

An attendant injects the hit.

Hector fades. "You're a turnip, Billy. And a champ . . . Leaping like a ballerina, smoking the bastards. Man!" The old eyes flutter. "I'm proud of you, Billy. You get the dough."

In tranquil aftermath, a warp voice announces the all-new fall lineup, with special offers on unlimited warpcon for one monthly fee and a joyful question. "Is this a great time or what?"

Fade on an antique Miles Davis spinning its erratic magic.

The End

But wait! What about the cold, rigored stiff of the formerly most powerful Republican on Earth? Could the font of military might, Hard Luckiness and World Dominion simply vanish? His H-

Oneness may bring only chump change on a Dust-to-Dust, but this bag o' fert is significantly artifactual, like Samson's short hairs, John's guitar, Bill's cigar, Rummy's Oija, Cheney's clot, Ashcroft's porn, George Jr.'s pretzel or a Man Tan aerosol empty. Dressing out for taxidermy would waste a stiff of historical magnitude. This Republican alone got the whole world to agree: *He's nuts!*

He played to win at all cost.

Leanne Longley lobbies to bypass taxidermy. It's deemed best to reveal vintage data in an RES. She might be a bit tetched, too, but she's a looker and swings some heavy dick. The Random Event Sampler is obtuse but factors probability at six-zillion-to-one on what might have been.

So, it came to pass three generations ago, that Aloysius Wenk filled out a loan app, but on this go he filled in the blanks with correct info.

A hundred fifty years later, a man stands on a curb with a sign: *Grand Opening No Money Down Ninety Years to Repay from $999,999.99!* If somebody yells, he dances a jig. His wild hair is orange and long.

Passing cubers turn their heads.

Leanne Longley says, "So be it!"

Retrieved and resuscitated, the once-High Republican is put on a curb to contribute. One couple per hour stops in for details on the amazing offer, and that is a *huuge* success.

Harry Wenk does not stop flopping but thinks *something is going on here. I'm going to find out what it is.*

Probability projection show he'll a better person for trying to find out.

The End

Corollaries (of the Republican Platform):

1: *We are. Attitude is all we have.*

2: *If you're on, they may love you.*

3: *Death is a great thing to cheat.*

3a: *Buy One Moon for the good of the many.*

4: *500 free miles with your pledge of fifty dollars or more.*

5: *Do what you must. Seek forgiveness.*

6: *You can't take it with you.*

7: *The warp gives. Absorb and be clean.*

8: *An open mind is best.*

9: *When it's time, don't go. Death to negativity.*

10: *Have a nice day.* 10b: Enjoy the rest of your day.

11: *Progress is our most important product.*

12: *Human* LIFE *is sacred.*

13: *Menstruation cannot be helped.*

14. *You have to share.*

15: *You should believe. 15a: You will believe.*

16: *Commercials are art.*

17: *We live in the corollative world.*

18: *Make it work.*

19: *Reality is real.*

20: *Vladimir knows best.*

21: *Q generates Q with proper coverage.*

22: *Home games are best, but the war must be away.*

23: *If threatened, we respond.*

24: *Don't worry about Kazakhstan.* 24a: *Drink Coca Cola.*

25: *Reality is real*:

26: *A man has to do what he doesn't want to do.*

27: *We shall maintain a worthy standard of worthiness.*

Political Forces

The Republic—That for which we stand, one nation, Under One Roof, with Liberty and Justice for all.

Under One Roof—UOR covers all denominations, sects and stray ideas with the Gospel of Jesus, who gave fishes and loaves to the many, no matter how many. With the Reverend Jimmy Grimm, all Hard Luck's children can pray together, as the Republic makes them free to do. Ninety floodlights shine on the crucifix tower at World HQ of UOR in Atlanta, Bubba Sector. Even the blind can feel the miracle, lighting the mini golf course below as well. Jimmy Grimm is Echelon advisor on the will the Many.

The NaySay Party—dispossessed by Hard Luck, without resources for gene splicing, suffering circumstance and the plight of the downtrodden. NaySayers want convenience to church, schools and shopping for all, not just the high mucky-mucks. Posing no threat to the Republic, NaySayers shore up the hohum and provide amusing grist for the warp. The Echelon deems the Party a non-force.

Bums and Misfits—underground in the Wyoming Wasteland since '44. Now thought to infiltrate. The Republic figments bum/misfit behaviors to fulfill fear quotient as necessary, so that the enemy remains them and does not become us.

The Law, as Written—The Book gives laws to live by, drive by, vent spleen, tune up, absorb, eat, sleep and work by. Not to be confused with regulations, which are unwritten.

Unwritten Law—Language Appropriate to the many shall be gender-neutral, including names of ships, boats and other items of bulk, like weather systems. Virtue and merit shall accrue in deference to family values, unless those values are negative. Negativity is bad.

Rosenfeld's Theory of Corollativity: $V= MQ^2$—Virtue equals Merit x Q squared. Negative Q has 0 Merit. But 0 Merit x negative Q will accrue ratings. Go figure.

Glossary

Cube—basic transportation. Primitive cubes in 2039 levitated on heavy metal batteries with DC propulsion. This modified swamp glider used gyrodiodes as bow and stern thrusters. Though Hector Moline designed and built it several decades prior, General Exxon/Mobile/TexaShell took over to rule the world in cube and gyrodiode manufacture.

Half-cube—same mode, in-line, two-seater.

Beef—animal protein, ® indicating high quality rodent parts, pigeon nutrients added as available. Other grades may contain nutrient below rodent level: grubs, slugs, roaches and seasonal favorite larvae. Taste the difference. Vegiburgers offer a recycled compound of chlorophyll and select friendly gastro-bacteria, so nominal they don't count as meat. Also in the hopper: Predigested matter with enhanced color, texture *and* flavor. Beef products are often consumed with B-1 Beef Sauce. NOTE: Reptile beef is technically an import delicacy from reptile farms in Japan and China.

Burgers—Chief staple of the many, providing carbohydrates, amino acids, enzymes, chlorophyll, biotin, thiamin, niacin, riboflavin and three times the daily recommended allowance of vitamins A, B, C, D and E. A nutritious meal = two patties and a pickle slice, sauce optional. Burgers help recycle nutrients at street level. In wasteful times, these nutrients were often wasted. Besides feeding the many, burgers sharply curb nutrient infestation in Memory Lane, home of the Zero Gentry. With burgers come full employment; the ZG can redeem pre-burgers @ 8¢/lb. Don't think it doesn't add up. Commercial burger farms are planned for the 22nd Century, or as soon as wild stock falls short of demand. The High Republican, Herself, calls this The Clean Eats Program.

Cheeseburgers—same as burgers with yellow melt on top.

Coca Cola—Drink of choice for the many. Its rich color, bubbles, sugar and caffeine will motivate an hour of warpage, minimum.

Pepsi Cola—Second choice, also habit forming, leading to body fat, stomach rot and other effects classified as harmless, in light of *PepsiCo*'s goodwill jingles, good cheer, the cherubic choir and contributions to the Republican Party.

Electrochem Dating Service—Once mandatory for citizens with three citations on eye contact in public. Proven efficacy put E-chem in the DOW 100. Ninety percent of matches stick at E-chem DS, whose motto is a household question: *Why take a chance?*

Hohum—The way things were, are and will be. The hohum provides. Eat, sleep, work, warpage. Live long and shop. Strive for convenience. Thank Hard Luck for weekends.

Community Property—WHEREBY one third of all assets, held jointly or by the party of the first or second part, shall accrue to the many. Rendered Off the Top means before legal fees, leaving the parties of the first and second parts to fight over what's left.

They—Capitalized in mid-sentence, the third-person plural pronoun takes the American Medical Association as antecedent. As in, *You wouldn't believe what They can do now*, or in casual deference, *The weather looks dry, but They say it might rain.*

Disneyland—Capital city of the Republic, home of the Pentawarp. The Shrine of the Ages includes the Mickey Monument and Goofy Enthroned. Site of the Beige House, former summer home of the High Republican, Natasha and Woof. Notably next door is the largest known amusement and thrill-ride extravaganza in the Earth-Sun System. Plenty of parking, free with validation.

Gene Splice—the process by which genetic re-coding retards or reverses the aging process. Splices include the 20, 10, 7, 5 and 3 and, since 2083, the 1-Moon Segment, installed in minutes. The 1-Moon comes with a latté for LIFE voucher (non-transferable).

Republican Grant—Republican Grants bear no interest. A single grant is worth six 1-Moons or a LIFE supply of Coca Cola, all you can drink. You may choose New Coke, New Diet Coke, New Caffeine Free Coke, New Diet Classic or Regular Classic (Classic never came in caffeine free). You may substitute other colas, including *Pepsi*, but you may not redeem for Coke (or *Pepsi*) for LIFE and then in a year or whenever, say, *Yuk, this stuff makes me want to puke!* And then try to change over to, like, trips to Disneyland or something. BUT you can change from Coke to *Pepsi* or vice versa or go Diet or Caffeine Free or Classic or New for a nominal administrative fee. Multiple Grant redemption depends on current catalogue offerings, like LIFE time cube power for three grants or unlimited Disneyland for LIFE for five grants. Tobacco products, prescription drugs and firearms begin at seven grants and are considered most beneficial to the Republican Party.

Subdivision—Single or multifamily dwellings in extreme density five stories maximum. It's your choice: condo or subdivision.

Condos—Multifamily dwellings in extreme density, no height restriction. Your choice yet again, subdivision or condo.

Memory Lane—(aka street level) those spaces among high-rise condos and cluster subdivisions. Restricted after dark to residents, Memory Lane cured the problem formerly known as homelessness. By numbering spaces in the Lane, persons residing there can feel counted. Addresses are claimed at street level. An address and access to public services in the Lane help the Zero Gentry integrate with the hohum, the many and the Republic.

Name Q-ing and Copyrights—grants legal claim to celebrity or place names. Name copyright enhances revenue for the Republic, like vanity plates. Name sequel registration fees are a function of the coefficient Q divided by the years from original to sequel. Fees are subject to change without notice.

Rimball—Took over when basketball dropped two points in Sports Q Overview. Average player height topped seven feet, but fan frenzy waned when back and forth, forth and back got tedious.

Rimball eases racial imbalance. Thirty percent of each team must show Caucasian descent, even if a more qualified player is cut, so sportspersons of Caucasian descent may realize their sport potential. The rim, at thirteen feet, is razor sharp in a six-inch frontal segment. The dunk gets dicey. Glass shards and nails obtrude from the goal post. A moat with crocodiles surrounding the court may add color to out-of-bounds play soon. The NRA is under advisement that croc moats will boost ratings, meaning more of everything for the many, the players and owners.

The Precious Few—Persons showing net worth to longevity ratio of $3 billion per year. If under eighty, PF status requires projected LIFE span of fifty more years *with no drop in annual income.*

The Republican Platform—gone since 2020, deemed inflexible—since the Republican sweep that did not happen. Most Republicans asked, "What?" The Republican Platform Steering Committee stands its ground: mistakes are impossible, a laughable iota of the Luckless past.

The Echelon—CEOs of top twenty-nine warp frequencies. With majority interest since 2050 in twelve top warps and major minority stock in nine more, plus sole ownership of thirty-nine of the next seventy-one, Time-Warner-Exxon-Mobile and TexaShell-Comcast-Halliburton-Disney-Fox rule the Echelon. TWEM & TSCHDF want to rename the United Sectors of America to the Sectors of Republican Unity, to include Third World and Pipeline Sectors. Disney opposes, favoring The Wonderful World of Disney. Disney flies the Fantasy Land flag, so the many can live happily ever after.

Disney strives to nominate Mickey Mouse as candidate for High Republican. At Q.7.99, their cute little rodent is the oldest living Republican. Disney says it's the office, not the man or mouse, that requires faith and allegiance to the Way of Unity.

Some say the Mickey scheme is a megacorp power grab. The cartoon candidate is a guy in a mouse suit who changes, one shift to the next. Mickey polls strong as the environmental, evangelical, pro-business candidate.

The PSE Award—for actors and jesters who capture hearts and minds of a gross demographic Q ratio 2.9 over a thirty share, three nights in a single season. The PSE Award (Perceived as Something Else) qualifies for worthy opinion and comment.

Olden Values—self-evident truths guaranteed in the Republican Platform and in *Corollaries 15 and 15a: You should believe. You will believe.* OV grant basic rights of convenience to church, schools and shopping for those with adequate down payment.

Electrosphere—Cyberspace for penal rehab. Egress requires six pass codes. Anyone can get in. Japanese spheroids, as seen on the Japanese channel in permanent song, dance and slapstick, may be former persons, imprisoned in the ES.

The War—It wages for appropriate resource allocation. Let Freedom Ring. The war is not discussed. Support our troops, especially those who didn't want to go and died and couldn't be retrieved. What, Emeretrieve should set up in a frikkin' desert?

Rumor—News on Warpanal till proven untrue or unratable.

The Warp—That which reflects, refracts, imitates, substitutes for and is THE LIFE. Holographic electrons jam neutrons in minimum two-inch radii, since the Radii Minimendment of 2052. Radii more commonly run LIFE size or better.

Warpanal—Warpanalysis programming other than sitcom, game show, soap, movie or infomercial. Family special on subdivision or condo LIFE may be Warpanal, depending on poignancy.

Warpanal includes forespin, analysis analysis, sub-, post- and diatonic analysis on what has been, can be and what it is. Shouting above wind and rain in hurricane sector gets a few more points if flood waters pour over the top rims of the waders.

About the Author

Robert Wintner has authored twelve novels, three memoirs, four story collections and five reef photo books. He crossed two continents on motorcycles, sailed four of the seven seas, dove tropical reefs around the world and rose from ashes to success in a place *Forbes* magazine called the most difficult business arena in America. Profiled in a dozen metro daily papers, interviewed on a hundred radio shows, he declined Leno when asked to arrive in mask, fins and snorkel. He is committed to style, story, entertainment and lasting value intact. He's Executive Producer of *The Dark Hobby*, an award-winning feature film exposing the aquarium trade's devastating impact.

Robert Wintner is the nom de plume of Snorkel Bob, Hawaii's reef outfitter, known for quality and hygiene in trying times. He lives on Maui with Anita, Cookie the dog, Yoyo, Tootsie, Rocky, Buck, Inez and Coco the cats, and Elizabeth the chicken.

Made in the USA
Las Vegas, NV
14 October 2023

79080434R00157